Nightfall in Mogadishu

Nightfall in Mogadishu

By

Veronica Li

ISBN: 1-58820-251-8

1stBooks - rev. 10/12/00

Prologue

Mogadishu, Somalia, 1990, the last year in the existence of Somalia as a nation-state.

The city's power grid had gone dead again. The street was pitch-black except for the occasional orbs of light fueled by private generators rumbling like distant thunder. One of these lights emanated from the back room of a house, which in daylight would show up as a white Mediterranean-style rambler, made of ceramic blocks shipped from southern Italy and protected all around by an eight-foot concrete wall.

At the front gate, a pair of small leathery hands reached in between the sweating bars and fumbled for the padlock. The link slipped off. Abdullahi muttered to himself, relieved that he didn't have to insert the blind key into its hole, but also dismayed that his master had forgotten to lock the gate again. Lately, he'd been cautioning Mr. Barnett to check the doors and windows when he was alone, but the Englishman would only smile that indulgent smile of his and say, "Yes, Abdullahi, have a good weekend." Mogadishu wasn't as safe as it used to be, Abdullahi had always wanted to say, but who was he to advise his master, whose counsel was sought by ministers, sheiks and presidents? Mr. Barnett was the World Bank's "res rep." Although Abdullahi wasn't sure what the title stood for, he knew its holder wielded great influence on the affairs of his country.

Abdullahi stooped to raise the bolt pegged to the ground. The iron creaked and the gate gave way. He closed it hurriedly behind him and shuffled as fast as he could toward the house, his hands groping ahead. His master would understand his reason for being late. As Allah was his witness, it wasn't his fault. He and his eldest had left early to get gas at the station, but after two hours of queuing, the pumps had run dry. The mood had turned incendiary, and angry drivers had hurled stones at the attendant. Abdullahi had ordered his son to drive away immediately. He wanted no part of any riot. The motorcar was a nice thing to have, but his own two feet were more reliable.

The length of the city was nothing compared to the distances he'd once covered with his camels.

"Mr. Barnett, I'm here," Abdullahi shouted the moment he entered the front door. After stamping the dirt off his feet on the doormat, he crossed the threshold into the dark house and pattered across the bare tiles of the living room. His stomach told him it was now long past dinner. His master must have helped himself to leftovers.

Light flowed from the bedroom. The door was wide open. The housekeeper stood respectfully in the hallway, an apology on the tip of his tongue. In a moment, there would be the sound of slippered footsteps and his master would appear, his hair tousled from pondering and a pair of wire-rimmed spectacles in his hand. The housekeeper waited. Moments passed. Abdullahi called again, but still no reply. He approached the door gingerly. After having served three foreign masters, he knew how much they cherished their privacy, especially when they were entertaining girlfriends during their wives' absence. He was always careful not to surprise them. Discreet as Mr. Barnett was, traces of his weekend escapades were as obvious as the stars on a clear night. He could have told Mr. Barnett not to bother about making the bed to pretend that it had been slept on by one person. It was only right for a man to take another woman when the existing one no longer satisfied his needs.

Abdullahi stepped across the threshold. The first thing he noticed was the haphazard manner the white cotton cover had been pulled over the double bed. Abdullahi frowned at the unprofessional job. He lingered at the foot, gripped by the urge to remake the bed even if it was going to be messed up again shortly, but decided announcing his return was more important. Abdullahi went around the corner of the L-shaped room into the study. The neck of the architect lamp craned forward, casting a shower of yellow light over the desk. There was Mr. Barnett, the blond wide dome of his head shimmering above the high-backed chair, deep in thought. Afraid to startle his master, Abdullahi tiptoed toward him, hesitated, but finding no other way to get his employer's attention, said gently, "Mr. Barnett, I'm back."

Mr. Barnett didn't respond. Abdullahi touched the back of the chair. It swiveled slightly to the left. Mr. Barnett leaned forward as if to get up. Suddenly his chest hit the edge of the desk, and his face fell into the pile of papers he'd been reading. A dab of caked brown dirt scarred the back of his neck. His left eye twisted up at an angle, flat and still as a fish's. Abdullahi groaned a low "aah" and fled.

Outside, the night crashed down on him. Darkness had never frightened him before. He'd grown up without electricity and had known darkness to be as comforting as a warm blanket. But this night was different; it was fraught with dangers he couldn't see, intentions he couldn't read, and out there was someone waiting for him, ready to pounce on him and—a shove pushed him forward. He tripped and fell, kicking and punching for all his aging body was worth. After a while he stopped. His adversary had disappeared, or perhaps there had been none at all, only the fear in his own heart. He got up and groped frantically for direction. His fingertips found a hard rough surface. It was the wall. He followed it, scraping his hands along the gritty concrete until he touched the cool iron of the neighbor's gate. The black void in front stared at him like an empty eye socket. Clutching the rails, he called out for help.

Chapter 1

Hot air poured into the 737. Susan Chen stepped out of the plane, blinking in the blinding sunshine. The ground below was dotted with pools of water, which she knew were only mirages since Mogadishu hadn't seen a drop of rain for the last five months. For as far as she could see, the world was blanketed with dust and sand. From the airport tower to the grove of palm trees and the dour-faced soldiers at the bottom of the steps, everything was crayoned in earth tones.

Soldiers were everywhere, heavily armed and surly looking. A group had cordoned off a path leading to a bungalow at the end of the tarmac. The passengers walked along the prescribed trail, and when a European woman broke off to wave at someone outside the fence, an irate soldier yelled at her to get back into the fold. The woman complied, for nobody was going to argue with a man brandishing an AK-47. The passengers plodded silently with their hand-carried luggage, the crunch of coarse sand the only sound. No wonder tourism never flourished here, Susan thought.

Inside the building, the arrivals milled around like a herd of bewildered cattle in a pen. A variety of tongues asked the same questions, but there was no one to answer them. The rickety fan on the ceiling swirled in a drunken stagger. It was doing its best, but the heat of more than a hundred bodies was fast increasing the temperature. Minutes went by; most of the passengers stayed calm, shifting their weights from one leg to the other and sweating a great deal. They looked as if they'd gone through this before. Patience, Susan had been told, was the foremost quality for working in the Third World.

Her life had never reeled in such fast-forward speed as in the past two weeks. Only Monday before last, she'd been a personnel officer at the World Bank's headquarters in Washington. Her task that day had been to prepare an announcement on a staff member's death. "It is with much regret that we inform you that Andrew Barnett, the Bank's

1

resident representative in Somalia, has passed away unexpectedly in his home in Mogadishu." Having been instructed by her supervisor not to divulge anything more, she'd moved on to a long and glowing eulogy of the forty-year-old Englishman. Hardly had the memo gone out when she got the phone call. Spring had come; it was time for the mole to crawl out of its hole.

The briefing had taken place at a safe house on the eastern shore of the Chesapeake Bay, in the heart of hunting country where gunshots were part and parcel of bucolic life. After a round of target practice, her boss had appeared. Alex Papadopoulos, a stubby, dark-eyed Greek American, was her commanding officer at the CIA.

"May I introduce you to Andrew Barnett," Alex said, displaying an eight-by-eleven portrait of the back of a naked torso. "See anything?" the chief asked, offering it up for closer scrutiny.

"There's a little incision here," Susan pointed to the dab just below the hairline.

"Neat, isn't it? Just a smidgen of blood. He's always been known to be tidy."

"Who?"

"This is the signature of a killer called Hamid, an Afghan guerrilla trained by us. There aren't many people in the world that can kill like that. Neat, isn't it?" Alex repeated with admiration, baring the gap between his two front teeth. "He was just a kid when his village was wiped out by Soviet missiles. His entire family was killed. He was away tending sheep or goats or whatever when it happened. After that, the mujahideen adopted him. Then when we got involved, he was one of the commandos sent to us for special training. He was only fifteen at the time, but already a seasoned fighter. Fast, precise, and quiet as a cat, he had all the qualities of an assassin. He mastered the techniques in no time and became a member of a small team assigned to knock off officials of the puppet government. You know how he does this?" The chief pointed to the dab of blood in the picture. Susan shook her head.

"Let me show you," he said and straightened to his full height, all five-foot-four of him. "He comes up from behind you and cuts off the wind in your trachea." He clinched his own with two fingers. "His other hand is holding a chisel, knife, or anything sharp. With surgical precision, he inserts the chisel between two vertebrae and cuts your spinal cord. You drop dead without a squeak."

"Pretty good," Susan said tentatively.

"You know what they practiced on? Goats. It's actually a very humane way of slaughtering animals, which is how it's done in some countries. Here, feel the bump on the base of your neck." His short, hairy arm twisted back in search of his own. "That's the seventh vertebra, the last in the cervical column. Just below it is a big gap. If you insert a chisel right in that crack, it would penetrate as easily as cutting cheese."

"Uh huh," Susan said, a chill going down her spine as she felt the soft skin between the two bony lumps on her nape.

"Hamid disappeared on one mission that had gone sour. We presumed he was captured and executed, but last year a PLO officer was murdered in Paris in exactly this manner. We had information that Hamid had resurfaced and was working for a terrorist organization called the Brotherhood. We even had a tip on his hideout in Paris. Unfortunately, the frogs bungled and he slipped the net. Here's a picture of him."

Susan studied the photo. It was a blow up so enhanced that it showed every pore and blemish. But what good were the minutiae when the totality was lost behind a tattered heap of turban and a shaggy beard? A hawk nose was all that stood out. A bank robber couldn't be better disguised.

"This is the only picture you have of him?"

"Fraid so. You're lucky we have anything at all. Remember, we're talking about Afghanistan. Our involvement with the mujahideen wasn't something we liked to advertise. We were there only as advisors. We had no authority over the locals, let alone personnel records." Pointing to the nest of rags on Hamid's head, Alex added, "He's gotten rid of that thing and shaved his beard, and who knows what else he's done to himself. The bottom line is, we haven't got much of a handle on him."

Susan pulled her eyes away from the photo. There was no need to clutter her memory with something that no longer existed. "What motive did he have for killing Andrew Barnett?" she said.

"I have my conjectures. Keep in mind that he's a professional. People like him don't kill for personal reasons. He was hired by somebody, and in the context of Barnett's position and the state Somalia's in, the murder smells like a political conspiracy."

Alex got up and walked to the map on the wall. Somalia, the horn of Africa, was highlighted in bright yellow. Alex explained the strange shape of the country: The hammerhead was once a British protectorate, and the crudely fashioned handle, an Italian colony. Ethiopia drove into its guts like a sharp wedge. This piece of land was called the Ogaden. Although Somalis had inhabited it in recent times, western powers had given it to Ethiopia to keep Addis Ababa on the right side of the iron curtain. In the Cold War balance of power, twenty million Ethiopians certainly carried more weight than six million Somalis.

"*This* is why we're neck-high in Somalia," Alex said as he put his finger on a red dot on the north coast of Somalia, marked "Berbera." "Right here in the middle of nowhere is an airfield with the longest runway in Africa. If you recall, a chain of events in the late seventies were undermining our position in that part of the world. In Ethiopia, rebels threw out Haile Selassie and established a Marxist government. In Iran, fundamentalists toppled the shah, and in Afghanistan, the Soviets seized control and set up a puppet regime. Our friends were dropping like flies. We needed any base we could get to bolster our defenses in the region.

"Around this time, the Somali president, Siad Barré, decided to invade Ethiopia. He thought he could take advantage of the chaos next door to get the Ogaden back. Somali troops made good headway in the first phase of the campaign, but at a critical moment, their Soviet friends shifted their alliance to the Marxist government in Addis. With a fresh supply of Soviet munitions, the Ethiopians counterattacked and pushed the Somalis back.

Barré was outraged. He renounced socialism, booted out his Soviet advisors and severed ties with the Soviet Union. He came to us and offered us access to airfields and ports in exchange for military aid. The facilities have given us an extra foothold in the region, and if you look at their proximity to the Persian Gulf, you can understand why we can't afford to lose them now. If Saddam Hussein doesn't withdraw from Kuwait soon, we'll have to go in and get him out."

Susan scribbled a few words on her pad. Blessed with an elephant's memory, putting things down in writing could do her more harm than good. However, she'd also learned that if she sat through a briefing with an idle pen, her behavior could be misconstrued as a sign of inattention.

Alex sauntered back to the table and sat down. "Somalia is sitting on a powder keg. Siad Barré has ruled with an iron hand since he seized power in sixty-nine. Anyone who dares oppose him has been thrown in jail, and the way he persecutes opposition clans is downright genocidal. He's bombed their city to ruins and destroyed water wells and grazing grounds, causing thousands to die of thirst in the arid country. Another one of his tactics is to send his goons to rape the women and bayonet them to death."

"Sounds like the kind of guy we love to support," Susan couldn't help but say. The moral dilemma of succoring dictators in the name of freedom had always bothered her.

Alex paid her no heed. "Barré's own clan, called the Marehan, is a small minority," he went on, "but it controls all the important sectors of the economy. Siad Barré is now old and sick. His diabetes is so far advanced that he's nearly blind. His throne is up for grabs. Members of his family, his former friends and current foes, the factions that call themselves united fronts or national movements, everyone's getting ready for a showdown. With the millions of dollars of military aid from first the eastern bloc and now the West, they've got enough

5

gunpowder to blow themselves up several times over. A tiny spark is all it will take."

Susan scribbled some more. She was beginning to get an idea where this was leading. The wings of her imagination fluttered, but her pen tied them down to the paper under her nose.

Alex went on, "Now, we're no fans of Siad Barré, but ever since he brought the country over to our side, we have to treat him like a friend. Our orders are to keep him safely in power until the matter of succession can be settled peacefully. That's why we have to go in and get Hamid before he takes out another aid worker. The Somali government lives on handouts. The moment the donors are scared into leaving the country, the government will cease to function, and the country will go up in flames."

Alex clasped his hands on the table. "We have to stop Hamid," he reiterated. "We created the monster. Now we need to find our Frankenstein and destroy him." Alex gazed straight into Susan's eyes. "I want you to apply for the res rep vacancy in Somalia."

A clatter woke Susan from her musing. The wooden shutter of a window opened. The crowd rushed toward it and fell into a messy line. Susan was swept into its midst.

The Somali at the window shoved a form at her and asked for twenty shillings.

"I don't have any shillings. Can I give you a U.S. dollar?" Susan said, rummaging for her wallet. "You can keep the change," she added quickly.

The Somali shook his head and insisted on Somali shillings. Susan explained again she had none. He refused to look at her. Giving up, Susan asked where the currency exchange was. The Somali flicked his head back and mumbled, "Outside." Keeping a lid on her rising agitation, she said, "Outside the building?" When the Somali nodded, she couldn't help letting out a cry of "What?!" The catch-22 was just too absurd: To get out of the building, she must fill out the immigration form, but to purchase the form, she must get out of the building. Unless she'd been to the country before and saved some shillings, there was no way to get in.

The clerk looked beyond her and yelled, "Next!"

Susan stood squarely at the window, her elbows defiantly anchored on the sill.

"Give me two forms," a voice behind her said. A slight man with a pale, pointed face pushed a couple of rumpled notes through the window. "One for me, and one for the young lady," he added.

He handed Susan the precious piece of paper. She proclaimed an emphatic "Thank you" and pressed the greenback into his hand.

The man refused to take it. "You can buy me a beer later," he said, tipped his head, and turned to make his way through the crowd. While his reedy body began to squeeze through with little difficulty, the camera case strapped to his shoulder was trapped among the mass of travelers. Susan stepped up and gave it a nudge, noting that this must be an expensive camera to deserve the protection of a combination lock. The case dutifully followed its owner. Too bad she hadn't had a chance to ask his name, but with that long, sad sack of a face, she was sure she could recognize him anywhere. The few words he'd uttered had also given away his nationality—an American from somewhere below the Mason-Dixon line.

Susan quickly filled out the form and went to the baggage chute. Luggage was being thrown about, and passengers were waving, jumping and yelling to claim their belongings. Putting her New Yorker instincts into gear, Susan elbowed through the mob, clinched one of the men behind the counter by the arm, and pointed out her maroon Samsonite. He hoisted the suitcase onto the bench. Susan felt the heat prick her scalp as he nosed into her bag of bras and panties, and when he opened her toiletry kit, the beads of sweat behind her ears started gathering into a rivulet. Her lock-pick knife was among her brushes and lotions, and although the casing looked like an ordinary pocketknife, he would know it wasn't once he pulled out the blades. Susan inserted a twenty-dollar bill into her U.N. *laissez-passer* and handed it to him.

He slipped the money into his pocket and zipped up the bag. Red-faced, Susan repacked her suitcase. Half a dozen men hustled to carry it, but she'd be damned if she'd let anyone take it from her.

Outside, a handful of people were waiting around, among them a lanky Somali holding up a name scrawled in bright red ink: "*Mrs*. Susan Chen." *Miss*, Susan corrected in her mind and dragged her suitcase toward him. When their eyes met, the anxiety on his face changed to a timid smile.

He was Mohammed, her driver, and on the curb was the company's Mercedes Benz, bedecked with ensigns of the World Bank on each side of its silver hood.

Chapter 2

In the backseat of the limo, Susan rolled down the window. The breeze felt good in her face. It was a dry heat, unrelenting under the direct rays of the sun but quite tolerable in the shade. The air smelled of baked earth. A desolate landscape rushed by: prickly bushes stripped to the skeleton, and now and then a jagged, flat-topped tree jutting out of the scrags in tortured formation, a harsh cry in the silent skyline. In the middle of the bleakness stood a rickety tent made of branches patched over by odds and ends of animal hide. Gathered around it were three naked pot-bellied children and a woman wrapped in black from head to ankle. In the weeks of frenzied action, Susan had sat up in bed reading about this little-known country. Somalia was home to six million people, most of them nomads who'd lived in the same way as their ancestors since biblical times. While the men roamed the land with their animals, the women and children waited at the camp. They were ageless, even the children looking old and wizened, the women of childbearing age toothless and desiccated. When the average life expectancy wasn't much beyond forty, the stages of life collided into one indistinguishable heap.

A while later, the texture of the air changed. Susan tasted salt on her lips. She'd entered Mogadishu, capital of Somalia and an ancient trading post on the shore of the Indian Ocean. The scenes scrolled past, and she sponged them all in like a child seeing the world for the first time: the sparkling blue ocean, the ancient octagonal fortresses protecting the shores, the tableaus of adobe houses, the Moorish arches and minarets, the colonnades and cupolas of an Italian *arc de triomphe*, and a gigantic poster of Siad Barré, his face long and morose, bottle-feeding a baby in his arm.

But of all the sights, nothing could compare to the apparition on the roadside. Susan watched with wonderment a young man walking behind his camel, his sun-blackened forehead close to the sky, a king on top of his world. His eyes were trained at a vision farther and greater than the scuttle of petty activity around him. The stringy, fat-free body was wrapped in a dusty shirt and coarse sarong, yet a person clothed in gold couldn't have expressed greater disdain for the commoners around him. The fiercely proud nomad represented poverty at its starkest; his rank was at the bottom of global statistics on every score. His only means of living was his camel, which fed him its milk and took him to places where no other man could survive. Susan could think of no poorer existence, yet looking back at the receding figure, she could barely suppress the flood of admiration welling up within her. If any man had a claim to freedom and independence, it was he.

When the Mercedes Benz stopped beside a sidewalk, Susan had no idea that she'd arrived at the hotel. There was no sign, bellboy, or even a door to indicate she was at the threshold of an establishment. She got out, watched Mohammed unload her suitcase, and waited to see what was going to happen next. A ponytailed woman walked out of a wall. Her face was long and horsy; she was forty-something and small, compact as a tightly packed bundle. Behind her shuffled an old, stiff-jointed Somali in a dirty white djellaba.

"Welcome to the Eden," the woman said. "I am Isabella Giuseppe, owner of the hotel, and you must be Miss Susan Chen." Reading from a hardcover ledger in her hand, she continued in the roller coaster ride of her Italian cadence: "And you are staying for two weeks."

After Susan confirmed her reservation, the aged bellboy hobbled away with her luggage. The proprietress led Susan to where the sidewalk opened into a courtyard restaurant. Engulfing it in a horseshoe was a two-storied white stucco building known as the Eden, Mogadishu's five-star hotel.

The women climbed the stairs. From the veranda Susan looked down into the courtyard and took in the view of the giant liana scaling the walls and the jungle of potted plants with leaves large enough to wrap her in. The first diners were taking their seats at a table.

"I hear you've come to replace Andrew," Mrs. Giuseppe said while unlocking the door to a room. "He was a very special man, the kindest man in the world, and so intelligent. His death was a great tragedy." Her ponytail quivered as she pressed down on the squeaky handle. After a thoughtful pause, she added with finality, "He was truly a gentleman."

Susan murmured assent. Everyone she'd talked to had sung Barnett's praises in notes beyond the call of courtesy toward the dead. While the men expressed admiration for his professional competence, the women went into hyperbole over his virtues. It was obvious that many of them had been head over heels in love with him. It was also obvious that they pitied her for trying to fill his shoes.

Mrs. Giuseppe switched on the light. Susan gave her accommodations a once-over: The carpet was the color of mud and smelled the same. The thick coat of white paint on the wall was as uncomfortable as a mask of excessive makeup on a woman's face. Even so, it failed to hide the bumps and scrapes. The furniture consisted of a scratched-up desk and chair, an armoire of the same material, and a double bed that sagged like a hammock.

"I hope you'll enjoy your stay here," Mrs. Giuseppe said.

"Oh yes, I'm sure," Susan said with more enthusiasm than she felt. She wasn't sure what she'd expected, but probably something better from the country's premier hotel.

The old man staggered in with her luggage. Mrs. Giuseppe told her the restaurant hours and wished her goodnight.

Susan decided to freshen up before going out to face her new world. A rusty showerhead jutted out of the wall, but there was no tub or stall or curtain, just a drain in the middle of the bathroom floor that turned out to be clogged. After a brief splash in the cold water, she stepped out of the flooded bathroom. From her suitcase she dug out a flowing floral skirt and white V-necked top that highlighted the bronze glow of her skin.

The night-backed window served as a mirror as she brushed out the knots in her hair. It was long and thick and best

11

presented by allowing it to cascade freely down to the middle of her back. Her face was open and uncluttered, and a slight upturn on her lips gave the impression of somebody who'd recently emerged from a happy childhood. Her physique had the tender plumpness of a teenage girl just on the far side of puberty, well toned and supple and subject to spurts of appetite. She was three months over thirty, yet most people treated her like a recent college graduate posing as an adult in her first real job. People's unwillingness to take her seriously had been the bane of her existence, but lately she was beginning to discover that to be underestimated had its advantages. No one in his wildest dream would suspect that she had the guile to lead a double life.

Susan checked her appearance once more in the reflecting window and sallied out of her room. The courtyard was full. A group of Italians, apparently blue-collar workers by their dress code and manners, were carousing at a long table. Smaller clusters of white men and women more elegantly dressed in tropical fashions occupied the others. Then she spotted a familiar face. It was the American who had rescued her at the airport. He was by himself, spooning soup into his mouth with one hand while the other held open a paperback. On the glossy cover a scantily dressed blonde was running away from an exploding jet.

"Excuse me, I think I owe you a beer," Susan said, gazing down at his thinning pate.

A small, pinched face lifted, displaying an expression so sorrowful that one would have thought that a close family member had recently passed away. With a deep sigh that shook the pasty flabs of his cheeks, he dog-eared the page and set his book aside.

"I hope I'm not imposing," Susan said.

"Are you kidding? Coming from a pretty girl like you, it's never an imposition," he said in a monotone that didn't match the banter. The man's bloodless lips curled with flirtation, but the compliment, coming from such an uncomplimentary source, was lost on Susan. He introduced himself as Hoyt Grimley, a salesman of agricultural machinery from Raleigh, North Carolina.

"I thought you were a photographer," Susan said. "Wasn't that a camera you were carrying?"

"Oh, that. I use it to take photos of farmers using my products. There's no better sales pitch than showing people what their neighbors have in their backyards. Keeping up with the Joneses—works everywhere in the world," he droned on. For no reason that Susan could see, his narrow chest heaved up and down in a profound sigh. An undertaker would die to have a face and voice like his, she thought.

"What kind of machines do you sell?" Susan inquired.

The man shrugged. "Nothing big or fancy. Have you ever used a three-pronged cultivator? Well, it's a handy little gadget for harrowing crusted soil. I've come up with a model specially designed for local conditions. The way it works is..." The salesman was about to demonstrate with three clawed fingers when the lights wavered and went out.

Several male voices shouted, then rang Mrs. Giuseppe's several decibels above them all. Footsteps pounded down the staircase. Someone was running into the back of the building. An engine coughed and grumbled. Lights flickered, the motor settled to a constant hum, and power was restored. All was motion again: The guests resumed eating, chatter quickly swelled to an indecipherable level, and Mrs. Giuseppe ran around, shouting instructions in Italian to the ancient waiters.

"I don't know what a nice girl like you is doing in Somalia," Grimley said under his breath. "It gets very dark here at night. Just a few months ago, the World Bank's rep was murdered in his home. I hope your company has prepared you for this."

Susan gazed at him, a number of thoughts crisscrossing her mind. "Oh yes, I know about it," she said.

Chapter 3

Susan tied her hair back and selected a somber gray suit befitting a Wall Street banker. It was probably overkill, considering the intensity of the tropical sun, but she'd rather err on the conservative side her first day. Fortunately, the walk would be short. According to Mrs. Giuseppe, the World Bank office was just around the corner, in a commercial building called the Savoy. Next to it was the ten-storied Ministry of Finance, a skyscraper by Somali standards, and she'd have to be blind to miss it.

At seven thirty in the morning, Susan marched out of the Eden, bouncing a satchel strapped on her shoulder. Across the street, a Catholic cathedral stood alone on the block, a world unto its own. She was just about to walk over for a closer look when a poster was thrust under her nose. A small grimy face stared up at her, mouthing incomprehensible words. She shook her head to say she didn't want any, whatever he was selling. But he persisted in shoving the crude painting of a beach and palm trees in her face. Instinctively she clutched her satchel and touched sticky, warm skin. A small hand was dipping into her bag. She grabbed at the spindly arm, but a snag at her elbow threw her off. A mob of children swarmed from behind, climbing over her back and swinging on her arms as if she was a human tree. Then as suddenly as they'd appeared, they jumped off and scattered in a gust of wind.

Susan looked into her satchel and discovered that her wallet was gone. She gave chase. She had no idea which one of the urchins had taken her wallet, but at this point she was ready to seize any one of them and wring his neck. Homing in on the smallest, she collared him and twisted his matchstick arm behind his back until he shrieked in pain. One jerk from her and it would break.

The patter stopped. The pack turned around, their waggling tails coming down faster than dogs' at the sound of thunder. They glanced sheepishly at a boy, the largest and meanest of the lot. His head held high and haughty, he swaggered up and reluctantly handed over the wallet. Susan observed a scar under his eye and a good padding of baby fat under the nasty façade.

Susan released her captive, but not before her wallet had been safely tucked into the bottom of her bag.

"Next time you do this, I'll get the police to lock you up," she railed at the miserable bunch. They probably couldn't understand a word of what she said, but the message was in the sternness of her tone.

Her eyes landed on her captive, who was rubbing the arm she'd wrenched. He was just a tot, about the size of a pre-schooler although his coordination indicated he must be a few years older. Susan felt a tug of remorse. Picking on a child wasn't her style, even if he'd asked for it.

"We are hungry, give us money," the pack leader said, his body suddenly going limp to demonstrate his plight. His companions echoed him in a chorus of "baksheesh, baksheesh."

"You look pretty well-fed to me," Susan said, mostly to herself and was surprised to hear the boy say, "I no eat ten days." She'd thought his English proficiency wouldn't extend beyond the well-rehearsed line.

"You mean you haven't eaten for ten days and yet you have the energy to snatch my purse and run off like a wild dog?" Susan taunted.

"Five days," the boy corrected himself, spreading the entire set of digits on his hand.

"Where did you learn to speak English?" Susan said, now that she was sure that he understood her.

"From you, from him, from her," he said, throwing up his arms at the silliness of the question. "Welcome to the Eden! Do you want a taxi? It's a lovely day. *Bon giorno, Io parlo italiano. Sta bene, signorina.*" The boy rattled off a string of phrases that sounded right out of Mrs. Giuseppe's mouth.

Susan was duly impressed. She could never learn a language without the whole gamut of textbook, teacher, and language lab. This child, who had probably never seen the

16

inside of a classroom, had absorbed the rudiments of two languages by pure osmosis.

"What's your name?" she said to the self-made linguist.

"Jamil," he said.

Susan fished out her wallet, keeping one eye on the gang as she pulled out several crumbling notes. "All right, Jamil. I'm going to forgive you today, but if you dare try any tricks on me again, I'll make sure that you'll be very sorry." Flinging her arm out to keep a safe distance from the mob, she forked out the money. "Here. Share this with your friends."

The boy's face broke into a grin, his scar deepening into an impudent dimple.

Susan reached the Savoy without further incident. She climbed the stairs to the fourth floor, where a gold-plated sign bearing the global World Bank logo flashed at her from the end of the veranda.

She took a deep breath and plunged in. "Hello, I'm Susan Chen," she said to the Somali woman at the desk.

The woman stood up slowly, arranging the resplendent wraps around her head and shoulders with serene dignity, and extended a long, slender hand.

"You must be Fatima," Susan said. Her secretary's personnel file came to life: thirty-eight-year-old mother of six, a graduate of the University of Somalia, one of the founders of the Bank's resident office, who'd seen a succession of res reps come and go. She had all the typical features of the Somali race: a high, ovoid forehead, straight proud nose, and slightly pouting lips that bespoke both humor and defiance.

Fatima showed Susan to her office. The room looked lived in, as if somebody had just stepped out and was coming back any minute to finish clearing his in-tray. Pieces of paper were scattered on the desk, a report was opened to a page, and a drawer was halfway out, revealing its contents of paper clips and yellow Post-it note pads.

"Everything is the way Mr. Barnett left it," Fatima said, her almond-shaped eyes glistening. Susan was dying to know whether they were really tears or just the sun bouncing off her dark pupils.

"Did the police come in here?" Susan said.

"No, I won't let them," Fatima said, her calm voice suddenly severe. "They'll mess everything up."

"Nobody's been here since?"

"Mr. Klaus was here. He's the chief of security for the U.N. I let him because it's his job to investigate."

"Did he take anything away?"

"I don't think so. He would have asked my permission first," she said confidently.

They went on to inspect the rest of the premises, which consisted of a library, conference room, and a spare room for visitors from headquarters. At the end of the hallway, Susan spotted the back of a man in the corner office. He was hunched over a desk and despite the commotion of her tour, he refused to turn around to see what was going on.

Fatima called his name and said something rude sounding in Somali, as if she was clearing her throat and about to spit it out. The man heaved himself out of the chair. Fatima presented Omar, the research assistant, a delicate, narrow-shouldered Somali who refused to look his new boss in the eye. Then Susan realized that he couldn't, for one of his pupils was encased in a milky-white film and edged so far outward that part of it had disappeared into his skull. In the mirror of his deformity, it was hard to tell the object of his gaze. He was staring at Fatima while answering Susan, and if that wasn't enough to disarm his new manager, he buried his words deep down in his throat. After saying "I beg your pardon" several times, Susan decided to postpone his debriefing to a later date.

As they passed the telex machine in the reception area, Susan noticed a long tongue of paper hanging out and almost touching the floor. "Don't tell me the telexes are coming in already," Susan said.

"Yes, I was going to put them in your tray. There are some urgent ones. The government has defaulted on its quarterly payment to the bank again, and Mr. Davar has set a deadline for repayment. He wants you to act on it *as soon as possible*—"

"Please don't bring them into my office yet," Susan interrupted. "I've got to clean up that desk first."

Fatima nodded, but Susan could see disagreement cloud her face. It was good to have a competent secretary who knew the priorities of the institution she worked for, and Fatima seemed to understand how seriously the bank viewed a default on its loan. However, Susan considered herself an employee of a different institution. Mr. Davar, her supervisor at the bank's headquarters, would have to wait.

Susan went into Barnett's office, now hers, lowered herself into the swivel chair behind the oak credenza, and immersed herself in the last days of the dead man. The correspondence was a month old, mostly requests from Davar for this, that or the other. Persis Davar, the Pakistani director of the East Africa Department, was widely known as the "ASAP Man," and she could see how he'd earned the reputation. She collected all his requests, which always ended with ASAP, and filed them in the wastepaper basket.

The desk calendar showed that Andrew Barnett had rendezvoused with "AH" three times the week of his death, held half a dozen meetings with ministers of all sorts, and posted a reminder to himself: "Check on Eastern Horizon." Susan couldn't remember coming across such a title throughout her perusal of the archives. After tucking it in the back of her mind, she noted the scheduled appointments that Andrew never had the chance to keep and went on to the hanging files in his drawer.

As she sat in his chair sifting through the remnants of his life, Susan was beginning to form an impression of the man. Andrew Barnett was discreet. The inundation of papers bore no trace of his personal troubles. He was a man steeped in the throes of a nasty divorce, yet the only hint was a note to himself to "send papers to lawyer." Andrew Barnett was also organized in a messy way. He'd be the type of person who could fish out a piece of paper from the bottom of one of numerous piles on his desk and give you exactly what you needed. His files were sloppy, the corners spiking out here and there, but they were neatly tabbed and ultimately logical. There was one file for each project, and there were two full drawers of them.

Susan walked her fingers through the dossiers and stopped at the thickest one, labeled "Auction." It was the foreign exchange auction, where hard currencies were sold to Somali businessmen to enable them to import the goods they needed for their enterprises. The World Bank was a contributor as well as the administrator for this pool of money, which came as grants or very soft loans from a number of wealthy countries. The purpose was to coax the formerly socialist regime into decontrolling the currency trade, one of the prerequisites for a freewheeling market economy. There were two conditions: The bid winners were obliged to use the hard currency to import commodities that the country needed, excluding luxury goods and firearms, and secondly, the goods had to originate from the donor countries. In this way, the Somalis got the foreign exchange to finance their imports, and the donors got an outlet for their exports. It was a clever deal that everyone seemed happy with.

As Susan grappled with the heavy file, a corner of a folder that had slid to the bottom jabbed at her wrist. She straightened it and was surprised to see that it was empty. The tab read "Eastern Horizon."

She went out to Fatima, waving the empty file. "Do you know what Eastern Horizon is?"

Fatima turned ashen, but it happened so quickly that Susan couldn't be sure. "Omar may know about it. Let me get him," Fatima said, a little too eager to pass the buck.

Omar soon appeared, his fists clenched nervously. To put the man at ease, Susan invited him to a seat on the sofa. As she sat down opposite him, he muttered to the chair next to her, "I don't know. I was sick."

"Excuse me?" Susan glanced over her shoulder to see whom he was addressing. Then she remembered it was she. "Do you know what Eastern Horizon is—a project, a company, a restaurant or what?"

"It's a company," Omar mumbled.

"I see. Do you know what it does, and why Mr. Barnett was interested in it?"

"It won a bid at the auction."

Susan had sensitized her ears enough to pick up the fine sound waves. A mosquito could probably speak louder than Omar. "Ah yes, the foreign exchange auction. So what does this Eastern Horizon import?"

"Drugs."

"You mean, cocaine, opium, stuff like that?" Susan couldn't help teasing the gnome-like man.

"No—medicine." Omar stamped his foot with annoyance.

"Do you know why Andrew was interested in the company?"

"I don't know," he said, his walleye wandering farther afield.

Just at that moment, the door burst open and a human hurricane blew into the room.

"Hello, hello, how are you, and you?" A three-dimensionally large man whipped around, pumping one hand after another. "I am Juergen Klaus, U.N. chief of security," he said to Susan, "and you must be Miss Susan Chen. Welcome, welcome to sunny Mogadishu."

Juergen plopped into the seat Omar had vacated. A pair of imposing eyes peered out of the salt-and-pepper jungle sprouting all over his face, chin and head. Nestled among the overgrowth were cheeks that glowed like red-painted Easter eggs. His chest was apple-shaped, the kind believed to be prone to heart attacks.

"I'm in charge of your safety as long as you're in Somalia. All travels outside of Mogadishu have to be cleared by my office. Even within the city, it will be to your benefit to report your whereabouts through this CB radio." Juergen drew the black box clipped to his belt like a six-shooter. "You are to carry it with you at all times. Here, try it," he said, shoving it at Susan.

The command, delivered in a thundering Germanic voice, was compelling. Susan took the radio and pushed the "on" button. Amid the crackles, two male voices were engaged in a discussion about ordering duty-free beer from some embassy.

"Let me introduce you to my staff," Juergen said, snatching the radio back. "Jean-Paul, this is Juergen. I'm at the World Bank office. I want you to talk to the new res rep." He passed her the radio.

Pretending she'd never used a CB before, Susan's eyes rounded in a startled, "What do I do?"

Juergen leaned over and pressed the talk button on her behalf. "Say something," he urged.

"Hi, I'm Susan Chen," she said awkwardly. "I just got here yesterday, and I look forward to meeting you."

In the easygoing manner of a seasoned broadcaster, Jean-Paul welcomed her to Mogadishu.

"Good, good, very good," Juergen said when the drill was over. "If you don't have any more questions, Miss Chen, I have to get back to my other duties."

"As a matter of fact, I do. And please call me Susan."

"Ah, Suzanne," Juergen repeated the name in his own pronunciation. "Very nice. I have a granddaughter called Suzette. She's ten years old and living with her parents in Cologne."

For some reason, the men she worked with, especially those over fifty, had a habit of mentioning their daughters to her. It was their subconscious way of saying, "Good God, I'm working with somebody my daughter's age!" Being compared with a granddaughter was a demotion by one generation.

To make up for her handicap, she put on a tone as officious as the security chief's. "I'd like to have an update on the investigation into Andrew's murder," she said.

"There's nothing to update. As far as I'm concerned, the case is closed. I sent my final report to Washington yesterday."

"Did you send it through this office?" Susan said, engaging the man in her stern gaze. No matter how old or young she looked, whether she had the I.Q. of a genius or an idiot, she was the representative of the World Bank. All communications had to go through her.

His eyes swam away. "Well, no, I didn't think there was any one here—"

"Can you make sure I get a copy today?" she asked with authority.

"It will be on your desk before noon," the chief promised.

"What's the gist of the report?"

"The *gist*? Well, it's very simple. The police have concluded it was a bungled burglary. Lacking any evidence to the contrary, we have to accept its findings. Andrew was unlucky. He was in the wrong place at the wrong time. It's now up to the police to catch the murderer. The matter is out of my hands."

"But nothing was taken from the house, I heard."

"The burglar probably got scared and fled," Juergen shrugged.

"It's a rather sophisticated way for a burglar to kill, isn't it? There was hardly any blood, I heard."

Juergen's bushy brows dipped into a valley of concern. Susan was glad that he was beginning to take her seriously. She watched him puzzle over where she could have picked up that piece of information.

"You seem to know a lot about the subject," he said.

"Just bits and pieces floating around the bank's corridors. Did the police fingerprint the place?"

"Fingerprints? You're talking about the Somali police, not Scotland Yard or the FBI."

"Was he with anyone that night?" From the way Juergen fidgeted in his chair, Susan knew she'd touched on a delicate subject.

"He had dinner with a colleague from USAID. At a restaurant in Lido. They finished around nine and his colleague believed he went straight home."

"Somebody with the initials 'AH,' isn't it?"

"Amanda Harper. Yes, that was the person he was dining with." Juergen squinted at her and added, "How long did you say you've been here?"

23

Susan glanced at the clock on the desk and did a quick calculation. "Fifteen hours and...twenty-two minutes, to be exact," she said nonchalantly as she swiveled about in her chair. "Have you heard of a company called Eastern Horizon? Andrew was investigating it around the time of his death," she added boldly, as though she knew more than she did.

Juergen hacked a dry cough and cleared his throat several times. "I wouldn't call it an investigation. He was merely inquiring about it."

"Why was he doing that?"

Juergen wagged his head in exasperation. "Andrew was a good man, a very good man, but he didn't know his limits." He glanced up at her with the same accusation. "If somebody in Somalia is winning many times at the auction, you don't ask, how is it possible? The answer is obvious. He's related to somebody important. Andrew has been here three years, he should have known that."

"But he did ask, and he was murdered for it."

"Wait a minute, you're jumping into conclusion. As I wrote in my report, it was a bungled burglary. The government and our chief of mission have cleared the report before I sent it to the bank. If you would excuse me, I have to return to my other duties." He got up, a mountain of an offended man.

"Let's have lunch some time," Susan said as a peace offering. It wasn't good to antagonize a man who was in charge of her safety. "I'd like to find out more about the place."

"You know enough already," Juergen said sourly. At the door, he turned around and shook an enormous finger at her. "Remember, let my office know where you are."

Chapter 4

For a people as homogenous as the Somalis, the divisions were numerous. Despite their common ancestry, which could be traced back to a man named Samaal, despite their common belief in Islam, which had been brought to them by a group of Arabian Muslims centuries ago, despite their common language, history and culture, their differences were irreconcilable. The nation was split into six major clans, which were further splintered into twenty subclans. Although the government had outlawed clan-based customs, everyone knew that in crucial matters of life or death, success or failure, a person had to rely on members of his own lineage group.

Then there was another group—expatriate workers of foreign legations, aid agencies and private companies. Among them tribalism took the form of nationalities. The Italians, British, Germans, and Americans had their own clubs and channels for duty free goods; the Chinese lived in their cloistered compound, but if one were none of the above and the sole representative of a small country such as Korea, his stay in Somalia could be quite lonesome.

Chang Soo Park had always built his own community. Wherever his assignment was—the Philippines, Uganda, or Peru—he'd managed to assimilate with the natives. Although his wife and two sons had always stayed back in Seoul, loneliness had never been his problem. Somalia, however, had proven to be the greatest hardship post he'd ever taken. Three months in Mogadishu and he still hadn't found himself a woman. His body was rebelling against the deprivation. It woke him in the middle of the night, aching for relief; it made him shout at his local staff; it drove him to drinking more than he should. He never liked drinking alone, but in a Muslim country, the selection of partners was limited. Expats partied in cliques, but he always felt out of place with them. Despite his Queen's English, his doctoral degree from the London School of Economics, he was still an outsider among the Europeans. The soul mate he'd been looking for, in the shapely form of a woman, had eluded him. In all the other countries he'd worked in, women had fought over him. Rightly so, for a man who worked for a prestigious international consulting firm and earned ten times more than a minister was a juicy plum indeed. He had done right by his mistresses, leaving one a lump sum to finish college, sending monthly stipends to another for rearing his son, and helping a third to get out of her war-torn country.

But where were the women in Somalia? The secretaries in his bureau seemed to be selected for their sullenness. Ugly, indifferent and ill-mannered, they cared as little for him as he did for them. The ones he wanted were the gorgeous receptionists decorating the front of the minister's office, but a number of people had told him they were off-limits. He'd spotted some stunning young women on the street, their voluptuous bodies undulating under togas knotted on one shoulder but oh so deliciously bare on the other. There were many ways to wear a chador, and they were wearing theirs as loosely as possible. But picking anyone off the street could be dangerous. Blackmail and disease must be avoided at all costs, and he could congratulate himself for having stayed clear of both so far.

Had he known there was another evil to avoid in Somalia, he would have suppressed his appetite and waited till Christmas to fly out for his R and R. This evil was murder, not random but targeted at a small section of the population, a section to which Chang Soo belonged.

Chang Soo poured two shots of whiskey, downed it in several gulps, and rushed out of his apartment. He was late for a party, or rather, a function that he was obliged to show up for. His Somali assistant, Hasan, was hosting a dinner in his honor, and knowing how stolid a Muslim he was, the night promised to be a dry, sorry affair.

Chang Soo swept a glance across the living room. A few people had gathered in the humble apartment. They were his two British colleagues—English and Scottish to be precise—and Susan Chen, the World Bank's new rep. How on earth they picked her was something he would never understand. She looked awfully young, and as a total novice to Somali affairs, she would be well advised to keep her ignorance to herself. Snooping into the affairs of a company everyone knew not to question was the surest way of getting into trouble. Nonetheless, he had to be nice to her, for her organization was paying his salary.

After Chang Soo finished shaking hands with every one present, his host pulled him away, saying, "I'd like you to meet my wife."

Chang Soo's eyes rounded, the muscles behind his ears pulled back, and every fiber in his body went taut. Before him stood the most beautiful creature he'd ever set eyes on: star-bright eyes, a playful smile on her sensuous lips, and a nest of curlicues flaming out of a seductively draped chador. He quickly recovered to take the exquisite hand. To his pleasant surprise, she held his in a belly-warming squeeze, and in those frisky eyes, he could see his own reflection: a man in his prime, with a square, confident jaw, broad chest and shoulders grown out of success, and a lean, tight belly craving for opportunity.

Her name was Abdia. A-B-D-I-A, she spelled it out while he held on to her hand.

"What can I offer you to drink?" Abdia said when Chang Soo had finally let go.

"Iced tea will be lovely," he said in his most Cambridge accent, pointing to the tall glasses on the coffee table.

A chorus of laughter burst out. Chang Soo looked from one to another in puzzlement.

"It's a very special kind of tea," Hasan said with a wink, "called Black Label."

"By jolly, I didn't know you were that kind," Chang Soo said, viewing his assistant with a fresh eye. He'd never dreamed that this chubby, plain-looking Somali could be imbibing alcohol and making love to the sexiest woman in Somalia.

At the dinner table, Chang Soo got the seat of honor at the middle of the long table, next to the hostess. The seating was rather tight, for the table was small for the six of them. Several times her hand brushed his lap. He wasn't sure whether it was accidental until he learned where she'd been, and then he knew it wasn't. Having spent six years on the Swiss Alps studying the hotel business, she must be bored to tears to be kept at home by a husband picked by her parents. From the way her supple body leaned toward him when he told a story, he could tell she was as hungry as he was.

Throughout the evening, Chang Soo told story after story of his travels, punctuated with the repertoire of crude jokes he'd collected from far and wide. Everyone laughed but the one who laughed the loudest was his hostess, who found them so funny that she elbowed him in the ribs, bumped her shoulder against his and slapped his hand. His host kept on replenishing his "tea," until finally, his merriment spilled over and he burst out in a song, "The Impossible Dream."

The next morning, he woke up with a vague memory of driving round and round the city and tumbling into bed. But the farther back he probed, the more his memory clarified. There was meaning in the woman's eyes, the scent emanating from her body, the haphazard, seemingly innocent touches. The ritual of courtship was no stranger to him. She was engaged in the first stage of it, and if he were right, they'd meet again within the next few days. But for now, he was glad he didn't have to see anyone that day. It was Friday, the Islamic day of rest, and rest was what he needed. He rolled over on his side and pulled the sheet over his aching head.

Already at seven in the morning, the siege at the Ministry of Finance was well underway. A throng crowded around the narrow entrance to the compound. Some were waving papers at the guards, but most were just trying to inveigle their way with pleas and bribes. Contempt was written all over the soldiers' faces as they pushed away the slips of paper that were being shoved under their noses. Occasionally, they would condescend to tip the net and allow one or two to swim through.

Chang Soo thrust his briefcase forward and wedged through the masses. The guards moved aside for him, closing the hole as soon as he'd passed.

Inside the building, more people milled along the corridor. Chang Soo could never understand what they were doing there. The talk about Somalia becoming a high-growth economy such as South Korea was farcical. The comparison was ridiculous, but ever since Somalia embraced market reforms, its western sponsors had been flagging it as a showcase of the superiority of capitalism. Being an econometrician, Chang Soo's job was to capture the Somali success with statistics. He knew which way his masters wanted the numbers to trend. It was a tightrope that he had to walk, and if he weren't careful, he might end up losing either his job or his professional credibility, or both.

He stepped into the common room where members of his team were already at their desks. Hasan greeted him with a twinkle in his eyes and asked about his health. Chang Soo thanked his assistant for the dinner, and began wondering what foolish acts he'd committed that night. But so what? A man was allowed to express his emotions. If he felt happy, he had the right to howl at the top of his lungs. If he were attracted to a beautiful woman, he had the right to drown himself in a deluge of desires. What was a man without passions? He might as well be dead. With that, he strode righteously into his office.

Around midmorning, a tap on his door interrupted him. Hasan entered, but instead of closing the door behind him, he kept it ajar. Then Chang Soo recognized her scent. Trailing behind was Abdia, intriguingly draped in a saffron chador bordered by black tinsel.

"My wife wanted to see if you have recovered," Hasan said. "She came to bring me my lunch," he added, his round cheeks twitching with pride.

Chang Soo stood up, his heart pounding like an infatuated schoolboy's. Aloud, he mouthed something about being good to see her again. Abdia returned the greeting with a demureness that was absent when she was in her own home. Chang Soo had never seen her concerned about her husband's sustenance before. Why the sudden wifely devotion?

"Thank you very much for the lovely dinner the other night," he said in a chesty bass, wishing his assistant would vanish. But Hasan didn't, and the three were forced to sit together chatting about the drought. Actually, only the two men were talking, for Abdia's participation was limited to an agreeable nod or a docile smile. When the visitors got up to leave, Chang Soo was torn between relief that the charade was over and a longing for her to stay.

After they were gone, Chang Soo pondered the meaning of her visit. Suddenly it occurred to him that he was right. What did he predict during the lucidity of his hangover—that they would meet again within the next few days? Little did he dream that she would come to him. Yes, she'd come to him. Chang Soo got up and paced the floor. His masculinity was crying for action. His head spun with excitement. He told himself to calm down. After all, this wasn't the first time he was establishing a liaison. But there was something special about this one—she was a married woman. The affair would have to be the world's best-kept secret. The thought excited him even more.

A while later, he opened his door and called to Hasan to step into his office.

"I have just finished perusing the surveys from Merca," he said, pointing his granny glasses at the stack of computer printouts. "There appear to be numerous inconsistencies in the data. Correct me if I'm wrong—it seems to me the surveys have been conducted by the local staff." As soon as Hasan delivered the expected reply, Chang Soo went on, "Please don't repeat what I'm going to say, but I truly, honestly do not have an iota of faith in these numbers. Somebody should go down and check them out. Frankly speaking," he lowered his voice in confidence, "the only person who can carry out this assignment, the only person I can trust, is you."

Hasan was too flustered for words, but Park had enough for both of them.

30

"I'd like you to make the trip as soon as possible, since we can't input the data until they've been verified. You have any objections to tomorrow?"

Hasan's brows jumped. Chang Soo squashed his excuse before he could use it: "Don't worry about the public expenditure report. I can give that to somebody else. Unless you have some personal engagement you have to attend to."

"No, no, I'm free to travel—"

"Since you'll be in the vicinity, why don't you visit Brava, too." Taking advantage of Hasan's stunned silence, Chang Soo added, "Don't forget to put in a request for your per diem," by way of reminding Hasan of his excellent terms of employment. Aside from receiving a monthly bonus many times his civil service salary, the assistant also received generous advances to cover his travel expenses. The message wasn't lost, for Hasan promptly thanked him and left to make the arrangements.

When the doorbell rang, Chang Soo knew exactly who it was. But in the eyes of the beholder, he couldn't have been more surprised if Marilyn Monroe had appeared at his doorstep.

"Abdia, what a pleasant surprise! Come in, come in."

She crossed the threshold and remained there, preventing the door from closing. "Am I early?" she said in her husky voice.

For the subterfuge to work, the next few steps were vital. "Not at all, you're welcome to my home any time," he said, gently guiding her out of the door's way. He put a hand on her shiny elbow and ushered her to the living room.

"Where's everybody?" she asked, refusing to sit down on the love seat.

"Who's everybody?" Chang Soo countered with a smile of good-humored bafflement.

"You invited me to a dinner party tonight," she said.

"It's *tomorrow* night."

"How can it be? Your invitation says Monday. That's tonight," she said, flustered. Her hand plunged into her purse and reappeared clutching a card. "Monday, yes. I was right, it says Monday."

Chang Soo bent over her shoulder to read his own handwriting. Apple green was her color tonight, and it brought out the earthy fertility of her complexion. "Goodness gracious, you're right. It does say Monday. It's my secretary's fault, oh, I'm so sorry. This is inexcusable. Wait till I see her. I am so terribly sorry," he said, slapping his head in distress.

"We all make mistakes. Please don't be too harsh on her." In her earnestness, she placed a hand on his forearm.

"Oh, you're too nice," he said gazing at her with admiration. "But now that you're here, you can't leave without giving me a chance to show my hospitality." His words shooting in rapid fire to stop her from protesting, he insisted that she stay for a simple fare that his houseboy had left him. Her protest did come, but it was mild and contradictory. For even as she was saying she couldn't dream of intruding on him, her curvaceous derriere was on its way down, toward the damask upholstery of the love seat. Persuading her to drink "tea" with him required greater skill. After alternately assuring her that he was old enough to be her father and gibing her to behave like the liberated woman she should be, she finally agreed to try a thimble full. When the drinks were laid out on the coffee table, she took hers down so smoothly that Chang Soo knew she'd need a few more to succumb. He poured her a double while she played with the corners of her chador. They talked about their parents, their childhood, their dreams, the earth, the sea, the heavens, and the planet Venus hanging outside the window. Dinner was accompanied by a full-bodied Merlot, which she guzzled like grape juice. When he lifted her out of her chair, her lamb chop half eaten, her body was as pliant as a sea anemone opening and closing its skirt to catch the organisms flowing its way.

Chapter 5

The taxi drove off, its taillights receding into two red pinheads. Its passenger was left standing in the dark. Susan's eyes adjusted to the iron gate, which appeared as a rack of spear shadows pointing toward a waxing half-moon. She gripped the cool iron rails and pushed. The metal clinked against the chain that held it. She sprang up from a horizontal bar, climbed over the spikes at the top and jumped off, landing with a barely audible thud. Her figure cut a black stencil in the gray surroundings as it moved soundlessly along the pool of shimmering water.

The door to the clubhouse was locked. The digital on her wrist flashed 9:02. Either her watch was fast or he was late. Either way, she was going in. She took the lock-pick knife from her satchel and pried into the hole. The lock was a European lever lock, an antique that had been long off the production line, and she could see why. Its innards were as simple as a block puzzle designed for children under the age of five. She selected the "skeleton" from her knife and inserted it. The tip probed the parts and hooked on to the lever. A satisfactory *click* reached her ears.

She walked into a night darker than the one outside. A hard object poked at her back.

"Don't move, or I'll shoot," a deep, throaty voice said.

The door closed, blocking out the last ray of moonlight. He must be as blind as she, she thought, and in a continuum of movement as effortless as the turning of a wheel, she lurched aside and dropped to one knee, her other leg kicking back to deliver a rude heel to her assailant's shin. Muffled shots pelted the room. Susan flattened herself behind a piece of furniture. In the blindfold of darkness, she could feel her body metamorphosing into one gigantic ear. He was shuffling farther and farther away, toward the door—the light switch. She crept with the footsteps, stopping with them, smelling the faint waft of dirt from his shoes, a picture of the next scene burning with severe clarity in the window of her third eye. In the same instant as the flip of the switch, the spark of electricity, her feet swept out in a smooth circle under his and slammed him backward on the ground. She threw herself on the sprawling figure and dug into his windpipe.

"Ugh, ugh," the man choked, apparently trying to speak. His face was as red and wrinkled as a sundried tomato.

Susan eased her grip.

The man squeezed out the words, "Nich-las Wade."

"Where are you from?" Susan loosened her fingers further. His Adam's apple vibrated as he blurted, "Twenty-seven miles south of Kabul."

Susan let go and stood up. Her assailant curled up on the floor in a fit of coughing. He pulled himself up after a while, tears streaking down the corners of his eyes. He was a stringy man with sharp features that might have passed for handsome once. Right now, however, he looked like a strip of meat that had been hung out for too long under the sun. His skin looked tough as beef jerky and his lips were parched and warped to a permanent leer.

With one hand massaging his bruised neck, he fell into a chair. "You didn't have to be so rough," he complained while smoothing back his sparse gray hair.

"You were the one who shot at me."

"They were only blanks."

"What did you do that for?"

"To see what metal you're made of. They've told me a few things about you, but they never told me you were that ferocious. Sit down and relax, we've got some acquainting to do."

Alex told me a few things about you, too, Susan thought. To outsiders, you're the manager of the American-run International Club, but to us, you're a specialist on the horn of Africa and the CIA's one and only station officer for Mogadishu. As one of the few people in the world who could speak Somali like a native, you were the best man for the job until you started taking it too personally. Since you fell in love with a local agent and fathered a child with her, your judgment had been clouded by your sympathy for her clan. She was an Isaaq, whose family had been wiped out by Siad Barré's bombs during the decimation of Hargeisa. You'd been told to cut off the relationship. You agreed, but your polygraph showed otherwise. Alex had been thinking of recalling you, but the swift deterioration of the country had saved your ass. Changing horses where the current was most rapid was unwise.

"I heard you're some kind of kung fu kid —"

"It's called *tai chi*," Susan said.

"Isn't that like aerobics for older folks? I didn't know you could fight with it."

The more Susan looked at him, the more she found his leer off-putting. "Would you like me to demonstrate some more?" she taunted.

"We'll save it for another time," Nick said. "I also heard this is your first assignment. You got in the Agency as a translator, and then somebody in Operations 'discovered' you"—his fingers scratched quotation marks in the air—"and transferred you over."

The way he slurred the word "translator" brought out his obvious prejudice against that class of humanity. "You got any problems with that?" Susan said.

"Who, me?" Nick pointed at himself as if she could have been addressing anyone else. "Who am I to pick on whoever Langley sends me? You guys are so smart, you can walk out of training camp one day, parachute into a country you've never heard of before, do your thing and make everything right again. If you mess up, you're not to blame. It's because the bozo at the station misled you. In any case, you're on the next flight out. What do you care about consequences?"

Susan had expected an ineffectual station officer, but not a hostile one. "Listen, you don't have to like me, just as I don't have to like you. But personal feelings aside, we have a job to do together, and I am all you've got."

"Don't get me wrong. It's nothing personal. I never said I didn't like you. I just wish the pompous asses at Langley understand how much is at stake here. We've supported Siad

Barré, given him arms, food and money to keep him away from the Soviet camp. We've given him the means to slaughter his own people, and now they've had enough of him. We can't just walk away and let them clean up the mess themselves. If we don't help them through this transition, there will be massive bloodshed."

That's why I'm here, Susan wanted to say, but remembered that *she* was precisely the problem. He wished they'd sent somebody else.

"Believe it or not," Nick went on, "Somalia's a good place to live, and there are many people who wouldn't want to live anywhere else in the world—"

"Such as yourself and your family," Susan said, sprinkling salt on the open sore.

Nick gave a mirthless laugh. "Apparently they've told you a few things about me too. They'll hold it against me forever. I know what you're thinking—" Nick wagged his finger at her. "You think you'll never make a stupid mistake like that. You'll find out, your heart isn't something you can control all the time. You'll see."

"I will take it under advisement. Can we go on with our briefing?"

Nick waved a go-ahead and slumped back in his chair, his white shirt crumpling like a windless sail.

"Andrew Barnett was investigating a company called Eastern Horizon when he died. What do you know about it?" Susan said.

"It cropped up from nowhere about two years ago. The registered owner is a Hawiye, a nobody in the clan hierarchy. He's just a front, of course, and the identity of the real owner remains a mystery. The company's loaded, that's for sure. It's won every bid it has submitted at the auction. It's supposed to use the foreign exchange to import medicines, but nobody's seen any of them on the market. Given the civil-war climate of the place, it's most likely a gunrunning operation. The owner is suspected to be a Hawiye, but if the elders know, they're being tightlipped about it."

The man's hopeless, Susan thought. He'd embedded himself in the wrong clan, the rebellious Isaaq from the British north who had never accepted the rule of southerners in Mogadishu. What a mistake. He'd cut off any possible connection with the inner circle.

"You have any other leads on this?" Susan said.

Nick shrugged, which Susan interpreted to be a face-saving way of admitting incompetence. "You can see what charm you can pull on the Hawiye leadership," he said, "although I have to warn you that some of them won't even shake hands with a woman. The best suggestion I can make, however, is this. Andrew was killed while he was investigating Eastern Horizon. Somebody didn't want him nosing into its business. If you pick up where Andrew left off, that somebody might want to go after you, too. He may think he's hunting you down, but it's actually the other way around. You've dressed yourself up as a juicy piece of bait, the tiger walks into the trap and the door crashes down. Question is, when you're trapped in the cage with the animal, can you take him on?" His lips crinkled in a rakish leer.

"I took *you* on, didn't I?"

A chortle escaped from his throat, which Susan found most annoying. "You sure did," Nick said.

He bent down and picked up from the floor the handgun that Susan had knocked out of his hand. It was a Glock subcompact, a 9 mm, snub-nosed pepper pot that one could stuff in a purse or pocket. He unscrewed the silencer, placed the toy-size firearm on his palm and offered it to Susan. "No matter how brilliant you are, it doesn't hurt to have this around. I've got some more goodies for you."

Nick unlocked a cabinet and took out a brown leather briefcase. He opened it, peeled off a strip along the edge and unscrewed a pair of nuts that held together the secret compartment. The paraphernalia was exhibited one by one: an escape and evasion kit, wristwatch camera, key-impressioning kit, a flaps and seals tool roll, and last but not least, a blue fountain pen.

"You know how to use this?" Nick said, holding up the pen.

Susan took it, slid the pocket clip aside and tapped on the little detent ball. "You press this and tear gas shoots out."

"That's right, and one shot is all you'll get. Keep it handy all the time. This baby may save your life. Remember, you're dealing with a seasoned assassin, trained by people at the top of the profession. This man has refined killing to an art, and his style is so distinct you needn't check the signature at the bottom of the painting. He could've gotten rid of Barnett with a pump of the trigger, but no, he preferred to do it manually. He wanted us to know that this was the work of Hamid, the man who can kill without a sound."

Susan returned his steady, unwavering gaze. If intimidation was his purpose, he wasn't going to have the pleasure. "How do we make contact in the future?" she said.

"Tennis lessons, once a week or any time you want. I'll give you a good discount, plus a guarantee that you'll learn to play a mean game within a month."

From her hotel window, Susan watched the red embers of dawn smoldering away at the fringes of night. The image of Nick was fresh in her mind, having haunted her dreams with his insults and cynical chortles. Sitting cross-legged on the floor, she closed her eyes and tried to concentrate on restoring her equilibrium. With hands resting on her thighs and palms facing the heavens, she let in the *ch'i*, the breath, the eternal power that moved the universe, a little at a time until her body expanded to a balloon about to float away. Her abdomen contracted and the *ch'i* gushed in all directions, radiating a stream of warmth through the tips of her extremities back into the universe. Her senses flowed to every corner, magnifying the presence of every element in and around her. Her eyes were closed yet she could see through a third eye that burned in the middle of her forehead, a penetrating vision of the essence of her being, one with everything around her.

To Susan, feeling the *ch'i* was as natural as breathing. Her father, a martial-arts instructor who had emigrated from Taiwan to New York, had trained her since she'd been a toddler. As a child, her self-control had scared other kids away. Her world revolved around her father's martial arts school and the tournaments and meets from which she would bring home still more trophies and medals to clutter a corner of the living room. She had no playmates her own age until ninth grade, when she discovered how she could use her fearful skills to make friends. She tried out for the cheerleading team and with her coordination and agility, the coaches welcomed her with open arms. Her popularity soared, and in her senior year the class voted her the friendliest girl.

She'd dabbled at karate and *tae kwan do*, but *tai chi*, known as a "soft school," was what suited her. It was most in tune with the philosophies of harmony and compassion that her upbringing had been steeped in. Her mother was a devout Buddhist and a vegetarian who would get rid of flies by trapping them in a jar and sending them out the window. Although Susan was a carnivore and had no qualms about swatting a bothersome bug, she was still her mother's daughter.

Tai chi was a passive-aggressive technique that involved neutralizing one's opponent with his own force. If a person were to throw a punch at Susan, she would grab his arm and pull him in the direction he wanted to go. The more vicious the offensive, the more energy there was to exploit. She'd tossed around a man twice her size like a pizza, and all she'd done was borrow the assailant's own momentum to launch him into orbit.

Susan released a long stream of air. When she opened her eyes, the world was a different color. The sun was a quick riser at the equator. At seven in the morning, it was already white-hot. Gone was the pall Nick had thrown over her, the self-doubts and the fear of going it alone, for that was what it amounted to. Nick wouldn't be of much help, but she could do it with or without him, and she was prepared to give it everything she was worth. Nick would see what "metal" she was made of.

Her first meeting of the day was with the finance minister, the bank's chief liaison in the Somali government. From what she'd gathered, he was a man loved by the international aid community. Cooperative, accessible, and understanding were the most common adjectives used to describe him. But as always, after the initial compliments, the snickers would sneak in, and she would learn that he was the richest man in the country, with bank accounts and villas all over the world. His ten-percent cut into donor funds was known by one and all, and the practice was seen as the grease that kept the wheels of progress turning and thus a necessary evil for the country's development.

With Omar ahead as her trailblazer, Susan waded through the crowd into the ministry compound.

"What are all these people doing here?" Susan asked her assistant.

"They want favors," Omar muttered.

"Favors from the minister?" Susan said.

"Sometimes."

"You mean sometimes from the minister and sometimes from other officials?"

Omar grunted a reply, which Susan interpreted as a yes. She didn't know what to make of her walleyed assistant. He was a good worker, a tremendous help in answering the flurry of telexes from Davar, but in his communications with her, Omar hadn't strung together more than three words. Every time Susan talked to him, she could feel him shrinking into himself, threatening to shrivel and vanish if she didn't let him off the hook soon.

Omar took her past a dilapidated box that was once an elevator and proceeded up the staircase. Susan had always thought she was quite fit, but as she set foot on the tenth floor, her lungs were whistling like a house full of cracks on a windy day. Omar, on the other hand, frail as he seemed, was intact as a rock.

They stepped into the antechamber to the minister's office. A ravishing Somali beauty sat at the desk. A number of men hovered around, joshing and batting flirtatious glances at her as she sat sideways, her legs crossed and eyes averted from them.

40

Susan announced herself. The secretary slowly lifted her pretty head, and with the languor of a cat forced to budge from a sunny spot, she stretched to the full length of her fashion model's figure and tripped away, flashing a pair of finely sculpted ankles under the long skirt. Moments later, she returned, uttering a surly command to the visitors to follow her.

Susan and Omar entered a rambling room. The secretary waved them to a seat in a corner. At the far end, four men sat around a desk, engaged in what seemed like collective meditation. After a while, a piece of paper was passed from hand to hand. Finally, the man behind the desk penned something on it. The other three got up and filed out in solemn procession.

Now the minister was moving toward Susan. Mohammed Mahdi Suleiman, one of the most powerful men in Somalia, stepped out of the shadows. A pair of gopher's teeth peeked out of a diffident smile, and a hand extended from the crumpled blue suit. Susan gripped it and abruptly let go at the unpleasantness of the touch. The minister's hand was soft and wet like overcooked spaghetti. As she turned around to take an indicated seat, Susan quickly wiped her palm on her skirt.

In a creamy voice, Suleiman opened the meeting with a eulogy for Susan's predecessor, praising him for his flexibility and understanding of the difficulties that his country faced. The underlying meaning, that Susan should be just as flexible, didn't escape her. But there was one matter where the rules were as stalwart as the door to a bank safe, which Susan could lose her job over if she didn't tackle it ASAP.

"Your Excellency, there's an urgent matter I'd like to draw your attention to. Your government's repayment on the bank's loans has reached the ninety-day overdue period. My director, Mr. Davar, has set a deadline for the end of the week."

The minister beamed a toothy smile. "We have just completed negotiations for a bridge loan from the Italian government. Please be assured that Mr. Davar's deadline will be met."

Susan recalled reading about the "bridge loans," which weren't for building bridges but for helping the government meet its debt obligations. When Somalia turned capitalist, it became the darling of the West. Lenders of all sorts came offering money, and like a kid given his first credit card, Somalia went on a spending spree. It became so mired in debt that it now had to resort to a game of credit roulette, borrowing from one to repay another.

The minister went on to talk about the government's austerity program. Although he understood the necessity of sacrifice, it pained him to think of the women and children suffering from the cutbacks in food subsidies. He outlined the steps he'd taken to avoid future defaults on loan payments, and in the same breath noted that success or failure depended on the donors' willingness to release more funds. The auction money was running out. When was the bank going to release the next tranche?

Drawing on her short apprenticeship at the bank's headquarters, Susan rattled off the shortfalls in Somalia's economic performance indicators, lectured the minister on the virtues of sound fiscal management, and in the style of a typical bureaucrat, passed the buck.

"The bank will be sending a team here to review the program," she said. "Based on their findings, our management will decide on the release of the next tranche."

"Ah yes, but the team only comes here for a few weeks. You live here. You know the situation better than anyone," Suleiman said.

Susan laughed in spite of herself. "This is only my second day here. I can hardly claim to be an expert." As the words left her mouth, she knew she had made what diplomats would call a *faux pas*. She observed the minister observing her, amusement in his eyes and an impression jelling: young, inexperienced, a pushover.

"But your assistant here is the best economist in the country," Suleiman said, reaching over to hold Omar's hand. "He can tell you everything there is to know about Somalia. I wish he would work for me, but I can't pay him as much as you do."

Omar squirmed in his seat, his lips moving in a soundless mutter.

"If you ever need anything, please do not hesitate to call on me. My door is always open to you," the minister said with a gallant bow.

"There *is* something you can help me with, Mr. Minister," Susan said. "Have you heard of a company called Eastern Horizon?"

A loud squeak sounded from Omar's chair. Everyone turned to see what he had to say, but he only looked down at his notebook and pretended to be elsewhere.

The minister's vision projected toward a faraway object, then zoomed back abruptly with a blink. "Eastern Horizon. Oh yes, Andrew asked me about it, a long time ago. I think I asked my assistant to get him the information. Let me send for him." He got up and called for his secretary.

A little later a thin, almost emaciated man slipped through the door. He approached with one arm folded back respectfully, but as he came closer, Susan realized there was nothing more behind the back. His arm ended just above the elbow in a smooth, rounded stub. An exchange in the harsh, guttural native language ensued. Susan was rather surprised that an underling would use such rude tones with a minister, but when the shouting ended with no apparent ill feeling on either side, she began to suspect that there was no argument at all. The rough texture of the Somali tongue could turn a friendly chitchat into a shouting match.

The one-armed man handed a file to the minister, who browsed its contents and passed it on to Susan.

"All the information is here. Yusuf," he pointed to his aide, "had the dossier ready a long time ago, but when the tragedy happened, he didn't know whom to give this to. I am sorry if the delay caused you any inconvenience."

Susan opened the file. "All" the information was a name and an address written on a scrap of paper.

"I copied this from the company registrar in the commerce department," the man called Yusuf said, bending and bowing with solicitousness.

"I'm afraid our registrar is quite primitive," the minister said. "It was established only a year ago with German technical assistance. If the information is insufficient, please feel free to ask Yusuf to help you."

"Thanks, but do you know why Andrew wanted this information?" Susan said.

"I suppose for the same reason you want it," the minister said cheekily. "Omar, you should know. You were here that day Andrew asked for it."

For a second, Omar seemed on the verge of fleeing. His body launched forward, and if it weren't for his hands gripping the rim of his chair, his feet would have carried him out the door. "He wanted some medicine," he managed to mutter.

"Ah yes, this is a pharmaceutical company, isn't it?" Turning to Susan with a reassuring smile that everything was as it should be, he explained, "You see, in Somalia, medicines are hard to come by. You can't just go to the store, as you do in America, and get what you want. Our country hasn't developed to that stage yet. So when Andrew was in need of a certain medicine, he had to go directly to the importer. That was why he wanted the company's address. I hope this answers your question," he said.

"It's a start, but I'm sure there's more to it than that," she said, putting everyone on notice that she wasn't through yet.

As Susan emerged from the finance ministry, a U.N.-plated Land Rover pulled up in front of her. The bulge of the driver's paunch came into view. It was Juergen Klaus, come to escort her to her next appointment. She parted with Omar and climbed into the four-wheel-drive vehicle.

Juergen maneuvered it expertly through the congested street and reached an open stretch of road by the shore. He stepped on it, and the vehicle zoomed along the seamless sheet of royal blue welding together the Indian Ocean and the Somali sky. After a while, the Land Rover careened inland onto the city's main drag, Afgoy Road. Unimpeded by traffic lights or stop signs or competition other than the occasional bus or jalopy, Juergen floored the pedal in *grand-prix* style. Because nobody in Mogadishu ever put on a safety belt, Susan had refrained from strapping herself in for fear that the driver might interpret it as an insult. But as the pace pressed on, she decided her safety was more important. She dug out the safety belt from behind the seat and snapped in the buckle.

At the circle, Juergen finally lightened his foot. This was the town's midpoint, he explained to Susan, and was called K-4 for the fourth kilometer from the beginning of the city. The whole of Mogadishu was organized in this way: The corner of K-5 was the blind spot where many accidents occurred, K-6 was the mosque, K-7 the U.S. embassy compound, and everything else was in between. Remember these key points and you would never get lost, Juergen said.

Somewhere after K-7, Juergen turned into a residential street. As the vehicle jolted to a stop in front of a pair of gates, he announced to Susan that she'd arrived at her home.

A small, wrinkled Somali came out of the house. Abdullahi, the "houseboy" who had discovered Andrew's body, was much older than Susan had thought. A man in his fifties was hardly a "boy," and just as Susan was astonished at his age, he seemed astonished at hers. In spite of the staid outfits she'd been wearing, she couldn't be a farther cry from the male and middle-aged res rep that people were used to seeing. Everybody she'd met so far had responded with a bemused curling of the lips, a lift of the brows, or a scratching of the nose.

"Have they started the renovation yet?" Juergen asked the housekeeper.

Abdullahi, an Isaaq from the Anglicized north, spoke in fluent English, "Somebody came yesterday. He looked around, measured here and there, and left again."

"That's all?" Juergen's voice boomed with impatience. "At the rate they're going, Miss Chen will never be able to move in."

45

As they walked from the driveway to the house, Susan observed her new home. The grass on the front lawn was turning brown, but it showed signs of having been well manicured not too long ago. The house was a rambling structure, white walls against brown roof tiles, simply designed and all the more attractive for its unpretentious grace. Susan was glad it wasn't anything like the mansions she'd passed.

A gush of cool air greeted her as she stepped into the house. The air-conditioners were rattling at full blast. Like a prospective buyer, Susan toured the place, marveling at the spaciousness of the rooms, the elegance of the ceramic floor tiles, and the servant's suite behind the kitchen. Most importantly, the bathroom had a small water boiler that was fueled by a propane tank independent of the city's fitful services. The thought of hot water for her showers gave her skin a pleasant tingle.

"When can I move in?" she said.

"Not for a while. You can't live here until the renovation is finished. Come with me. I'll show you something." Juergen crooked a finger at her.

Susan followed him into one of the bedrooms, protesting all the way that the house was perfect as it was.

"This here is the guest room," Juergen said. "And this window was where the murderer entered. See how it was pried open?" Juergen pointed at the dent on the metal frame. "The landlord has agreed to install bars on all the windows and doors. You're not moving in until that's done," Juergen ordered.

The men were hard on her heels when Susan entered the master bedroom. Boxes and packing tapes were strewn around the floor. The queen-size bed had been stripped. Susan rounded the corner into the study, and the first thing that entered her vision was the leather chair. She could imagine Andrew sitting in it, reading a World Bank report and penciling remarks on the margin.

"If you don't think this is suitable, you should telex your headquarters immediately," Juergen said, seeing the ghost in her eyes. "Andrew has paid a year's rent in advance—don't be surprised. There are too many expat workers around, and the landlords know how to gouge. However, considering the circumstances, I'm sure some refund can be negotiated."

"The place is perfect," Susan said, but as her eyes landed on the leather chair again, she felt a chill at the base of her neck. "I'll have to rearrange the furniture. The desk, for example, should be turned around. There's more light this way." What she meant was she wouldn't want to be caught from behind as Andrew had been.

After Juergen had left, Susan and Abdullahi sat down in the living room to discuss housekeeping details. Lime sherbet was the color scheme of the upholstery in this room. There were several sets of the same furniture arranged in separate clusters, an appropriate seating for a large party that was expected to break into smaller, more intimate circles. Parties, parties, parties—they were an essential part of her duties. Already her calendar was filled with events every evening, and when she moved into her house, she must provide her share of entertainment.

Abdullahi sat ramrod straight in the chair opposite her, hands folded neatly on his lap. His eyes were moist and anxious. He seemed as uncomfortable with her as she was with him. Susan thought he'd be relieved to know that he didn't need to live in, but his reaction was quite the opposite.

"Oh no, you cannot sleep here by yourself, madam. It's too dangerous. I will sleep here every night, and on Friday, my wife and one of my sons will come here to stay with you."

"That's really not necessary. After the iron bars are put in, this place will be safer than a prison."

Abdullahi shook his head vehemently.

"You're supposed to be spending time with your family on your day off. But if they're here when you're home, how would you ever meet up?" Susan said.

"There are many in my family—twelve children and eight grandchildren. We will all take care of you," the housekeeper said.

Susan was inclined to turn down the generous offer, but the grip of the old, wrinkled face told her that the only way to change her housekeeper's mind was to fire him.

"Let's give it a try," she said cautiously.

"Don't worry, madam, I will keep you safe," Abdullahi said.

"Call me Susan."

"Yes, madam."

Giving up on this issue, Susan moved on, saying, "I heard you were the one who found Mr. Barnett. It must have been awful."

Abdullahi lowered his head. "It was my fault. If I had come back on time, Mr. Barnett would still be alive." He poured out the bits and pieces of the fateful day, from his awakening with a fear in his heart to his escape from a riot, the discovery of the body and the manhandling from the police. If it hadn't been for Juergen's intervention, the police would have given him the routine workout until he confessed. He was lucky to get away with the loss of something as minor as a tooth.

"Mr. Barnett was a very kind man. He did many good things for me and my family." A litany of the Englishman's good deeds followed. There it goes again, Susan thought. The more people sang praises of Andrew Barnett, the more she wanted to dislike him. Nobody could be that good, unless he was an insecure wimp who needed to be liked by everyone. Her ears shut themselves off, her lips muttering "mmm hmm" once in a while to put on a show of listening, and then something caught her ear—the word "medicine."

"He tried his best to get the medicine for my daughter Mariam, but it was too late." Abdullahi shook his head sadly.

"What did Mariam need the medicine for?" Susan said.

"It was like this. One Friday, when I went home, Mariam was lying in bed. I thought it was strange because Mariam was a hard working girl. On Fridays she would be studying, not lying in bed like other people. I touched her and her skin was burning. I took her to the hospital immediately. The doctor said she had typhoid and needed a special medicine to make her well. I said, 'How much? I'll pay for it." And he said, 'It's not how much.

48

We don't have it.' I said, 'Write it down, I'll think of a way to get it.' Then I took the paper to Mr. Barnett and asked him to help. He said, 'Don't worry, Abdullahi. I know a company that should have plenty of medicine. I'll talk to the owner right now.' But when he came back, his hands were empty. His face was red and he was very angry. I've never seen him angry before.

"He went to the phone and called the American doctor. She was very good, she went to the hospital right away, but..." Abdullahi heaved a great sigh, his eyes misting over. "It was too late. Mariam was in a deep sleep.... she never woke up. She was only eighteen."

"I'm so sorry," Susan said. After pausing to allow the servant to blink away a tear, she pursued gently, "The company that Mr. Barnett told you about, was it called Eastern Horizon?"

"I don't know," Abdullahi said. "Mr. Barnett was so angry I didn't dare ask him anything."

Susan imagined Andrew's frustration and for the first time, felt a surge of warmth for the man. He was no longer the insipid, indiscriminate nice guy but a man of flesh and blood, who could be provoked to passion by the loss of a young life. Was that what prompted him to open a private investigation into Eastern Horizon, to overstep the boundaries of the unwritten rules and ask indiscreet questions that led to his death? Susan imagined Andrew to be the kind who would withdraw into himself when he was angry. Too bad for her, for if he'd vented off more, her job would be much easier. However, one person would know, the person who knew the private side of Andrew Barnett.

The company's Mercedes Benz was waiting for her in the driveway. Mohammed held open the door to the back, but Susan walked past him and seated herself in the front. She'd never been a backseater, and if she had her way, she'd rather be driving herself.

"USAID," she told her driver.

49

The concrete wall was high, and made higher by a growth of glass shards on its coping. It stretched the length of the entire block, a solid barricade that yielded not a crack of a peek to the other side. The gates were a pair of metal plates sturdy enough to withstand a battering ram. In a potentially hostile environment, the U.S. government had gone to great length to protect its diplomatic corps.

From inside her limo, Susan could see the eye of the camera studying her. She waved her World Bank I.D. The heavy gates clanked open, and a rosy-cheeked marine peered into the car and waved it by. The vehicle wound around an anemic lawn, above which the Stars and Stripes hung like a leaf withering from drought, and cruised toward a low huddle of buildings. After climbing a flight of stairs, Susan found herself in a veranda outside a row of offices. The sound of American efficiency pervaded. Telephones rang, computer keyboards clicked away, and hard-soled shoes clacked from one workstation to another. There were no loafers or moochers here. Everyone who was here worked here, except for people such as Susan who wore a tag pinned to her chest that said, "Visitor."

Amanda Harper, the sign on the door read. Susan knocked; a faint voice invited her to enter.

The shades were drawn. The room was dim except for the shower of light over the desk. In the high noon of the tropics, the woman at the desk was relying on a lamp to read. Amanda Harper looked up, her face bathed in the soft glow of the lamp. It was the kind of face that Romance poets raved about: the flaxen hair, ivory skin, wide, generous lips, and mournful sea-green eyes glittering with golden flecks. Susan was surprised to see how young she was. Mid-twenties at most, which meant more than a dozen years younger than Andrew.

"Yes?" Amanda said, businesslike.

The moment Susan introduced herself, Amanda's iciness melted. She rose to greet Susan, saying she'd heard of Susan's arrival and had been looking forward to meeting her.

"I'm sorry to barge in on you like this," Susan said. "The telephones in this city don't seem to work very well. I figured for the time it takes to make a connection, I can hop in my car and get myself over here." Her excuse was unarguably true, but the real reason was that she preferred spontaneity to manufactured statements. The truth, or a glimpse of it, was more likely to emerge when a person hadn't had time to prepare for questioning.

"It's quite all right," Amanda said, folding her lily-white hands on the desk. "What can I do for you?"

"I'd like to ask you a few questions about Andrew's death."

The young woman stiffened. Susan sensed a defensiveness, which she could well understand. In the close-knit expat community, the heated Amanda-Andrew affair was popular grist for the gossip mill. The combination of being pretty and single made Amanda a threat to all the expat wives, who often left their husbands to tend to matters back home. They hated all the Amandas of the world, the young, unattached, independent women who would let nothing stand in the way of what they wanted—career, adventure, and romance.

"I thought the case was closed," she said coolly.

"The official report calls it a botched burglary, but there are too many loose ends for such a conclusion. A number of people in the bank have reviewed the report and found it unconvincing," Susan told a little white lie. "I don't feel it's right to drop the case. I was hoping you could shed some light," adding in a softer tone, "as you were the last one to see Andrew alive."

Amanda sank her teeth into her lower lip. Her eyelids fluttered, her professional-woman façade about to be dropped. Susan felt the deepest sympathy for her. Not only had this woman lost a lover, she was deprived of the right to grieve. The prerogative belonged to the woman who was still legally tied to Andrew.

Suddenly Amanda was composed again. She straightened her swan-like neck and gazed down at Susan. "I've gone through this with Juergen Klaus before. He should have a transcript of the interview in his files. I'm sure he'd be happy to show them to you."

51

"Amanda, I know this must be painful for you," Susan said quietly but firmly. "But Andrew deserves better than a sloppy investigation. The evidence I've seen points to the possibility that he was murdered because he was making inquiries into some shady deals. By finding out what happened, we may be closer to finding the killer."

Amanda sat back, away from the lamplight. Her hand wandered over to a pen, picked it up, and stood it on one end, then the other.

Slowly she sat forward, showing her clear, unblemished face. "We had dinner at the Blue Marlin that night," she began. "He wasn't feeling well." She hesitated a moment, then her lips pressed together as if steeling herself for an ordeal. Susan had a hunch that what she was about to say would be said for the first time. "He was actually very depressed that night. His wife had been using their daughter to play this guilt trip on him. You know he'd filed for divorce?"

Susan gave a deep nod that indicated that she'd heard about the strident marital strife that had spilled out of the home into the bank's hallowed corridors. Mrs. Barnett had barged into Davar's office, demanding that the bank recall her husband to Washington or be taken to court for ruining her marriage.

"Jenny had written him a letter telling him how irresponsible he was to leave her mother. I'm sure his wife had put her up to it because no ten-year-old would use those words. He was feeling really down and saying he didn't want to lose his children...I, well, I thought he was trying to back out of our relationship. I got mad and left him." Her fine lashes dropped. "If I'd been with him that night, he'd be alive today."

The young woman bit her lip again, but Susan wasn't worried about her falling apart anymore.

"You shouldn't blame yourself," Susan said. "Somebody was out to get him, and if it wasn't that night, it would have been another. Have you heard of a company called Eastern Horizon?"

Amanda looked up, her watery eyes clearing. "It's a pharmaceutical company, a very successful one that was always winning bids at the auction."

"Do you know why Andrew was investigating it?"

"He suspected the company wasn't importing medicine as it claimed. If it were any other company, Andrew wouldn't even dream of interfering. But because it was using auction money to finance its imports, Andrew felt he couldn't turn a blind eye. Andrew was a man of integrity. He couldn't have let that go."

Susan heard a defensive note again. The matter must have been subject of debate between the two, and most likely among the expat community at large.

"Did Andrew have any idea what the company was importing?"

"I don't think so. He was going to talk to somebody at customs about it. There's this Swiss guy..."

"Belmont?" Susan prompted. He was a name on Andrew's calendar, a person he was supposed to have an appointment with the day after he died.

"That's right. He's the consultant hired by the government to revamp custom procedures at the port. A big, tall guy with brown hair and brown mustache."

"I haven't met him yet, but I will."

"Please be very careful," Amanda said in earnest. "There are certain people in Mogadishu you can't cross. There've been stories about people disappearing, and days later, they'd be found floating in the harbor, half eaten by sharks."

"Do you know which one of those people Andrew crossed?"

Amanda was silent for a few heartbeats. "You mean do I know who killed Andrew?" she said. The women's eyes locked. Amanda blinked first. "No, I don't. Rumor has it that Eastern Horizon is owned by somebody very powerful, somebody close to the president. But nobody knows for sure." Amanda picked up a paper clip and started straightening it. "If you want to work in this country, you have to observe certain taboos. We can't change things overnight, but if we pack up and leave, the country will be plunged right back into the dark ages. It's important we maintain a presence...no matter what happens." Her eyes never left the paper clip that was now a piece of wire in her hands.

Chapter 6

It seemed as if the sky had opened one day and plopped down a fortress in the middle of the flat never-ending no man's land. Tinged with the reddish hue of the surrounding sand, it looked more like a butte in the desert than a man-made structure. Some decades ago followers of a popular religious sheik had constructed the bastion to safeguard their lifestyle against the winds of moral erosion. In recent times, however, one of Siad Barré's fiercest supporters had taken it over and renovated it into a base for his army. The fortress now belonged to General Ahmed, a clan outsider who had wormed his way into the president's heart.

Inside the walls, a bustling town unfolded. Tidy rows of mud and wattle huts flanked a paved road, followed by a stretch of workshops noisy with the whining of electric saws and crackling of blowtorches. At the center of town, a wall rose within the walls. In the core of this double protection squatted a chock of undecorated concrete. There were no windows, just gashes to allow a minimum of light to flow in and eyes to see out, like machicolations in a medieval castle, to be used by the defenders to drop hot liquid and heavy stones on their enemies without exposing themselves. This was General Ahmed's residence.

Scattered around it were several cottages of friendlier design, with ordinary doors and shuttered windows. Inside one of them, a man was shaving in front of a wall mirror. The razor grated on the black matte of stubble. His head jerked back. A drop of blood oozed out. He grabbed a washcloth and clamped it tightly on his chin, as if it was a gaping wound that he was stanching and not just a nick. After a while, he eased his grip, but when he saw a new drop of blood seeping to the surface, he slapped the cloth back on. He hated messes of any kind.

Hamid took the washcloth off slowly. Good, the blood had clotted. He snapped on a pair of plastic gloves, poured two capfuls of bleach into the basin of water, and dipped his head in.

His gloved hands combed through his hair a dozen times, making sure no patch was left untouched. Then he lifted his head, hooded it with the towel draped on his shoulders, and rubbed with vigor. When the towel fell off, the crop of ruffled hair was a colorless gray. It had been bleached so many times that had it not been for the growth on the rest of his body, he would have forgotten his hair used to be raven black.

Hamid browsed through the assortment of bottles on the shelf, ticking each off with his index finger, and settled on one that read "Sahara—light blond." He applied the dye to his hair and massaged it in. Satisfied with the evenness of the tone, he parted it along a neat line on one side. Next, he opened a flat plastic box lined with two columns of tinted lenses. Gray blue was his eye color today.

The door opened. The mirror reflected a woman carrying a tray and staring at him with open-mouthed wonder. He told her to put his breakfast on the table. The sound of his voice brought a glimmer of recognition to her eyes. With a petulant smirk, she set the tray down and continued to watch his grooming.

Somali women were an irreverent bunch. They covered their heads after a fashion, but never their faces, and they loved to tease. His comrades in the Brotherhood would throw stones at her, but he rather enjoyed their boldness, which, however, had to be kept in check. Men have authority over women, because God has given the one more than the other. A woman who disobeys her man should be banished to a separate bed and beaten. So it was written in the *Koran*.

He brushed past the woman and sat down to the breakfast of camel's milk and bread. She took a seat next to him, her eyes tenderly playful from the frolic of the previous night. He must teach her some manners.

"Get up," he said. She looked at him with a catlike indifference that infuriated Hamid. "Get up," he repeated, louder.

"Why?" she retorted.

He nabbed her by the front of her tunic and flung her against the wall. "Stand there," he ordered and turned around to finish his breakfast.

The camel's milk had a smoky taste and was as thick as cream. It was no wonder Somali boys grew into strong, towering men. Hamid himself wasn't a large man, a disadvantage that had irked him when he started combat training. But he soon learned that mass and power weren't directly related, and it was because he was small and swift that they selected him for the assassination squad. The other boys used to laugh at him for hardly leaving footprints on the ground he treaded, but when the leaders chose him over them, they were no longer laughing.

While others toted guns and rifles, the elite team carried silent weapons such as daggers and garrotes. A typical mission involved sneaking into an enemy camp in a group of four. Their target would be a high-ranking official of the pro-Soviet puppet regime. To get to the man, they would have to get rid of his guards first. Hamid would always remember his maiden attempt. He'd clamped a chokehold on the soldier from behind and plunged in the knife the way he'd been taught—right under the rib cage with an upward thrust aimed at the heart. The resistance jarred him. The guard was wearing a bulletproof vest. In a panic Hamid slashed at his face and fled. His comrades never made it out. Just as well or they would have ratted on him.

Hamid concluded that the neck was the most vulnerable part of the body. It was the connection between the body and its master, without which the body was nothing but a lump of meat. Best of all was that the neck was always exposed. Unhindered by layers of clothing, a piece of strong wire was all that was needed to cut through the thin coating of skin and tissue. The only drawback was the god-awful mess it created. A slit artery could spurt like a fountain, and Hamid would smell the stink of blood on himself for days after.

For a while, the mujahideen seemed hopelessly pitted against its superpower neighbor. Soviet fighters drove Hamid and his comrades into Pakistan. The group was falling apart when the Americans came with their big guns and taught them how to launch ground-to-air missiles. They also brought along a small, quiet man who rounded up the remnants of the assassination squad and demonstrated a new method of dispatching the enemy. He flicked open a switchblade and held it over the neck of an old brindled cow. While the animal was still chewing her cud, he gave her a gentle pat on the side and inserted the point of the blade into the raggedy pelt. The cow slumped to the ground without a moo. The knife had slid in easily, almost gracefully, and when it reappeared, it was amazingly immaculate. The merits of the method struck Hamid at once. He could eliminate an enemy without a sound, prop him up so that anyone who saw him from a distance would think the man was merely resting. The assassins would be long gone by the time the truth was known.

Hamid became a star pupil, and when the American left, he gave him his switchblade as souvenir. It was a great honor, which Hamid deserved because his mastery of the art had surpassed the teacher's. Hamid could perform the operation blindfolded. As if with eyes of its own, his blade knew where to glide down the cervical contour and slip into the weakest spot of the human body. From there on the grip of the vertebrae was as fast as magnets, drawing the blade in until it touched the cord and snipped it in two. His arm was always ready to catch the falling body, but the soul he let go, soaring and liberated from the pain of life.

How easy it was to die, yet how hard. On his last mission, a traitor within the mujahideen had tipped off the enemy. He walked right into their arms, and in the days that followed there were many times when he wished his captors would be as kind to him as he'd been to his victims. The soldiers strung him up by the thumbs and thrashed him with iron pipes. He felt every bone in his body break, and there was nothing more he wished than for his spirit to break away and free him from the agony. But they always knew when to stop. They dunked his head in sewer water, and when his lungs were about to explode, they lifted him for a catch of air and shoved him in again, over and over. They left him to die on the cold floor of the cell.

He prayed to God to take him away, but a halo of light appeared before him and told him his work on earth wasn't over yet. The jail door creaked open and he was lifted off the floor. When he awoke—he knew not how many days later—he was in the house of an agent of the Brotherhood. He later found out that his rescuers had bribed the prison guards and smuggled him out. When he was well enough to travel, the Brotherhood arranged his passage to its base in Khartoum. God had saved him through the Brotherhood, and his life from then on was theirs to use or take.

His talent had proven to be a financial asset to the organization. Every mission completed brought a hike in his price. He'd never dreamed that the work he used to do for free could now rake in such rewards. An enormous sum had been paid to the Brotherhood for his current job, although he failed to understand why the lives of a few aid workers could be worth that much. Perhaps there was more to come. He would know as needed.

The door burst open and a fat Somali in uniform barged in. His fleshy jowls quivered as he screeched in a shrill voice, "A fine time you're having here. We didn't hire you to sit around and have tea with our women. Come on, let's go, we've got work to do."

His voice pierced Hamid's nerves. It wasn't just the pitch but also the needling. How he would like to strangle the bloated buffoon. But he held himself back, for as much as he hated to admit it, he was at the mercy of the jackass. The Somali had been Hamid's only contact since he'd been whisked from the airport to this fortress in the middle of nowhere. His rank was that of a colonel, and his job was to deliver messages to Hamid and chauffeur him around. He was a good chauffeur, that much Hamid would grant him, and if he would only keep his bucket mouth shut, all would be well.

Hamid slowly got up and went to pick up his briefcase. Passing the mirror, he couldn't help stopping to admire the reflection. What he saw was a foreign aid worker dressed in a natty polo shirt and carrying a portfolio of documents. He could show up anywhere in Mogadishu and nobody would dream of asking what his business was.

Tearing himself away, he said with a mocking grin, "My dear colonel, I am at your service."

Chapter 7

The auction office was on the top floor of the Ministry of Finance, across the open atrium from the minister's. The office was a spacious but bare room that contained two wooden desks facing each other, an equal number of chairs, and a tall gray metal cabinet with sharp, rusty edges. A computer sat on one of the desks.

"How do you like my office?" Clive drawled in a soft Scottish lilt. He was a stocky man in his fifties with sleepy eyes and the appearance that he was always holding back a yawn.

"Very nice. That's the most highly rated computer these days," Susan said, astonished to see state-of-the art technology in this corner of the world.

"It's a handy little machine," Clive said, the cloud in his eyes lifting somewhat. "Let me show you my data base." He sat down, switched the machine on with a flamboyant flick of the wrist, and poked out his commands with a finger from each hand. A table appeared on the screen, showing names of companies and dollar amounts. Standing over him, Susan scanned the page.

She pointed to a line and interpreted, "So this company won this amount of dollars in this auction."

"Right," Clive said. "It's pretty clever, isn't it? And if you want to see what the total is, go to the last column." He moved the cursor to the far right. Susan noticed that the sum had been typed in manually, not tabulated automatically by the spreadsheet's functions. Clive was using the computer as a typewriter. Nothing he'd done so far had tapped into the machine's vast computing capability.

"That's great," she lied through her teeth. "Can I show you something?" She leaned over and entered a formula. Presto, the sum of the string of numbers appeared.

"That's clever," Clive said slowly, not quite sure what to make of it. "But I don't trust the machine. It makes mistakes sometimes."

"Yeah, I know, you have to watch what it does," Susan said with tongue in cheek.

Suddenly, a harsh voice shouted from the doorway, "Mr. Clive, you made me lose again! I'm going to kill you!"

Susan turned in the direction of the speaker. The business end of a magnum revolver was staring her in the face. Its owner was a hulking Somali with a wide, angry face.

"Put away your gun. We can talk about this," Clive said in his singsong cadence.

"Three times I put in bids, and three times I lose. If I don't get the foreign exchange, my supplier will cancel my shipment of spaghetti. I'll have to close my shop, and how am I going to feed my family!" The Somali gestured excitedly, waving his gun and snorting like a mad bull.

"I know who's winning the auctions," the gunman went on. "The Marehans! They're getting all the foreign exchange. We Hawiyes can't take it anymore. One day, we're going to kill them all. The auction money will be ours." He thumped his thick chest.

"Well, now," Clive said. "When it comes to that, I don't think there will be any more auctions. Miss Chen here is from the World Bank. She can tell you that."

Susan stared at the Somali. Hell, what was she supposed to say? She cleared her throat to buy time. A piece of paper taped to the wall caught her eye. "The auction is conducted according to rules," she said. "They're posted right there in black and white. Let me read them to you." She walked toward the wall and stopped an arm's length from the gunman.

"But the rules are not fair," the Somali protested.

Susan windmilled around and sliced his wrist with the edge of her palm. The gun scuttled across the floor to where Clive was standing. The Somali stumbled back in a daze. Clive gaped at the gun at his feet and then at Susan. She motioned him to pick it up. He bent down and lifted it with such dread that one would have thought that it was a live, ticking bomb.

"Give it to me. It's my gun," the Somali said.

Clive put it in a drawer instead.

"Why do you think the auction rules are unfair?" Susan said to the Somali.

"Only some people can win," he said. "Others, like me, will never get our foreign exchange no matter how hard we try."

"The bids are submitted in sealed envelopes, so there's no chance that anyone can rig it."

"You don't know, Miss. The Marehans have all the shillings," the man retorted. "They can afford to bid high because they can walk into the Bank of Somalia any time and ask for a loan. We can never bid as high as they."

Susan could see he had a point, but she hadn't come here to solve the problems of the auction. "I will personally look into the matter," Susan said. "Be assured that everything will be done to make the procedure as fair as possible."

"What about my gun?"

"We'll leave it here for safekeeping."

The Somali spouted smoke like a frustrated dragon, but seeing that there was nothing more he could do, he declared, "I'll be back," and lumbered out.

Clive let out a sigh of relief. "The next auction is in a week. What if he doesn't win?" Susan posed the disturbing question. "Will he be back with another gun?"

"Probably."

"Can we tell the guards not to let him in?"

"He's probably one of their friends."

"You mean he can't be stopped?"

Clive raised his shoulders. "This is *Somalia*," he crooned out the word as though it was the title of a love song. "It's the Wild West here, and the Somalis are a bunch of cowboys. They'll do what they want. Can I ask you a question?" Clive tilted his head in puzzlement. "When you knocked over his gun, was that deliberate?"

Susan laughed. "What do you think? No, I'm not that brave. Let's say it just *happened*."

Clive chuckled along with her. "Now, is there anything else I can show you?"

"Um, yeah, sure," Susan said. She'd almost forgotten what she'd come for. "I'd like to see the supporting documents for the winning bids."

Clive sauntered over to the cabinet and showed her the stacks of cardboard boxes.

"They're all here. Which one would you like to see?"

"The latest one," Susan said, having noticed on the database that Eastern Horizon was a winner in the last auction.

Clive lugged the heavy box to the desk.

"Don't let me keep you from your work," Susan said. "I'll sit here and browse through it."

While Clive returned to his computer, Susan winnowed the files until she found a tab that read "Eastern Horizon*tal*," obviously a typo. She glanced across at Clive, who was staring intensely at the screen, so absorbed that he was biting the tip of his tongue without knowing it. Susan took out the file. The first page was an invoice for two hundred thousand dollars worth of drugs. She leafed through the papers and found a copy of the bill of lading, which contained multisyllabic names such as Garamycin and Levothyroxine. The shipment was to have arrived two days ago. As she raised her head to ask Clive a question, she discovered a pair of eyes glaring at her. Immediately, the skin on the face pulled back. The wrinkles on the finance minister's forehead disappeared and a pair of gopher's teeth peeked out amiably.

"Miss Chen, how are you? So pleased to see you again," Suleiman said.

Susan stood up and explained that she was educating herself on the intricacies of the auction.

"Very good. Do you have any particular questions? I or Clive will be most happy to help you," the minister said. "Let me see, which file are you looking at?" He picked up the invoice laid open on the desk. "Oh yes, Eastern Horizon."

Clive's eyelids lifted. Susan saw alarm in his eyes.

"Oh yes, Yusuf gave you some information on the company. Is there anything else we can help you with?"

"Not now, thank you very much," she said, deciding that pursuing the matter through official channels was as useful as chasing her own tail.

"Fine, fine," the Minister repeated, nodding his head like a doting parent.

"Please carry on." Turning to Clive, he said, "Can I see you for a minute?"

Alone, Susan checked the computer for the previous auctions. Eastern Horizon was one of the regular winners together with several importers of food and construction materials. She went back to the cabinet, guessed that the second box down was the one she wanted, and carefully eased it out.

"What are you doing?" Clive said. She hadn't heard him return. "I just wanted to look at other examples," Susan said, her voice strained by the weight of the box that had slid out halfway. Clive helped her carry it to the desk.

"You know, Miss Chen," he muttered, "I don't mean to tell you how to do your job, but because you're new here, I thought I should give you a piece of friendly advice."

"By all means. I'd be most grateful." She gave him her round-eyed innocent look.

"Well, you know,"—his body swaying melodically with his accent—"as you've witnessed today, people here are used to doing things their way. You kind of have to go with the flow if you want to survive. Don't tell anyone I said this," he lowered his voice to a whisper, "but I think Andrew was killed because he was sticking his bloody nose where it didn't belong."

"You mean Eastern Horizon?"

Clive put a finger to his lips. "I didn't say that. Please don't put words in my mouth."

"I'm sorry, I didn't mean to do that. Thanks for the advice anyway." In the same conspiratorial tone she said, "A shipment of drugs was supposed to have arrived two days ago. Do you know whether it has cleared customs?"

"You're talking about Somalia. Nothing gets done that fast."

"Glad to hear that," Susan said with so much intention that Clive frowned.

Francois Belmont was a browner Swiss than Amanda had described. He had tawny skin, auburn hair and mustache, and wore various shades of chocolatry from milk to dark on his safari suit, socks and sandals. Even his mood blended into the color scheme. It was a chocolate of the darkest and most bitter kind, that hung over his head like a storm cloud as he sat opposite her in his office-cum-living room, recounting the causes of his wretchedness, which outnumbered the fingers on his hands. Susan felt like asking: What did you expect? When your employment was crammed down the government's throat by donors, when your job was to clean up customs and close the funnel of millions of dollars to smugglers and corrupt officials, did you expect them to lay out the red carpet, provide you with an office and the staff to run your operation, and kiss your cheeks like a brother?

Enough was enough, especially when he was beginning to repeat himself. Susan decided it was time to butt in. "I noticed on Andrew's calendar that he had an appointment with you," Susan said. "Do you know what he wanted to talk to you about?"

"I have no idea. He never showed up for our meeting. I was waiting for him all morning, his secretary didn't even call—"

"I think I know what he wanted," Susan interrupted. "Have you heard of a company called Eastern Horizon?"

The Swiss shook his reddish-brown head.

"It's a pharmaceutical company, and it has won foreign exchange at almost every auction," Susan said. "If it had used the money the way it should, the country would be flooded with medicines by now. But I've talked to doctors at the hospitals, and the shortage is as acute as ever. Nobody knows where the medicines went."

Belmont's brows shot up with a question: "So? What's that got to do with me?"

"My guess is, Andrew wanted you to inspect one of its shipments."

"Precisely. If they would only let me do my job, this country will have no problems. But no, they won't even give me a pass to get into the warehouse. How am I expected to carry out my responsibilities? At the end of the year, the minister would say, this fellow Belmont, what did he do all year? Where are the taxes and duties he was supposed to collect?"

"A new shipment has just come in. It's still sitting at the port. Can you get permission to open it?" Susan said.

A climatic change came over the Swiss. The nimbostratus over his head blew away and a calculating cool front descended. "What do you think is in it?" he said.

"I don't know. But I have a strong hunch it's not medicine."

"Do you know it's very dangerous, what you're asking me to do? If it's contraband, then fine, good, excellent. Then maybe the minister will know how important I am and let me do my job. But if it turns out to be nothing but medicine, it would be *most* embarrassing for me."

"The World Bank is the administrator of the auction. According to the legal document, we're obliged to ensure that the funds are used properly. We have every right to carry out spot inspections." One of the first lessons she learned at the bank was that quoting from the legal agreement was equivalent to calling on God.

"Fine." Belmont said and jumped up. "Let's go to the port now."

Chapter 8

Chang Soo dialed the number again and again. The odds of getting a call through in Mogadishu were slimmer than striking a jackpot at Monte Carlo. Normally, his secretary would be dialing on his behalf, but this was a liaison that couldn't see the light of day. After a dozen futile attempts, he got up, snatched his briefcase and rushed out of his office, hollering to his secretary that he was going to a meeting. In the corridor, he bumped into Hasan. The young man was radiant.

"I've filled out the application," he said. "Can you please take a look, especially the section on work experience—"

"Put it on my desk. I'm late for a meeting," Chang Soo said and dashed out. Lately, he hadn't been able to stand the sight of his assistant, yet he couldn't take his eyes off the radiant face either. Every morning Chang Soo would scan Hasan's face for a reading of the kind of night he'd had. Chang Soo had known women of all shades of skin, but never one as erotic as Abdia. Her presence exuded sex, in the way she walked, sheathed herself in sensuous fabric, concealing the dark rose of her womanhood as fertile as volcanic soil. But why wasn't she a mother yet? She'd been married for more than a year. She should be breast-feeding a baby and swollen with another by now. Could there be something missing in Hasan's virility? Chang Soo himself sucked on a bit of ginseng every day. At forty-five, his hair was still black and bushy, and his trim waistline could put any young man to shame.

Chang Soo got into his black sedan and drove out of the ministry grounds. One side of him told him he was being indiscreet, while another side, the stronger half, propelled him forward. Since Hasan came home, he'd seen Abdia only once, in her husband's presence, which was worse than not seeing her at all. He felt like a lovesick teenager. It was dangerous, but what was a man without emotions? He must let them burn, if he was to live fully.

He'd nominated Hasan for a six-month course at the London School of Economics. With his usual eloquence, he'd convinced the ministry that lacking an assistant of such training, his analysis would take much longer to complete. But the term didn't start till January. How was he going to live through almost the whole of December without her?

He glanced left for oncoming traffic. Snatching a judgment, he zipped into the main road without stopping. Not far behind, a cross-country Pajero followed suit. Chang Soo spotted the vehicle in his rearview mirror, but the impression made no dent in his preoccupied mind. He'd actually seen it once before, when he was driving out of the ministry, but he'd been too busy with his own thoughts to register the sight.

Chang Soo's heart was pounding in his ears when he hammered the door three times. Abdia gasped at the sight of the wild-eyed Korean. She admitted him quickly, hustled toward the window, hips rolling like an easy ocean swell under her batik muumuu, and dropped the blinds.

"What are you doing here?" she said, her voice hoarse with tension.

"I've been trying to reach you, but your bloody phone doesn't work," he cried out in frustration.

"Not so loud." She clasped her hands in front of her chest, imploring. "You should have sent me a message."

"Who's going to do that? The messenger boy in the office?"

Abdia's eyelids batted. She knew that wouldn't do. Even the most generous bribe couldn't keep a messenger boy's mouth shut. "Let me think of something, but right now, you have to go." She placed her dusky, svelte hands on Park's chest and pushed him toward the door.

The warmth of her touch sent an electrical current down his groin. His legs jellified, Chang Soo could no longer restrain himself. He took hold of her shoulders.

"Hasan won't be back till late afternoon. He has a meeting at two, it should last till at least three. We have enough time!"

"Oh no," she shrank back in horror. "Not here. We can't, not here." She pushed him harder, but his hug only became more passionate. Barely able to breathe, she wheezed, "I'll go to your place."

The embrace eased. "My place? Really?"

"I can pretend to go to the market. As long as I'm home before dinner, Hasan won't suspect anything." A plot was hatching in her amber eyes. "I'll go to the market right now, pick up a few things, and then...one o'clock," she said, her face uplifting with the boldness of her decision. "But I can't stay long," she warned.

"Lovely!" Chang Soo said. A hungry man could wolf down his meal in no time.

Shortly before one, a black sedan rolled into the parking lot of a six-storied apartment building. A Korean man in a crisply starched safari suit got out and sprinted up the open stairwell. Across the street a Pajero pulled up against the curb. The two men in the vehicle peered up through the windshield. The driver, a large Somali man whose belly touched the steering wheel, pointed at the lampblack clouds as they stampeded out the sun with the fury of a herd of humpbacked bisons. In the drought-ridden country, a phenomenon such as this was as close as it got to a miraculous apparition. The driver's jaws dropped, and his eyes bulged with wonder. His passenger, however, only gave the sky a darting glance and leveled his gaze at a particular balcony on the second floor. His hair was blond and his eyes a vacuous blue, pupil-less, like a marble sculpture.

A taxi stopped in front of the building. A veiled woman stepped out. She, too, looked up at the sky and ducked into the staircase. At the sound of descending footsteps, she pressed herself against the banister, lowered her head and let the other person pass. Her burlap wrap was soiled and worn. Most of the residents in this expat housing complex would take her for a maid. She knocked on a door on the second floor and slipped in.

Around two in the afternoon, the sky ripped open. Water slammed down, sending people scurrying for cover. Rivulets ran down the street to seek outlet in the modern sewerage system

71

that had been built with funding from three international aid groups. At the mouth of the drain the water swirled around, but finding no place to go, it regurgitated back onto the road. The grill cover had long been removed and converted into some more practical utensil by the citizens of Mogadishu. In its place, debris had plugged up the culvert as good as concrete. One heavy dousing was enough to flood the low-lying city.

A while later, a man and a woman came out of the building. Leaving the woman under the eaves, the man dashed into a black sedan and drove up. The woman tiptoed out of the shelter, her skirt hitched to mid-calf. The water was already ankle high. She got in, and the sedan splashed away.

Chang Soo cursed the sky. Why of all the bloody days in this bloody country did it have to rain today? Abdia had been so distracted that he could hardly get any enjoyment out of it. Barely had he caught his breath when she sat up and asked to be taken home. Navigating the rivers now, he could understand why. The rain was still coming down in buckets, and the heaviness of the sky promised plenty more to come. The city was fast filling up into one large swimming pool. Nothing worked in the goddamned place, Chang Soo cursed. He kept his foot relentlessly on the pedal, afraid that once the car stopped it would never start again. He had to get her back, or their secret would be blown and the six months of promised bliss would evaporate into thin air.

Her apartment was finally in sight. The car plowed on through the water, passing others that had given up.

"Stop here," Abdia said a block from her home. Without a kiss or goodbye or word about their next meeting, she threw open the door and braved the muddy knee-high water.

Chang Soo moved on immediately, steered a wide turn and pointed the prow of his four-wheeled boat toward home. Several miles down the road, his worst nightmare came true. The engine died and refused to be revived. Cursing the country, the people, the woman, he rolled up his trousers, said goodbye to his pair of oxfords and stepped into the disease-infested water that now reached his waist. The carcass of a goat floated past. Not far away, a frantic rat was paddling toward him. He beat the water with all his might until the current carried the animal away. Half wading and half swimming, he fought his way upstream.

Darkness was fast descending. The city's power supply, unreliable at the best of times, was nonexistent that night. Even the private generators had been soaked and rendered ineffective. Chang Soo had no idea where he was going, but just as he was swearing to return to Seoul and get a cushy university post, two dots of light penetrated the cascading curtain. He waved and hollered at the top of his lungs. The lights came closer and closer and stopped a short distance away. Between the high beam and the water stinging his eyes, he could make out the silhouette of a large man in the driver's seat.

"What a night," Chang Soo exclaimed as he deposited himself next to the driver together with some gallons of sewage. "I'm terribly sorry to dirty your car," he said when he realized what he'd done.

The driver was silent. Chang Soo could see that he was an unusually fat Somali, who looked cramped even in the spacious four-wheel-drive vehicle.

"I live just a couple of kilometers down the road, in one of those garden flats that expatriates live in," Chang Soo said in his most British accent. "I'd be much obliged if you can give me a lift home."

Without a word, the driver shifted into gear.

"That's jolly good of you. I really don't know how to thank you enough." Eliciting no response, Chang Soo blabbered on, "This is a splendid vehicle. What make is it?"

"Pajero," the driver said curtly.

"Jolly good," Chang Soo said, making a mental note to talk to the minister about getting one for the office. His admiration grew as the vehicle parted the body of water and planed down the street. When they got to his building, Chang Soo shook the driver's hand and found it to be as thick as a bear's paw. "I wish I could invite you up for a drink, but it will take me a while to clean myself up. I really must take down your name and address, so I can thank you properly once this bloody rain stops."

The Somali turned his face away and wagged his hand. Well, nobody could say he didn't try, Chang Soo thought. He thanked the man again, jumped into the water, and waded into the building. He bounded up the staircase, unbuttoning his shirt en route. Once inside the apartment, he flipped the switch on the wall. As expected, nothing happened. Accustomed to finding his way in the dark, he moved nimbly through the living room, tearing the vile clothing off his body and leaving a trail of wet garments on the parquet floor. By the time he reached the bathroom, he was stark naked. The water in the shower was cold. He scrubbed up a lather and scoured every nook and cranny of his body with such vim that his skin prickled and the cold no longer bothered him. He dwelled on the scratch on his calf, stretching open the skin to make sure that the soap got to the flesh. A colleague of his had died of an infection from wading in floodwaters in some godforsaken land. Who knew what deadly disease he could catch here? After a thorough cleansing, he stepped out of the tub, groped for a towel and rubbed himself vigorously. He then reached out for his robe that usually hung on the bathroom door. Not finding it, he swore at his housekeeper and walked into the bedroom, toward the battery-operated lamp by the night table. His bare feet probed the cool tiles, careful not to stub his toes. He'd done it once too often since he'd come to Somalia.

Suddenly he felt the warmth of another body behind him, an iron clamping his throat, and a sharp, icy point on the back of his neck. Before he knew what was happening, the darkness sank to the bottom of a deep, cool well and he couldn't even feel the pain of his body hitting the floor.

Chapter 9

A tugboat chugged toward the berth, towing behind it a cargo several times its own tonnage. The barge was so loaded with containers that the waterline came dangerously close to the gunwale. From a distance, the giant boxes seemed to be floating on their own in the inky sea. The heavy sky was a monotone similar to that of the water. Standing on the edge of the berth, Susan looked up and thought the same thought as the people around her. Any time now, the firmament was going to crack open.

Belmont hopped on the tugboat as soon as it had docked. After conferring with the ship's captain, he shouted to Susan, his fist raised in triumph, "It's here. We've got it!" Like a seasoned stevedore, he did a quickstep on the gangplank to the barge and disappeared behind the cargo. When he reemerged, he was smiling and pointing to the red container on top. Susan waved a thumbs up. A drop of water fell on her arm, and without further ado, the sky released its reservoir. The score of workers fled for shelter. Susan jumped into the cabin of the boat, converging with Belmont, who had run in from the barge. Together with the ship's captain, they conferred on what to do next.

"I say let's go on with it," Susan insisted. "We've gone as far as we have, I'm not sure if we can pick up the momentum another day." Indeed, whipping the disgruntled port manager into action had been no mean feat. An outright bribe would have been more effective than all the cajoling and threatening they'd done, but it wouldn't have been correct coming from proponents of clean government.

"I've never been able to unload so fast in this harbor," said the small Dutch captain in a loud voice. "We normally have to wait around for weeks. I don't know how much time and money my company's lost in this goddamned harbor. Excuse my language," he apologized with a chivalrous nod at Susan.

"You better be right about this," Belmont said, wagging a tobacco-stained finger at Susan. Turtling his head into his collar, he leaped ashore into the rain. Susan held her breath as if she was about to dunk her head into a pool and dove in. By the time they got to the warehouse where the workers had gathered, they were drenched to the skin. Conscious of the men's ogling, Susan fluffed out the blouse plastered to her chest. The port manager was grinning like a Cheshire cat.

"Rain is good. We need rain," he proclaimed, flashing gold in his front tooth. Both Belmont and Susan knew the real reason for his happiness. The heavens had answered his prayer to stop the foreigners from taking over his port.

"Come on, we've got work to do!" Belmont shouted above the thundering rain. The men looked to their boss for a go-ahead. He stood there, arms folded in passive rebellion until Susan opened her mouth and let out a stream of World Bank gobbledy-gook about cancellations and suspensions and obligations. He clamped his hands to his ears and shouted something in Somali. The workers laughed and rushed into the rain.

Shadows fleeted behind the watery curtain and a motor revved. Susan was craning to see what was going on when a spray of water slapped her in the face. She jumped back and saw a row of mammoth wheels splashing past her. She took off after the huge vehicle. In the gray slate ahead, the fuzzy outline of a giant red box dangled in midair. Inside it were crates carrying the contraband that Barnett had been trying to uncover. In a few minutes she would expose it for the world and especially Nick to see. A bit of respect was all she asked of her station chief, but a bit of admiration would be welcome, too.

A dozen arms stretched up to guide the container onto the bed of the truck. Metal clanged and creaked and rested. The men slapped the nearest surface and shouted in a universal language for a job well done. The truck forged through the fast-rising water. The workers chased after it like children running wild in the rain. Susan found herself laughing as the waterfall tumbled on her. She couldn't be wetter if she were standing naked under a shower. She wiped her eyes to see where the others had gone and went sloshing after them.

The truck was backing into the warehouse, and at the angle it was going, the wall was about to go with it. Bangs and shouts overrode the thundering rain. The driver stopped in time, spun the wheels forward, and straightened them. The monstrous tail zigzagged in. By the time the workers shouted approval, most of the truck was inside the shelter.

The container door opened to reveal a number of neatly stacked crates. One by one, a forklift inserted its arms under the boxes and lowered them to the ground. Belmont checked the serial number on each. When he finally shouted "Bingo!" Susan felt the blood drain from her head. Hugging her sopping self, she walked up to the wooden crate, which was as high as her chin. Two workers jimmied open the lid. Layers of bubbly packing material billowed out. Belmont burrowed into them and pulled out a carton.

"Careful, careful," he shouted as knives slashed the masking tape. He took out a plastic bottle labeled with a long Latinic name, broke the seal and removed the cotton. With a chemist's steady-handed deftness, he shook a measure of its content onto his palm. Capsules of red and white glided out. He opened one, grazed the powder with the tip of his tongue and spat it out. He looked up, searching for someone. When his eyes found Susan, the caramel pupils darkened to a murderous shade. "I think it's medicine," he growled.

"This one is," Susan said spunkily, while inside, her stomach was twisting into a knot. She'd expected to find pieces of hardware, ammunition, anything other than medicine.

After dumping twenty-four inches of rain in as many hours, the storm moved out of the capital, swelling rivers and inundating more land. The drought committee, comprising aid workers from six bilateral and seven multilateral organizations, quickly hung up a new shingle and became the flood committee. The drought disaster areas became flood disaster zones and an emergency meeting was called to rally support for the rescue.

A steno pad in hand, Susan skirted around the puddles in the courtyard of the United Nations complex. After a day's respite, most of the rainwater had found its way to the sea, and life in Mogadishu began to resume once again. For Susan, the hiatus in official functions was a godsend. Her bruised ego needed a little time to grow a protective scab. Belmont was mad at her for sending him on a wild goose chase, but the worst part was that Nick was going to hear of it. She couldn't help thinking about his leer and the contempt on his face when he uttered the word "translator" as if it was some sort of contagious disease.

Inside the conference room, a dozen aid workers were chattering excitedly. Susan inserted herself in a circle that included the only other woman beside herself.

A Swede with a handlebar mustache was postulating: "What did he have in common with Andrew Barnett? They're both in the development business. Therefore, it has to be somebody who wants us to get out of the country, somebody who wants to topple the government."

"There's something else they have in common," a tall, sleek Italian said with a naughty wink. "Ext-rramarital affairs," he said, rolling his tongue as if it was luxuriating in a mouthful of fine wine.

"They've both crossed the line of decorum; that's for sure, each in his own way," the Swede said.

Susan whispered to the sari-clad Indian woman from UNICEF. "Who're they talking about?"

"That Korean economist called Park. He was found murdered in his apartment."

"What? When did it happen?"

"They're not sure. They found him today. He was naked," she mumbled the last word behind the shield of her hand.

"What's the connection with Andrew Barnett?" Susan said to the Swede.

He stared at her, noticing her presence for the first time. "I'm afraid it's confidential information I cannot divulge at this point. The investigation is still ongoing, but I'm sure Juergen

Klaus will make the necessary announcements at the appropriate time."

A series of claps interrupted the discussion. "Ladies and gentlemen, please take your seats. The meeting is starting now," a portly, older man said from one end of the room. Several people made halfhearted motions toward the table, but the hubbub over the murder continued unabated.

"The agenda for this meeting is the flood situation in Somalia, not the security," the chairman called out again with good humor. "The meeting on security will follow this one, and will be chaired by Juergen Klaus in the auditorium. So now, ladies,"—he nodded toward the two women—"and gentlemen, let us begin."

Susan had never seen any meeting move as swiftly. An FAO expert laid out the scope of the flood damage. The representatives promised to report back to their respective headquarters. There were no questions asked, no pontifications on logistics or philosophy. Within half an hour the chairman capped his pen and declared the meeting closed. The gathering rose as one body and headed toward the auditorium.

The room was already packed. Juergen Klaus directed delegates of the flood committee to the last empty seats.

"This morning, Mr. Chang Soo Park, the economist who worked for the statistical unit of the Ministry of Finance, was found murdered in his apartment," Juergen announced from the podium. A frisson of angst shook the audience. Although the information was no longer news, the bare announcement brought a fresh wave of shock.

Juergen went on: "Mr. Park was reported last seen two days ago, several hours before the rains started. According to his houseboy, Mr. Park had gone home around noon that day and told him to take the rest of the day off. The following day, as you all know, the flood had immobilized the city. The houseboy couldn't report to work until this morning. He got into the apartment," Juergen paused, his face red with heat despite the air conditioning, "and found Mr. Park's body in the bedroom."

"Are there any suspects?" a question was shouted.

"None yet. A linkage with the Barnett case is suspected, due to certain similarities."

"What might those be?" somebody asked.

All eyes were on Juergen, pressing the same question. These were diplomats and bureaucrats, seasoned in the art of distributing the truth in calibrated portions. They were watching Juergen, wondering how much he would give them, which might well depend on whether he'd had the chance to consult with his superiors in New York.

Juergen stepped down from his podium, pulled up a flip chart and in one continuous squeaky stroke of his felt pen, drew a simple outline of a head and neck. He penned in two vertical lines for the spinal column, and subdivided it into tiny ladder-like rungs.

Juergen pointed to the space between two upper rungs and said, "In both cases, a sharp knife was inserted between two vertebrae at the base of the neck. The incision is very small, but deep enough to sever the spinal cord." Gasps resounded from the audience. "This is not official yet," Juergen cautioned. "An autopsy will show the exact cause of death, time and so forth."

"Don't you have to be very precise to commit a murder like that?"

"I would think so," Juergen answered.

"Doesn't that mean the murderer is a professional killer, and not just a bungling burglar?" the same interrogator pressed, triggering another round of murmurs.

"That's a possibility," Juergen conceded, in essence challenging his own conclusion on Andrew's death. A number of questions flew out at once. "Please, please, one at a time," he said and pointed to a raised hand.

"What's the motive for the murders?"

"That we don't know yet, but we have a few theories, and it's inappropriate to divulge them at this point."

"Are we talking about a serial killer?" somebody spoke out of turn.

The inflammatory term fell on the audience like a squirt of gasoline on a fire. Of all the categories of killers, this was the one that struck the most fear in people's hearts. A serial killer would stop at not one or two but an insatiable number as high as he could get away with.

"Please, there's no need to scare ourselves," Juergen shouted above the uproar. "What I urge you to do is follow security rules. Every time you go from one place to another, you should radio my office. These rules have been in place for two months now, but the majority of people have failed to follow them."

"What's the use of telling you? Both murders took place in the victims' homes."

Juergen was speechless for a second, and no more. "We have drafted guidelines on how to secure your home. I hope to complete them by the end of the day and distribute a set to every one tomorrow. We can even visit your home and advise you on the devices most suited to your residence."

"Do you plan to issue an evacuation advisory for families?"

"Not at this point, but we will keep close track of the situation and inform you accordingly."

Another question was raised: "How effective have the Somali police been in the investigation?"

"They're doing the best they can," Juergen said, wincing at the weakness of his statement. "But as you well know, they lack the equipment and expertise for forensic investigation—"

"They're probably in on it," somebody muttered. Only his immediate neighbors heard him, but his words seemed to have hit just the right wavelength and were soon bouncing back and forth, rippling through the entire hall.

"Why hasn't Scotland Yard, Interpol or the CIA been called in?" a voice shouted over the others.

"As a matter of fact, the CIA is already involved," Juergen said. Immediately his face flamed to the color of a fire engine, and his eyes shifted around like a culprit caught red-handed. "I'm not supposed to tell you this, so please don't ask me any more questions. But be assured that everything is being done to protect the community."

Susan lowered her head. The meeting had disintegrated into pockets of private discourse. She peered up from the corners of her eyes. As far as she could see, nobody was casting knowing glances her way. Juergen called for adjournment. As he got off the platform, people zoomed in on him with more questions and theories on the crimes. Susan slipped away.

She went straight to Park's apartment. A tall policeman opened the door. Susan explained who she was and that as the World Bank had been footing Park's salary, she had to write a full report on the circumstances of his death. She dropped the names of all the Somali bigwigs she knew, but in the end the winning argument was the twenty-dollar bill she palmed into the moist hand. The door opened wide. Another policeman came out of the kitchen, his fingers dipped in a white powder that looked like flour. His colleague shooed him back to the kitchen.

Susan stepped in and almost stumbled on a pile of clothing on the floor.

"No touch, No touch," the policeman said. The stripes on his sleeve indicated he was a sergeant.

"I'm not touching. Just looking," Susan said.

"Absolutely," the sergeant said with an emphatic nod.

With hands clasped behind her back, Susan bent down for closer scrutiny. A sewer stink gushed up her nose. The piece of clothing was the top of a safari suit, and it looked and smelled as if it had been laundered in the gutters. The sergeant fanned the air with his hand, and Susan scrunched up her face in agreement. Then she saw that a few steps away was another heap, the pants of the same suit. Pursuing along the trail, she came upon one shoe, kicked off with its laces still tied, and then another. The last item, a man's briefs, lay curled in front of the bedroom.

The sergeant went into the room, beckoning her to follow. "We find body here," he said, pointing to a spot in front of the bathroom.

The parquet floor showed patches of watermarks but no sign of violence. The police hadn't bothered to outline the body, but she had to be thankful that at least they had a "no touch" policy on the material evidence.

"Did you see the body?" Susan said.

"Absolutely. I was first person here," the sergeant said, his chest puffed with pride.

"Really? Can you show me how the body was lying?"

"Absolutely," the policeman said and collapsed on the floor. He arranged his trunk sideways and twisted his limbs this way and that in various poses.

"That's fine, that's great, thanks a lot," Susan said, delivering numerous verbal pats on the sergeant's back. The general direction was all she needed to know. Park was facing the bed, his back toward the bathroom. Susan imagined him coming out of the bathroom, and Hamid waiting for him, clinching his trachea from behind.

"I heard he was naked," Susan said as the sergeant scrambled to his feet.

His eyes slid away, too embarrassed to broach such a subject with a young woman. In a voice robbed of its usual gusto, he uttered his favorite word, "Absolutely." Susan could have sworn he was blushing beneath his brown skin.

"May I go in?" She indicated the bathroom. A gallant bow was the sergeant's reply.

A navy-blue towel caught her eye. It was draped over the toilet, one corner trailing the floor. She was tempted to touch it but remembered the policeman watching her.

"Just looking," she said, tucked her hands in her pockets, and stooped toward the towel. Her nose probed the odors of soap and a sour male musk. She imagined Park coming home on the day of the storm, soaked and dirty—his car must have stalled somewhere, otherwise he wouldn't have waded in the stinking flood water—tearing off his clothing the moment he got in, kicking off his shoes, scrubbing himself in the shower, toweling, and walking out of the bathroom, finally clean, ready for a drink.

Susan came out of the bathroom and stood on the spot where Park had fallen. She swiveled around hundred and eighty degrees. Hamid stood against the whitewashed wall, cool and collected. He'd been waiting for his quarry to come out to the clearing. Waiting, for how long?

83

"How do you think the killer came in?" Susan said.

"Oh," the sergeant laughed at the elementariness of the question. "Come, I show you." He took her back out to the living room and opened the door to the balcony. "This open," he said.

"You mean this was open when the police arrived?"

"Absolutely."

Susan bellied up to the railing and looked down. It wasn't far to climb at all. A person could easily find his footing on the brackets fastening the downspout. The paint on the wall near the railing was chipped, probably where he'd kicked off to grab hold of the bar. Susan looked up. Above and beside her, the same shoebox balconies jutted out of the face of the building. A woman was hanging her laundry in one and children's voices chirruped from another. There were people everywhere. The intruder must have climbed up at night, or on a day when nobody was on the balcony. The rain.

He must have brought water into the apartment.

"You mind if I look around some more? I promise I won't touch anything."

"Absolutely. Look around," the sergeant said, sweeping his hand magnanimously across the apartment. His companion came out of the kitchen, an apron tied to his waist. The smell of baked bread wafted into the living room. The sergeant excused himself and shambled into the kitchen.

From the balcony—assuming that was where the killer entered—Susan retraced his steps, scrutinizing the ground, the walls, the furniture. She imagined him dripping with water. If he'd entered the apartment before Park, he would have had time to wipe off traces of his intrusion before his victim got in. She went into the kitchen, apologizing to the policemen for disturbing their meal of freshly baked bread, and entered the servant's quarters. A basket of dirty laundry stood against the wall. On top was a blue towel, a match with the one in the bathroom. Looking behind to make sure that the sergeant wasn't on her back, she touched it. It was dank. She held it up by its corners. A few spots of dirt had caked. A golden strand

84

gleamed at her. It was no longer than a piece of dog fur, but it stood out plainly against the midnight blue. She pinched it with two fingers and placed it between two pages of her address book.

Chapter 10

Hamid stood behind the half-closed shutter of his window. A Pajero pulled up, disgorging the colonel and his quivering bowl of fat. Hamid's focus, however, was on the other man, who had come out the other side of the car and was now stalking across the yard, lopsided under the burden of a black case strapped to his shoulder. He was as white as they came. European was Hamid's guess, for the Americans he'd known had been much more hale and hearty than this colorless weakling.

Hamid withdrew from the curtain, put a Panama hat on his bleached hair, and went out to meet his instructor. The two men shook hands in silence. No words were exchanged, just a hard look into each other's eyes and a handgrip of understanding. The subtle communication, however, was beyond the colonel, who babbled on and on until the other two had to shut him up before he gave away any names.

They drove through the walled city, past the rows of mud houses, and exited through the back gate. Over the flat sun-scoured land a sea of olive green tents rose and fell like waves in a seascape. Around it, the land was stripped; whatever flora there was had been stomped out of existence by the thousands of booted feet. The hardscrabble landscape was filled instead by blocks of manmade greenery—soldiers in spinach-green fatigues.

Soon they came upon a stony plain where a raggedy group in civvies had gathered. The car stopped and the fat colonel waddled out to talk to the officer. Hamid surmised these were new recruits. One of them, a boy with a dimpled scar under his eye, must be younger than Hamid at the time of his initiation into the mujahideen. In a week, the baby fat would be burned off and replaced by hard muscle. The younger they were, the easier it was to train them. The best killing machines were eight- or nine-year-olds.

The captain shouted an order. The ragtag bunch fell into a crooked line, all except the boy, who took a step toward the car and squinted with a mixture of astonishment and familiarity at the white man in the front seat. The captain jabbed the burning end of a cigarette into the boy's thigh. He gave a sharp yelp and scurried away.

The colonel hauled a life-size target out of the back of his vehicle. Hamid pulled down the brim of his hat and got out. The white man was standing by the hood, mopping his forehead with a handkerchief. The scorching rays traced a web of red veins under the paper-white skin, and his breathing was as heavy as if he'd walked a mile in the desert.

With a deep sigh the white man held up his camera and said, "The maximum range of this weapon is thirty feet. Beyond that, the level of inaccuracy becomes intolerably high." To Hamid's surprise, the way he rolled his words together was distinctly American. "For practice purposes, you should try it from different distances. Now, let's start with the real-life scenario. If this was the scene of action," he paused to sigh again, "and the person pulling the trigger is standing where I'm standing, where would the victim be?"

"Bring the target over there," the colonel squawked at Hamid in his high-pitched voice.

A cord of muscle popped out along Hamid's jaw line. Who did the hippo think he was? Hamid wanted to tell him to go to hell, but one glance at the white man reminded him this was no time to pick a fight. With a clench of his jaws, he lifted the target with one hand and marched forward, grinding his heels into the dirt as if it was the colonel's face. After twenty-five steps, he heard the shriek to stop.

The American set the black case on the hood of the vehicle and dialed the numbers on the lock. His hands trembled like an old man's. After pausing long enough for Hamid to memorize the combination, he fumbled open the case and handed the camera to Hamid. Digging deeper into the case, he slowly hauled out a long tubular object wrapped in a soft felt bag. This was handed to the colonel. Next he reached into a side pocket and retrieved a small box. Inside, cushioned against the sponge lining were half a dozen sewing needles of the finest gauge.

The American exhaled with the exhaustion of a laborer who had completed a strenuous task. "You ever used a camera before?" he said to Hamid.

Hamid nodded, happy to be able to say he had, even if it had been only once. During his days with the mujahideen, his American trainer had let him peep through the hole of a camera and told him to press down on a button. The mighty peaks of the Hindu Kush had looked puny in the constricted frame. He could never appreciate the esthetic value of the contraption.

"This is a telephoto lens," his new American instructor was now saying as he screwed the tubular instrument onto the camera. "What you see through the viewfinder is exactly what you're pointing at. For short distances such as this, your target is your point of aim. Here, see for yourself."

The camera, with its bulky extension, felt as solid as a weapon in Hamid's hands. Through the small square hole, a set of cross hairs appeared against a blue backdrop. He panned to the right and found some blurry scratches. Without prompting, Hamid adjusted the focus until the scratches sharpened into branches. He might not be much of a photographer, but he was good with weapons, any weapon.

The colonel seized the camera from him and whipped it around, crying with astonishment at every object that entered his vision.

The American picked up the needle with two quavering fingers and raised it toward the sun. A minute bubble rose to the tip. It wasn't a sewing needle after all, but a minuscule vial filled with liquid. "Inside this is a chemical called curare, a poison that South American Indians rubbed on their arrows for hunting. They were pretty clever, those Indians." The white man's bloodless lips curled in a wry smile. "It's a wonder how they discovered juices of certain plants could be used as a muscle relaxant. In larger doses, it can paralyze. The substance we've prepared is so concentrated that all it takes is a very small amount to make you really relaxed, so relaxed that your heart forgets to pump. Within ten seconds of entering your bloodstream, your heart would shut down, and you wouldn't even know what killed you."

His marketing job complete, the salesman reverted his attention to the mechanics of the device. He ran his finger along a ridge on top of the lens and said, "This is the rascal that will do the job for you. Think of it as the barrel of a gun, or a miniature cannon. Watch how I load it." He held down a button under the lens, inserted the needle in the ridge, and tilted the camera backward. Hamid heard a click. "Next you aim and shoot as you would any camera. By pressing on the shutter, you release the gas compressor, and the needle flies out like a bullet. The principle is the same as an aerosol spray. You know, when you press down on the nozzle of a can of shaving cream, the stuff froths out like a volcanic eruption. Well, that's aerosol."

Hamid stroked his chin. Yes, he knew how shaving cream worked.

The American went on: "Your target will most likely be wearing a bulletproof vest. You'll have to aim for the face. Funny how we cover ourselves against the cold and rain, but our faces are always naked. I've always wondered about that. Anyway," he sighed, "the moment the vial penetrates the target, you can start the countdown. The beauty of this baby is that it makes no noise and hardly any mark on the victim. People would think it's a heart attack, and in the confusion, you'll have plenty of time to get away."

"Let's try it," the colonel said with the impatience of a child itching to lay his hands on a new toy. He tore the long-nosed device out of the American's hands and looped the strap around his thick neck. With one hand to support the trunk and the other ready at the shutter, he took aim at the face of the black silhouette, right where the nose would be. His finger came down. A wind whooshed across the desert. The three men walked briskly toward the target, excitement in their gait.

"Not a bad shot," the salesman said, fingering the pinhole dotting the target's chin. The colonel's tail fanned out like a peacock's. Hamid wiped his hands on his pants. It was his turn now, and whatever he did had to be better.

Hamid placed the cross hairs on the center of the head, zooming back and forth to different perspectives of his target. Suddenly he saw a goat wander into his path. It was grazing on a brush behind the silhouette, possibly beyond the thirty feet optimum range, yet his heart was pushing him to try it. He shifted his focus.

"What are you doing?" the colonel shouted. But before he could intervene, Hamid pressed the shutter. The goat's head jerked up and immediately drooped again, hanging and lolling like a drunk. It remained standing for five seconds, then the front legs buckled and its belly landed with a puff of dust. Its rib cage heaved for three more counts, then all was still.

Chapter 11

Susan walked through the gates of the International Club. At this time of day, the only people around were a handful of bikini-clad mothers puttering with their pre-school children in the baby pool. The sun was all over the sky, baking the earth on a high and even heat. Vapors shimmered over the path leading to the clubhouse. The asphalt was soft as fresh-baked cookies under Susan's feet. The duffel bag in her hand felt as if it was stuffed with bricks when, in fact, it contained just a pair of shorts and a T-shirt. The racket in her other hand was already slippery with sweat. Nobody in his right mind would play tennis at noon, which was probably why Nick had chosen this time for her tennis lesson.

A wave of relief swept through her as she entered the air-conditioned clubhouse. Several club staff in their yellow sport shirts had also discovered this was the coolest joint in town. Susan asked them about tennis lessons. One of them got up reluctantly and opened a book to sign her up. She was told to go to the learner's court, where the coach would join her shortly.

After changing into her tennis outfit, Susan stepped back into the steamer. The learner's court was at the lower tier, away from all the others. As the searing sun beat down on her head, she could think of a dozen cooler venues for the meeting. The sunscreen on her skin was already sizzling like oil on a barbecue. Before long, a rangy figure capped with a baby-blue bonnet approached. In his hand was a bucket brimming with lime-green balls. Tennis had never been Susan's kind of sport. In her book, no human activity could be as pointless as hitting a ball back and forth.

"It's impossible to teach me to play tennis. I have a block against the sport, mental, physical or both," Susan said as she looked up at the desiccated face, studying it, comparing it to the image captured from their first encounter. The insolent eyes were hidden behind a pair of sunglasses, and under the shade of the comical hat, the leer didn't seem so cynical. But it was still there.

"Let's see about that. You'll never know until you've tried," Nick said. "By the way, that was quite a performance that you put on at the port."

You don't have to be so sarcastic, Susan thought. She'd been chiding herself for barreling down a dead end, so cocksure of her own nose, but she'd be damned if she would admit this to Nick.

"A shipment for Eastern Horizon had just come in," she said. "I thought this was the time to find out what's in it —"

"Never mind what's in the shipment. It was your bumbling foreigner act that stole the show. The whole town is buzzing about you. They're calling you a bull in a china shop, blundering around and smashing teacups left and right. I like that." Nick's lips crinkled in an acerbic grin. "They're talking about you the way they talked about Andrew and Park before the two were cut down. You're beginning to stand out from the rest of us common expats."

Susan was surprised to find that Nick's compliment was sincere. The only sore spot was that she hadn't staged the scene. If she appeared clumsy, it was because she *was*.

"Our game plan isn't working, though," she said. "Nobody seemed interested in this bait. The Korean was the one who got bitten."

Nick set his bucket on the service line. "Our lesson today will focus on the basics," he said. "Never mind what you learned or didn't learn before. The important thing is to get the form right, and the rest will follow with hard work and *patience*." Susan could sense him winking at her behind the shades. "Now, the most basic of all forms is the forehand grip. Let me show you. Pretend you're shaking somebody's hand, like this." Nick took her hand and placed it on the racket handle. "Of course they got to the Korean first. He had a head start over you, but if you keep going at this rate, I bet my life that you'll be next."

Susan pulled an envelope out of her pocket. "There's a piece of hair in it. I found it on a towel in Park's apartment, and it's obvious that it doesn't belong to Park. I want it analyzed."

Nick slipped the envelope into his pocket. He pried loose her grip and moved her hand farther down the handle. "Park was playing with fire. In this country you don't defile a man's honor and expect to get away with it. I've seen a Somali shoot his wife's lover in front of the whole village. Afterward, he laid down his gun and turned himself into the police with an angelic smile on his face. Justice has been served, and although he broke the law, most of the villagers thought he'd only done what a man should."

"But would he hire an assassin to settle the score for him? I thought part of the ethics was the man-to-man confrontation."

"It's too late to ask him now. Hasan and Abdia have cleared out of their apartment and nobody's telling where they went." Nick adjusted her grasp some more. "I don't think it's Hasan, though. It's more likely somebody who can't stand the relationship. In Somalia, the place to start with any investigation is the clanship of the people involved. It's amazing how much that reveals. Siad Barré can preach all the brotherhood and national unity he wants, but what he's been doing has been the age-old tactic of 'divide and conquer,' arming one clan and setting it against another. The country is more divided than ever, and although Somalis won't admit it to foreigners, they still depend on the clan for everything from finding a job to getting married. Okay, now, watch me."

Nick set one foot forward, opened his body sideways, and scooped the air with his racket.

Susan swung out halfheartedly. Nick's didactic attitude was beginning to chafe on her, but in all fairness she had to recognize the beauty of a tennis lesson. She and Nick were as close as they could ever be—he was gripping her hand and guiding her through an exhaustive follow through—and in the isolated learner's court, nobody was within earshot.

"Hasan and Abdia were both Hawiyes, but so is the majority of the population in Mogadishu," Susan said.

"What else do you know about them?"

She searched her memory of the evening at the couple's flat. Abdia's bewitching face floated before her. The Somali was the most gorgeous woman Susan had ever met. There was also a wild and wicked otherworldliness about her, in the dazzle of her amber eyes, the beguiling laugh and the husky voice talking about vacationing at Suleiman's villa in Italy. Wait a minute—

"I think she's some relation of Suleiman, the finance minister. You think he might be involved?"

"I won't rule it out. Suleiman's been a thorn in the side of the Barré family. The only reason he's still in power is that Siad Barré has a special bond with him that dates back to their revolutionary days. Also, the donors love him, or at least that's the image he projects. His enemies haven't succeeded in removing him yet, but they haven't given up, either. Suleiman may want to stir things up to throw his enemies off the scent. I've been keeping close tabs on him, but so far nothing out of his usual wheeling and dealing has turned up."

"What about Suleiman's villa in Italy? I heard he goes there at least once a month. I think we should keep an eye on what goes on there."

Nick dropped a ball and spanked it with his racket. The ball traveled in a perfect arc just above the net and deep into the opposite court. "See if you can do that."

Susan did what Nick had just done, but the result was quite different. The ball flew like a crippled bird into the net. Nick adjusted the angle of her racket and told her to try again.

"I heard it's just outside Rome. You think you can arrange it?" Susan said, straightening from her tennis pose to face Nick squarely. She could see the reflection of her insistence on Nick's shades.

"I can ask for it, but whether Rome cooperates is another matter."

Susan looked away with a tight smile of triumph. She'd suggested something Nick hadn't thought of, and he was willing to take it seriously, after a fashion. She bounced the ball off the ground and hurled herself into the motion of the stroke. This time the lime-green sphere shot across to the opposite baseline.

Her face glowing from the hour under the sun, Susan walked into her office to find an apparition waiting for her. She shook her head once to clear it, but still the specter refused to leave. He stood up and stalked toward her. Rawboned and arid, his skin tanned to a leather, his hair hanging like Spanish moss over his shoulders, he looked like an ascetic returned from a desert retreat. Judging from the stubble on his chin, he hadn't shaved for at least a week. His clothes were dusty and thin from use, his eyes a pale, translucent blue which Susan found disarming.

He introduced himself by a name so complex that Susan couldn't catch any part of it. Fortunately, before she could show her total fluster, he presented her with a calling card. She recognized the name at once. It had appeared in many of the project reports she'd read. Jacobus van Voorthuizen was the manager of the semi-mechanized agricultural project. A slew of data from the man's résumé flooded her memory. Education: doctoral degree in agricultural economics, citizenship: Australian, birthplace: Amsterdam, marital status: married.

"I've discovered something unusual in my project accounts," the visitor said in a neutralizing blend of old and new world accents. "I think you should be the first to know."

"Hold on, I can't talk about project accounts without my disbursement book." Susan got on the intercom with Omar.

A few minutes later, Omar appeared, a black tome in hand. The two men had met before, saving Susan the task of introducing the visitor whose name she couldn't begin to pronounce.

"I ordered some spare parts about a month ago," the project manager said. "I tried to pay for it from the revolving fund, but the bank wired me to say the account had been completely withdrawn. According to the last statement, there was a balance of $1.3 million as of the end of the month. I'm not aware of any other expenditure since then."

"What?" Susan exclaimed. "You mean $1.3 million is missing?"

"That's what it seems like," the project manager said cautiously. "I've telexed the bank manager in Rome. He telexed back, saying the last withdrawal occurred last week and it was for the entire balance. As usual, it bore the signature of the minister of finance."

"What does our black book say?" Susan said to Omar.

The assistant opened the voluminous binder and was soon rustling up a paper storm. The sheets flew back and forth, a number of them in danger of tearing off their rings. Finally, he stopped at a page. His finger ran down the lines to guide his good eye along. Addressing the invisible person next to Susan, he confirmed that the last recorded balance of the revolving fund was exactly what the project manager had said it should be.

"I better go over and talk to the minister right now," Susan said. "Where can I reach you, Mr..."

"Call me Jack," he said.

"Jack?" she repeated with a bewildered grin, incredulous that such a complicated name could be distilled into a simple "Jack."

"Short for Jacobus," he explained, his pallid eyes directed straight at hers. She pulled away with embarrassment, as if she'd intruded on his privacy in some way. "I'm usually stationed in Kurtun Waarey," he added, "and I come to Mogadishu once a month, or whenever business calls. When I'm in town, I usually stay at the Eden."

"I'm staying there too," Susan said, adding with a grimace, "unfortunately."

She hadn't meant to be rude, but the extended hotel living was getting to her. Her house was still being renovated, although every time she showed up, the workers were somewhere else.

After Jack had left the office, Fatima heaved a heartfelt sigh. "I feel so sad every time I see this man. I always think about what happened to his daughter."

"I knew there was something tragic about those eyes," Susan said. "They're so transparent and defenseless...." She paused to find words for the uneasy feeling he'd stirred up in her. "Like he's been hurt so much he's not afraid of getting hurt anymore."

"His daughter was killed by a shark, right here at the beach in Lido," Fatima said. "Both Jack and his wife were there. They saw it happen right in front of their eyes. His wife left after that, but he stayed. It's not good for a man to live all by himself. Look how thin he is. He should have gone with her."

"He's crazy," Omar said.

Both women looked at him with astonishment. It wasn't often that the assistant volunteered his opinion.

"What's the basis for your diagnosis?" Susan said, half teasing.

"Living in Somalia. That's crazy."

"Why are *you* here?" Susan egged him on.

"I was born here."

"You can still leave the country. Many Somalis have done that," Fatima chimed in.

"Maybe I will."

"Just don't leave before me," Susan said by way of a compliment. Omar's eccentricity was beginning to grow on her. Besides, Omar was a diligent worker and a genius at telex compositions, which Susan attributed to his naturally succinct style. Without his help, the ASAP telexes from Davar would have inundated her desk.

Either unable or unwilling to recognize the praise, Omar harrumphed and tramped back to his office. Susan went out, wove through the bystanders and arrived at the entrance to the Ministry of Finance. The guards opened the gate for her. They knew her very well by now, as she was in and out an average of three times a day. Yusuf was in his office, working hard as usual with his one arm. When Susan told him about the missing money, he replied in his diplomatic way that he would raise the matter with the minister the minute he returned. Suleiman had gone to Italy and was scheduled to be back the next week. Susan tried to pry more out of him, but despite the stream of words promising the utmost cooperation, he was tightlipped as a clam.

Halfway down the stairs, Susan heard a hurried trot of footsteps behind her. She looked up and saw the baggy pants of Clive from the auction office. Panting, his sleepy eyes livelier than ever, he called out, "Miss Chen, can I have a word with you?" Susan waited for him at the landing.

"The minister can explain everything when he comes back. There's no need for alarm," he said between breaths. "Yusuf told me about the missing money."

That was fast, Susan thought. Yusuf must have run down the corridor the moment she left.

"What do you know about it?" Susan said.

"Oh nothing, really, nothing. It's just that you have to understand, this is Somalia." His tone settled back to its somnambulant rhythm, the vowels and consonants in "Somalia" swelling and lapping like lulling waves. "People here believe money belongs in the same big pot. I'm sure the minister had good reason for using it. He'll replace it as soon as possible."

"You seem to know a lot about it."

The Scot stopped swaying and switched to kicking the side of the step. "Well, you know, you're new here; you have to put things in context. This is the way they do things here. But if you're an outsider, you can get alarmed, and if you report back to headquarters, they'll get alarmed, too."

"I should hope so. A million dollars plus isn't peanuts for a poor country like Somalia."

"Well, the thing is, the auction money is running out soon. If the missing funds blow up into a scandal, the bank may refuse to release the next tranche for the auction. Then you and I would be out of a job."

Susan did a quick appraisal to see if he was joking and concluded he wasn't. "What do you suggest that I do?"

"Well, now, I don't want to tell you how to do your job, but if I were you, I'd wait till the minister gets back. Have a word with him privately. He's a very reasonable man. I'm sure he'd be more than happy to patch things up.   There's new money coming in from the Italians, so you see…"

Susan nodded.   Yes, she was beginning to see how the country's accounting system worked.

Chapter 12

The scenery outside General Ahmed's fortress was a far cry from that of a few days ago. Surveying the perimeter from his watchtower, Captain Osman marveled at the green gossamer that had sprung up from the previously jaundiced earth, now turned a rich cocoa color. The mirages of yesterday were now actually pools of water glittering like scattered gold coins he'd love to have jingling in his pocket. Through his binoculars, the captain spotted a family of baboons scampering toward a destination. He projected his view farther down. Of course, that was where they were heading—the water hole. On his last watch, it had been an ugly crater with a dry, cracked bottom, but today it gleamed at him like an oval mirror in a sultana's dressing room.

The captain raised his lenses toward the horizon. A stir in a clump of bushes caught his well-trained eyes. The movement was too localized to be caused by the wind. Another family of baboons, maybe. He kept his eyes on the spot until a figure cleared the top of the hillock—an upright animal moving on two legs and carrying a spear. The Ogadenis! After being chased out of their territory by the Ethiopians, this group of nomads had drifted south and laid claim to the water hole. General Ahmed had expelled them from the vicinity of his fortress, but time and again they had returned. The captain estimated a dozen men and about as many camels in the caravan. At the pace they were moving, they'd be at the water hole in an hour.

He hurried down the tower and charged into the colonel's office. Although the colonel wasn't the highest-ranking officer present, he was General Ahmed's nephew. If anyone could make a quick decision, it was he.

"Don't you remember the general's orders?" the fat colonel shrilled. "When people are uncooperative, we must deal with them decisively. This land belongs to General Ahmed now. They can't come back and leave their camel shit everywhere. Don't just stand there, go do it!"

As the captain took to his heels, the colonel shouted after him, "Take some new recruits with you. It would be good training for them."

The captain spun around, saluted "Yes, sir," and galloped away. Close to the training ground, he slowed down to catch his breath. He straightened his uniform, wiped the dust off his closely shaven head, and assumed the strut of a man larger than himself. Shoulders swinging and elbows jutting to extend the aura of his potency, he approached the cadets. After a word with their commander, he inspected the ragged line. What a sorry bunch, he thought. But what could he expect when the recruiters were pulling anyone off the street? The captain viewed the rookies with disdain. They all had cigarette burns on their arms and legs, but some had more than others. As one burn represented a misdeed, the trainees carried their report cards on their skin. He picked four of the cleanest, then at the end of the line, his eyes almost popped out at the spectacle. Below the hemline of the shorts, conveniently within the swing of a smoker's arm, bloomed a bouquet of black roses with overlapping layers of tiny round petals. On them all clung a film of sticky orange sap. The captain looked at the owner of the masterpiece and found a husky, round face sassing him with open rebellion. Scorn and hatred leaped out of the deep scar below the boy's eye. The captain pursed his lips. Breaking in a recalcitrant recruit was a challenge he couldn't resist.

"A week ago, I would have said no, you can't have him," the drillmaster said. "But these days, he's been behaving better. He hasn't tried to run away in three days, isn't that so, General Jamil?" He thumped the boy on the back. "He claims to have his own army in Mogadishu. A beggars' army with a battle cry of 'baksheesh, baksheesh,'" he whimpered in the manner of the street urchins of Mogadishu.

"I've got just the right lesson for him," the captain said. "After today, he'll know what happens to people who disobey General Ahmed."

The boy glanced warily at the smoke coiling out of his commander's hand.

104

The captain gathered five recruits into a truck and sped off into the scrub. At a copse of budding bushes, he stopped the truck and ordered everyone out. Flourishing his Kalashnikov rifle, he prodded the recruits toward the water hole. At the edge of the pool, he distributed what appeared to be one-pound sacks of sugar. He cut open his sack and dumped the contents into the muddy water. A pungent odor rose from the powdery fumes. The captain cupped his hand over his nose. Stepping back, he ordered his men to empty their packages. The water fizzled for a while and settled back to a thick brownish yellow.

They retreated behind the copse, where they were ordered to lie down on their stomachs. The captain checked his rifle to make sure it was loaded and stretched out next to the cadets.

"Keep your eyes open. This will be the experience of your life. It's going to make men out of you girls," the captain said. "Don't make any noise now, or I'll send you all to hell."

Tears were welling up in Jamil's eyes. The hot earth scorched the burns on his thighs. Yet he dared not squirm, for the captain was lying right next to him. Then he felt the earth tremble below him, a steady tremor that grew stronger and stronger until a phalanx of camels and men emerged from the shrubs. Jamil watched the leader plant the blunt end of his spear in front of every step. It was true that desert men never smiled. If they found out he was the one who spoiled their water, they'd skin him alive. The stuff was foul smelling, whatever it was. No matter how much his sores hurt, he must keep very quiet.

As the caravan closed in, several boys broke step and ran toward the water hole. The leader shouted at them; reluctantly, they fell back in rank. Alone the elder came forward, a lean dry man in his twenties and already bearing the scars of a lifetime. Carrying his spear like a wise old man, he stalked from one end of the pool to the other. Then he was standing full-faced in front of Jamil. The boy pressed his cheek to the ground. For sure, the herder had seen him. Jamil held his breath. The captain was as still as he was, a finger on the trigger. Seconds passed, but the shout Jamil was expecting never materialized. He lifted his head and saw the white-callused heels of a pair of bare feet receding.

The animals came first. Some were led into the water hole for a bath while others drank from the rim. Finally, when all the camels had gained access to the pool, the leader lay down his spear and sprinkled a handful of water on his neck. The boys jumped in, splashing the animals and themselves. They scooped the murky water in their hands and slurped it down. The leader squatted on the edge to fill his gourd. Soft tongues lapped the water. For a moment, the only sound was aquatic, ripples and gurgles of contentment.

A plash and shout interrupted the bucolic scene. Jamil saw a plume of spray. One of the boys was trying to get out of the water. His fellows pulled him back; he fell in and disappeared. The other boys laughed, but the horseplaying ended abruptly when the boy failed to resurface. They reached into the water, searching for their companion. Cries rang out from the other end of the water hole. A boy stumbled out and fell on his side, twitching and clawing at his throat. A camel brayed and thrashed its legs in the water. It was a harsh, jagged cry that could cut straight to the soul, and when a dozen of them joined in the cacophonous bellow, the noise could drive a person insane. Jamil clamped his hands over his ears, but the violent vibrations penetrated the flesh of his palms and rocked the innermost core of his being.

Satisfied that his mission had been accomplished, the captain and his men returned to the fortress. After boasting of the success of his operation to the colonel, the captain rounded up twenty men and a gas tanker to return to the scene of carnage. The corpses couldn't be left to rot, for an easterly breeze would blow the stench right into the fortress.

Dead camels littered the ground. Islands of humps floated in the water. The recruits jumped off the truck, eyes wide with terror. At the blow of a whistle, the men lined up in single file. Jamil glanced around to search for the bodies of the boys who had drunk the water, but they were nowhere to be seen. Enough of the nomads must have survived to drag their stricken

106

comrades away. There were only the angry eyes of animals staring at him, their double rows of lashes sprung back in accusation. Jamil begged their forgiveness. He'd always been told to be respectful to camels. They were ill-tempered creatures that never forgot a gripe and could turn around and bite you when your guard was down. Jamil grappled with a pair of legs. He'd never thought about how much a camel weighed, and now trying to move the dead weight of one with the help of five others, he appreciated the size of the animal.

One by one, they hauled the camels to an open area and piled them up. Very soon, the accusing eyes didn't bother Jamil anymore. He could only feel the sweat trickling down his neck and an agonizing dryness in his throat. It hurt to swallow. He looked longingly at the water but knew better than to touch it. Then he saw one of his companions wade into the hole, a lasso in his hand. Four others held on to the other end of the rope, ready to haul up the animal. These were men who hadn't participated in the earlier mission. Jamil dropped his burden, ran to the edge of the water and shouted, "Be careful of the water. It's been poisoned!"

The crunching of an officer's boots told him he was in trouble. Jamil spun around and saw the captain striding toward him.

"What's the matter? What's wrong with this water? Don't you want to take a bath in it?"

The captain moved so fast that Jamil barely felt the shove on his chest. He only knew he was falling backward into the deadly water. He pinched his nose and pressed his lips together. The water gurgled in his ears. He stumbled to his feet, leaped off the soft bottom, and clambered to dry land. He spat and spat until there was nothing left to spit. His eyes stung, but the more he rubbed them, the more they hurt. The officers were laughing their heads off.

Jamil was ordered back to work. The taste in his mouth was bitter. Any time now, he was going to fall to the ground and writhe in pain. Then his body would shake uncontrollably, his teeth would chatter and his eyeballs would turn inside out. He

107

thought of his companions in Mogadishu and wanted to cry. But the captain's whip was on his back; he had to keep on going until the poison hit him. He placed both hands on the camel's rib cage and pushed with all his might. When he got it to the pile, his sweat was pouring in a torrent, but neither the writhing nor shaking had started yet.

The sun was a low pink disc when the tanker rolled up to the mountain of legs and humps and dead eyes. Gasoline sprayed out of the hose. The fire had several false starts, but after a couple more generous soakings, the fat began to crackle and feed the flame. The bonfire lit the men's faces, although away from the radius of the glow, night was falling fast.

The recruits lined up. The officers took a head count and herded them into the truck. Jamil wedged himself into a corner. He was so tired he could sleep standing. His eyelids fell, and a delicious unconsciousness overtook him. He had no idea how long he'd been sleeping when the truck stopped and everyone was jumping off to the urging of shouts and whistles. Through the fog of sleep he saw the silhouettes of his companions running into the light of the tanker's high beams. Jamil roused himself and jumped down the truck.

The tanker's wheel was spinning noisily in the gully. The recruits swarmed around the tanker, pushing as the driver gunned the engine. But the harder they worked, the deeper sank the tire into the rut. The captain yelled for everyone to stand back. The vehicle reversed and attempted the climb from a different angle. Jamil held on to a side rail. He pushed as best he could, but it was hard to see whether he was making any difference. Suddenly the tanker surged forward, the rail was ripped out of his hands, and triumphant shouts echoed. People were running again, back to the truck. Jamil ran after them. He was falling behind. If he didn't step on it, he might miss the truck. He stopped, looked around and saw that he was outside the beam of the headlights. He dropped to the ground. The earth rumbled beneath him. After a while, all was quiet except for the pounding of his heart. He was alone.

Chapter 13

In Mogadishu, a document passed from hand to hand. At the back of a shop, inside a living room, in a corner of a restaurant, a car, the pen became a powerful weapon. The text had been typed on an antique Remington with a misaligned ribbon that produced letters black on top and red at the bottom. It was only one page, but the attachment of signatures was five times as many.

"What does this say?" Juergen said to a local staff in his office. Always the first in the office, he was the one who found the envelope. Someone must have slipped it under the door late last night, because when he'd left the office at 9 pm, it hadn't been there. The only word he could make out was "Manifesto" in the title. He also recognized some of the signatures at the back. They belonged to prominent citizens, including several former ministers and a chief of police.

The Somali translated: "We...concerned citizens of the...Democratic Republic of Somalia, would like to..."

"Skip all that. Just tell me what they want," Juergen said impatiently.

The Somali skimmed the first paragraph. "They want the president to resign," adding as his eyes roved down the page, "they also want an interim government made up of members of the opposition...and a timetable for multiparty elections."

"Ah yes, of course, thank you very much," Juergen said. He went through the list of names again. These weren't leaders of rebel clans but revered members of society who were once supporters of Siad Barré. Their signature on this document was a more devastating blow to the regime than an armed uprising in any other part of the country. This rebellion was right here in Mogadishu, the heart of Siad Barré's power base.

Heads were going to roll, Juergen predicted. Barré would never allow dissent in his own lair. Juergen started thinking about what it meant for the expat community, the safety of which he was responsible for. He could send out an advisory to batten down the hatches. If nothing were to happen, he would be criticized for being an alarmist. The government might even request his removal. On the other hand, if he did nothing and something did happen, the consequences would be far more serious.

He buzzed for his secretary. Although Juergen had a computer that he turned on every day as part of his morning ritual, he couldn't type, and he wasn't going to start learning a year before retirement. With his competent British secretary seated before him, he dictated an informal "Dear Colleagues" bulletin. From his Angola days, he'd learned the emergency guidelines so well that he didn't have to consult the manual. Or perhaps his knowledge dated farther back than that, from the time he'd been a small boy in Frankfurt. The rush to bomb shelters under the scream of air raid sirens, playing hide and seek in the rubble as grownups dug for bodies, scrounging for food and water—yes, he'd had some training in handling emergencies. Juergen finished his dictation and instructed his secretary to have the dispatch hand delivered to every organization under his jurisdiction.

He then called a meeting of the two other members of his staff—Ali, a young, strapping Somali, and Jean-Paul, a slender, artistic Frenchman who dabbled in watercolors. Juergen warned his staff to be prepared to work round the clock. Aside from the usual twenty-four-hour monitoring of the CB radio, they would have to function as newscasters as well. The CB would be the only means of keeping their constituents informed of fast-breaking news.

Toward late morning, Juergen heard a door slam, followed by a padded clomp that he'd recognize anywhere. He got up to greet his wife, Gertrude. A thickset woman with cropped hair walked in, her apple cheeks bobbing above an armful of paper bags. Juergen stubbed out his cigarette to help her.

"What's this for?" he said, inspecting the loaves of bread and canned meats. "There's going to be a riot. If you're going to be stuck here, you'll need some food," she declared.

"Who says there's going to be a riot?" Juergen said. His wife's declarations always got him into a counter-declaration mode, no matter whether he agreed or not. Gertrude waved him aside and crouched to put the groceries in the mini-fridge under his printer table. She pulled the two six-packs of beer out of the icebox and began stocking it with more substantial food.

Juergen spent the afternoon dropping in on the ministries and embassies. Nobody had heard of any arrests. The Somali officials he met with assured him there would be no reprisals against the manifesto signatories. Foreign diplomats, however, were less sanguine in their conjectures, but still they were only conjectures. Some thought it would be suicidal for Siad Barré to arrest his opponents, while others thought he had no choice but to clamp down in full force. The weather vane gyrated from person to person. Even the Italians, who as the ex-colonial masters had access to the highest echelons of the country's rulers, couldn't offer a more definite forecast of the weather to come.

Disappointed, Juergen headed back to the office. The streets seemed quieter than usual, yet again what was usual? He had to watch himself, for he could be hypersensitive at times.

When he got back to the office in the late afternoon, Ali was on duty. All seemed quiet. Juergen checked his Reuters teleprinter, which by now had filed a dispatch on the manifesto. President Barré, to whom the manifesto was addressed, still hadn't reacted in words or action. Juergen took his shift at monitoring the CB. At midnight, Jean-Paul showed up to relieve him. Juergen puttered around for another half an hour before saying goodnight.

The next morning, Juergen tiptoed out of bed at five. His wife was still snoring, an envious sound to a person who had been tossing and turning all night. If it hadn't been for the nightmares, he would have thought he hadn't slept a wink. After wolfing down a piece of his wife's chocolate cake—he could get coffee in the office—he drove off. The morning in the tropics was the best time of the day. The air was pure enough to drink.

Juergen rolled down the window and took a deep breath to clear his stuffy head.

The radio was crackling when he stepped into the office. Ali's voice was on the air. Juergen caught the word "soldiers." He quietly took a seat by Jean-Paul and tuned in.

"Ali, this is Juergen. Where are you?"

"On the roof of my house. A truck full of soldiers just stopped in front of my neighbor's. He's Abdulrahman Farag, one of the people who signed the manifesto. They've surrounded the house now. The truck is backing up...no, it's driving in...it's ramming down the gate..."

The radio went dead. "Ali, are you there? Ali, Ali."

The airwaves sizzled, and Ali's voice returned, "The soldiers have gone into the house. There are shouts...women crying...They're coming back out now. They've got somebody with them...it's hard to see...I think it's...yes, they've got Abdulrahman!"

"Shit," Juergen said. The pencil holder jumped as his fist landed on the desk.

More arrests were reported as the day wore on. Around noon, Juergen issued another bulletin summarizing the situation as best he could. He also advised everyone to keep his CB on. From his experience in two evacuations, a situation could turn ugly fast. That night, Juergen set up camp in his office. While he was proud of his team and trusted them to do their jobs without supervision, he felt he'd better be there. It could be a long wait, and although he kept warning himself not to wear himself out before the action started, he couldn't stop the rush of adrenalin. In a way, Juergen wished it would happen quickly, whatever would happen.

The night passed peacefully. Aside from two calls from parents looking frantically for their teenage children, who eventually showed up, the citizen's band frequencies were quiet. The next morning, the three men took turns to go home for a shower, a shave, and a catnap. On his way home, Juergen took a detour around the city and ran into a traffic jam near the stadium. He remembered there was going to be a soccer game that day.

Susan could understand Fatima's nervousness. She was a member of the Siad Barré's Marehan clan. If there were a riot, she and her family would be prime targets. None of her children had gone to school that day. Susan was willing to give her emergency leave, but Fatima's loyalty was dogged. She knew better than anyone how Davar could react if his telexes weren't returned promptly.

Omar was grumpy as usual, but with a difference. While his crabbiness had been a quiet, passive kind before, today it was loud and aggressive. He threw the files around and even yelled at Fatima when she asked him to fill out his time sheet. Susan knew he was a Hawiye, most of whom were resentful of the privileges granted to the minority Marehans. However, a number of Hawiyes had been co-opted by the ruling clan, and Susan didn't know whether Omar was one of them. It was hard to tell anything with Omar.

Around late morning, pounding footsteps in the corridor gave voice to the unspoken anxiety. Fatima sprang up from her chair. Omar and Susan came running from opposite ends. The door flew open. It was Mohammed, the driver, shouting in Somali. Susan had no idea what he was yelling about, but his gestures indicated a catastrophe. Omar dashed out with Mohammed on his tail. Fatima picked up her basket, muttered something about her children and bustled off. Susan turned on the radio. Between the crackles she recognized Amanda's voice.

"I hear gunshots…People are running out of the stadium…They're pouring out!"

"Amanda, get away from there. Go back to the embassy." The baritone was Juergen's.

"Don't worry, I'm several blocks from the stadium. I'll drive away the moment there's danger. Hey, wait, there are troops coming from the other side of the road…They're headed for the stadium…No, they're not…. They're just standing there.

I'm not sure what they're doing... Oh no, oh no, they're going to shoot at the crowd...."

The gunfire spoke for itself.

"Amanda, get the hell out of there!"

Omar ran into the street. A horde of young men was spilling down Via Somalia. His feet ached to sprint after them, but his intellect told him the stadium was several kilometers away and he was in no shape to race these youngsters. An idea crossed his mind. He ran to the back alley where the company Mercedes was parked, and found Mohammed engaged in spit-flying jabber with his friends.

"Let's go to the stadium," Omar said, pointing with his chin at the shiny silver limo.

"In that? What will the boss say?" Mohammed raised his eyes at the upper reaches of the building.

"She's not leaving yet. Just take me close to the stadium and you can drive back."

As Mohammed hesitated, Omar spat out, "You call yourself a Hawiye! They're slaughtering your brothers and you stand here and do nothing!"

His head hung in shame, Mohammed got into the car. Omar hopped into the front seat. Meandering around the side streets, they managed to avoid the crowds until the Afgoy Road intersection. Bands of irate men swirled around the car, forcing Mohammed to slow to a snail's pace. Omar shouted out the window to identify the clanship he shared with the demonstrators. He shook his fist, yelling and cheering them on. Bodies gave way to the limo. Fists banged its sleek, polished body in a show of solidarity rather than hostility. To Mohammed, however, every blow inflicted personal pain. How he wished he could step on it and go, but instead he had to tap the gas pedal as if it was made of eggshell. If he so much as brushed anyone, the crowd would tear him limb from limb with their bare hands. His calves were cramping up, and he was gulping shallow breaths through his mouth.

After many minutes of painful restraint, the Mercedes' broad nose emerged from the crowd. The way was clear. Mohammed tested the pedal, and in an instant he was beyond the reach of the angry mob.

On Via Lenin, Mohammed slowed down in front of a row of gold shops. The windows were smashed and looters were stuffing their pockets. He recognized one of them as a neighbor, normally a quiet, honest man. Mohammed's wife would never believe him if he told her what he saw. The whole town had gone berserk. A machine gun barked not far away. Mohammed jammed on the brakes. They were getting close to the stadium.

"We've gone far enough. Let's go back now," he said.

Omar flung open the door and got out.

"Hey, come back, don't be foolish!" Mohammed shouted after his friend. "There's nothing you can do."

Omar refused to look back, his bowlegs hurrying along.

He had no idea what he was going to do. The one thing he knew he couldn't do was hide at home. Anger seethed in him, the anger that he'd lived with since his eldest brother's arrest. On a blanket charge of "plotting to overthrow the government," Siad Barré had thrown his brother in jail and left him to rot for ten years without a trial. By the end of it, he was blind, his skin festering with sores and scabies, and his once brilliant mind eaten away by the worms of solitary confinement. He'd been a Member of Parliament, the best and brightest in the family, but the man who had returned home bore no resemblance to the brother Omar had loved. A few months later, he'd faded away. Nobody had dared mention his name since. Yet now, it was pounding in his head, *Hussein, Hussein, Hussein.*

A group of looters were lugging furniture out of a home. "Brothers, what are you doing?" Omar cried. The enemy is killing us and all you can do is grab for yourself?"

"We're taking from our enemies. They're Marehans," shouted a youth balancing a television on his head and clutching a bundle of clothes.

A blast of gunshots ripped the air. Omar clapped his hands over his ears and closed his eyes, certain that the end was near.

When he reopened them, he found himself still alive and the looters still carrying away their plunder, now with heightened frenzy. The skirmish was getting closer. With every shot, Omar could feel a body falling.

"They're killing our brothers. We've got to do something!" Omar cried. He waved his skinny arms and stumbled head-on into a gang toting a variety of homemade weapons.

"The stadium is that way," Omar yelled to them. But they pushed past him, their vision closing in upon an affluent compound a block away. Omar recognized it as the home of one of the wives of a prominent businessman, a Marehan.

"Please, this is not the way to take revenge," Omar pleaded, running to catch up with them.

At the gate, a man carrying an axe sprang up on the locked hands of another and vaulted over the wall. From the other side, Omar could hear the harsh clang of metal hitting metal. Tears poured down his cheeks and a flood of words tumbled out: "I lost a brother. He was the best person in the world and they put him in jail and tortured him, but it's still not right—" A final blow split the bolt and the gate yawned open. The gang charged in, sweeping Omar with them. The men fanned out into the wings of the mansion. As Omar stood in a daze at the center of the courtyard, the chilling sound of a woman's wail traveled down from the upper floor. People ran out of different parts of the compound like a pack of bloodhounds converging for the kill. With a flurry of yelps they chased up the staircase. Sputtering a jumble of exhortations, Omar staggered after them.

An old man lay in front of the doorway. The top of his head had been cracked open, and a glistening white mass was creeping out. His eyes dangled out of their sockets, one staring at Omar and the other at the ceiling. Omar felt his knees sag and his stomach churn. He wanted to get away, but a push from behind sent him leaping over the body into the room.

A woman and child huddled in a corner. The woman was shaking uncontrollably while the child clung to her, his face burrowed into her skirt.

116

"Where is your husband now, the rich man who can give you everything?" taunted the guardian of the axe. "What a beautiful bed he bought you. You think he'd mind if I tried it?" He pulled the little boy away from her. The shrieks from mother and child were piercing, and then the act happened so quickly that Omar only noticed the swiping gleam of a knife. The child fell to the ground, blood spurting out of the plump folds below his chin. The men threw the woman onto the bed and tore off her clothes. She struggled for a while and then became strangely quiet, her eyes still as a corpse's. Omar saw that she was pregnant, not far advanced yet, but pregnant.

Omar felt his stomach do a somersault. The wall spun around him; he put out his hand to hold it still, but it kept on swirling faster and faster until everything was a blur. He closed his eyes to shut it out.

Chapter 14

Mrs. Giuseppe shouted in her Italian voice, which was several decibels louder than her English. Around her, the guests scurried back and forth the courtyard restaurant, carrying the solid wooden dining tables and chairs to the hotel front and stacking them like Lego blocks across the defenseless entrance. Mr. Giuseppe, a short and stocky man who seemed happy to let his wife do the talking for two, sat in a corner, quietly cleaning his rifle.

"Everyone who knows how to shoot a rifle, please step forward!" Mrs. Giuseppe ordered. Taking his cue, her husband came to her side and held up his weapon. The rifle, with a stock of finely carved walnut and the slim long barrel of a musket, was more like an antique that deserved to be displayed on a living room wall than used as a weapon.

The volunteers numbered half a dozen: two Italian workers, the American salesman of agricultural tools, the Dutch Australian called Jack, Mr. Giuseppe himself and—everyone stared at this draftee with disbelief—Susan. She explained that her father used to take her hunting—a lie so blatant that she knew she couldn't blame people for rolling their eyes skyward. But when the Italian workers started snickering and exchanging wisecracks in their own language, she grabbed the gun from Mrs. Giuseppe, slapped back the trigger guard with expert flair, and pointed at the clock on the wall.

"I believe you!" Mrs. Giuseppe cried, either convinced or concerned for the welfare of her clock. "My dear, I believe you," Mrs. Giuseppe said, calmly now that Susan had lowered the gun. "It's a dangerous job, I don't want you to get hurt. But if you must insist, I will accept your bravery."

The volunteers were paired up. Susan got Jack for a partner, the Italians stuck together, leaving Mr. Giuseppe with Hoyt Grimley, the American salesman. He'd just returned from a trip to the rural areas to promote his wares and had obviously spent some time in the sun. His pasty complexion had turned a raw salmon pink, and his skin was flaking off like the scales of a sick fish. According to him, the embassy's travel warning was a gross exaggeration. The village he'd visited had been as safe as a fortress.

As the first team took its position, Mrs. Giuseppe improvised a tripwire alarm by tying pots and pans to a rope laid across the sidewalk. There was also a reshuffling of rooms. Tenants who could help in fending off an attack were moved to the ground floor, while others, mostly women, got rooms on the upper floor. Weapons consisted of all the household hardware Mrs. Giuseppe could gather. The Italian workers were bucking for action, but when the hotelier brought out a tray of freshly sharpened kitchen knives, their effervescence flattened instantly. This wasn't going to be a barroom brawl. If the scuffle got out of hand, the police wouldn't be there to break it up.

The day passed quietly. As time ticked away, the opening and closing of doors became more frequent. Residents converged on the veranda to speculate about the storm that might or might not hit. Cautious laughter punctuated the serious deliberations, but when night descended, and Susan's CB radio crackled with desperate S.O.S. calls from expats whose homes had come under attack, the residents returned to their rooms and locked themselves in.

At three in the morning Susan and Jack mounted their guard. For the longest time, they kept an unrelenting watch on the darkness. Neither made a sound, but suddenly Susan couldn't hold it anymore. She yawned, a soulful, unconditional yawn that said everything that needed to be said. Immediately in its wake a pronouncement equally profound escaped from her partner as Jack yawned, too. An eruption of soft chuckles pulsed through the tense night air. Jack pulled his chair closer to Susan.

"How are you holding up?"

"Fine, but that yawn was long overdue."

"So was mine."

They fell silent again, and then a small smacking sound came from Jack as his tongue parted from the roof of his mouth.

"I keep telling myself I'm going home next year," Jack said, "but the government keeps on renewing my contract and there's always another next year. I'll probably end up dying here."

"How long have you been here?" Susan said, turning toward him. His face was lit by a three-quarter moon, but all she noticed was the eyes, the pale, translucent windows that promised to reveal everything if she only dared look.

"Six years and three months," Jack said.

"That *is* a long time!" Susan couldn't help exclaiming.

"I should have left the first year, but given the fact that I didn't, I might as well stay here the rest of my life."

Susan chewed on his words for a while. "Excuse me, I don't quite understand your logic."

"You know what happened to my daughter, don't you?" he said. Instead of admitting that Fatima had been gossiping about him, Susan pretended total ignorance. "Sarah was six when we moved here," Jack said. "She was such a pretty little thing."
His voice melted and Susan thought she saw a smile, the first that she'd noticed. "My black beauty, I used to call her. My wife is Indonesian and Sarah took after her mother. It was our first year here, in fact, the third month of our stay. It was a hot day, and everyone was at the beach. You know, the beach at Lido." Susan nodded yes, she'd been to the scruffy strip of sand between Mogadishu's best seafood restaurant and the abattoir.

"She was playing in the water with three of her friends," Jack went on. "The water was only up to her belly button. I thought it was as safe as playing in a bathtub. When the kids screamed and ran out of the water, I thought they were playing." Jack paused. Susan couldn't stand the suspense, although Fatima had already told her the ending.

"There was blood in the water," Jack continued with the detachment of an unconcerned narrator, "and a little black head bobbing up and down, and I knew it was Sarah. I got in and pulled her out. Her belly had been ripped open. The shark had bypassed the dozens of other people and gone straight for her."

Susan's heart went out to Jack. "I'm sorry," she whispered.

"Some people say it was due to her dark skin," Jack continued in a bodiless voice. "There's an old wives' tale that sharks go for dark skins. I doubt if it's been proven scientifically, but that's how some people explain the attack on Sarah. Three other kids were with her, and they were all white. Maybe it's just plain bad luck, but you know what I call it?" Susan thought for a while, but nothing came to her mind.

"The cold war," Jack said. "My daughter was a victim of the cold war."

Susan turned to look at him, wondering what lunacy could be brewing under the calm surface.

Jack continued: "There've always been sharks in these waters, but they've never come so close to shore before. It all began when the Soviet Union sent a team to Mogadishu and helped the Somalis build an abattoir right by the water. It was convenient, because at the end of the day the butchers could dump the offal into the sea. The sharks loved it, but the coral reefs kept out most of them. The tide turned when Siad Barré switched camps. A group of American experts came and told the Somalis they needed more shipping lanes to serve the budding economy. A company was hired to blast a hole in the reefs, and from then on it's been an open highway for the man-eating monsters."

Susan regretted she ever thought the man was crazy.

"You know, this is the first time I ever told anyone," Jack said.

His eyes met hers, but this time Susan didn't turn away. The ghost had been purged.

A clatter of pots and pans resounded. Jack knelt down on one knee and cocked the rifle. Susan went down with him.

"Who's there?" he shouted. They peeped through the cracks of the makeshift barricade. Shadows flitted in the moonlit night. Somebody was out there. "Don't come any closer or I'll shoot!"

Gunfire was the response. Jack and Susan went belly down on the ground. Wood chips flew. Susan could recognize an AK-47 when she heard one. Footsteps pattered from behind.

122

She turned around and saw a figure running out of the hotel. It was Mr. Giuseppe.

"Get down!" she cried as the Italian braked and fell with a thump. Giuseppe was hit.

His wife called out. Susan shouted to her to stay in her room. A sputter of bullets re-enforced her warning. Susan peered out, searching for the source of the fusillade. From the wild dispersal of the slugs, she could tell it was the AK-47 that was deciding the aim, not the person pulling the trigger. The sniper was an amateur who hadn't mastered the art of taming an AK-47. Neither had he learned the art of sniping, which was to change his roost from time to time to avoid detection.

At the first break, Susan grabbed the rifle from Jack, stood up, aimed at the source of the gunfire and pulled the trigger. A metallic ping pealed, a cry, shouts and a rush of footsteps. Susan dropped on one knee and fired between the running legs. The pavement pounded, and the clamor rose and fell as the attackers fled into the night.

"I'll see to Giuseppe. You're in charge here," Jack said and parted with a comradely slap on her back.

When he returned to Susan's side, day was breaking. He reported on Mr. Giuseppe's condition: A bullet had grazed his shoulder and a physician staying at the hotel was attending to him. He was in no immediate danger but would have to be medi-vacced out of the country for decent medical care. Susan radioed Juergen, who was already in the throes of chartering a plane to transport the injured to Nairobi.

Around ten the next morning, the government announced that the army had regained control of the capital. Shortly after, a vehicle pulled up in front of the Eden. At the sight of Juergen and his assistant, the hotel guests opened an entrance in the blockade. Mr. Giuseppe was helped to his feet and escorted into the vehicle. Mrs. Giuseppe kissed her husband goodbye. She was staying to hold the fort.

Bit by bit, people ventured out. Susan decided to go to her office and was thankful for Jack's offer to drive her. His vehicle had been safely parked in the Giuseppes' private driveway, or it would have suffered the same fate as the gutted cars they saw along the way. In front of the Ministry of Finance, Susan and Jack showed their I.D.s to a platoon of soldiers and were allowed to pass. Susan directed Jack into the back alley where the Mercedes Benz was usually parked. To her surprise, it wasn't there. She'd expected it to be beaten and battered, but not absent. Not knowing what to make of it, she went into the building. As Susan entered her office, a tousled head raised itself from the sofa.

Mohammed jumped to his feet, buttoning his shirt and rubbing his toes against each other to hide their nudity.

"You've been here all this time?" Susan exclaimed.

"I'm sorry, Miss Chen. I'm very sorry..."

"How come you didn't go home?"

"I'm very sorry, Miss Chen," Mohammed repeated, his eyes downcast. "I told Omar we shouldn't go there, but he wouldn't listen to me. I know I should ask you first, but he was in a hurry..." The story of his driving Omar to the stadium trickled out. On the way back to the office, a gang of looters had surrounded Mohammed. They'd hauled him out of the car and knocked him about when one of the looters recognized Mohammed as a distant cousin and convinced the others to let him go. He'd turned on his heels and run all the way to the office, never once looking back to see about the fate of his beloved Mercedes.

While Mohammed begged for forgiveness, Susan's concern was for her assistant. What was Omar doing, hurling himself into the midst of a riot?

"Do you know where Omar lives?" Susan said.

"Yes, I can take you there." Mohammed brightened, but his face dimmed again the next instant. "We don't have a car—" Before he could complete his sentence, Jack was jangling the key to his Land Rover.

They passed several checkpoints, and every time they sailed through, Susan was grateful to Jack for more reasons than giving her a lift. Without him, she was sure she couldn't have traveled that far. The soldiers showed a quiet menace that she'd never seen before. In their bloodshot eyes, the distinction between expats and locals had blurred. The embassies could protest all they wanted, but these men were in no mood to think of diplomatic niceties. Fortunately, Jack knew how to handle them. He greeted them in Somali, passed cigarettes around and displayed a male camaraderie that eased their nervousness. Without Jack, she definitely couldn't have made it past the first checkpoint.

Around K-5 on Afgoy Road, Jack stepped on the brakes. The remnant of a vehicle was sprawled across the road. As Jack steered around it, everyone gawked at the bareness of the shell. It was lying on its side like a butchered turtle, its head and limbs chopped off, its insides eviscerated, stripped of every piece of flesh and organ. The paint had been scraped, but the odd streak of silver revealed its original color. When Mohammed gasped, Susan saw the horror on his face and knew this was the company car.

Past K-8, Mohammed guided Jack into a narrow dirt track into a part of town that few expats would have reason to set foot on. After numerous twists and turns between rows of modest houses, they stopped in front of a green wooden gate. Mohammed knocked and shouted in Somali. A woman replied. The gate opened, and there stood a spitting image of Omar, except that it was female and her eyes were straight. Susan kept glancing over at the house, hoping to see Omar's gnome-like figure lollop out in that awkward gait of his. But what came out was yet another version of Omar, this time a generation older. The elderly woman hobbled up, and an earnest exchange followed. The younger woman was shouting in the old woman's ear. Comprehension was slow, but when it came the reaction was instantaneous. The woman wailed and wrung her hands.

As Susan had feared, Omar hadn't come home.

"Tell her not to worry. I'll find Omar and bring him home," Susan said to Mohammed, who translated the message. The crying stopped. The old woman clutched Susan's hands and mumbled blessings. Susan was amazed that she could have made such a promise.

Back in the car, Susan suggested it was time for Mohammed to go home. There, the scene was that of a joyous reunion. His parents, his pretty wife and numerous other relations lined up to thank her. They offered her tea and biscuits, and at the risk of being rude, she declined.

The next stop was the U.N. compound. The place was a madhouse, in particular Juergen's office, which was doubling as an asylum for expat refugees too scared to return home. Nobody had information about Omar. Juergen jotted down his name and promised to do his best. His grayish hair had faded a few shades since Susan had last seen him.

Once again in the car, Susan and Jack looked at each other and simultaneously said, "The hospital." By process of elimination, their options were becoming dangerously few.

More bedlam greeted them at the hospital. An overflow of patients had spilled into the corridor and were moaning and bleeding on the ground while doctors and nurses swooped about like barn swallows. Susan and Jack went from bed to bed, mat to mat. Having seen what bruises could do to a person's face, she was careful not to go by her memory of what Omar used to look like. One feature would identify him for sure: his left eye. The moment she peered into a patient's eyes, any shadow of a doubt would be gone, and she would move on. There was one whose entire left face was swaddled in bandages, but his legs were so long that they stuck out of the cot. Omar, the runt, couldn't have grown overnight. At the end of their inspection, Susan was glad that none of the sick and maimed was her assistant. Her relief, however, quickly turned into a stone-cold dread.

She stopped a nurse and asked the ultimate question: "Where are the dead taken?"

The nurse pointed glumly to the east wing.

"Susan," Jack said at the entrance. The mention of her name was endearing. She felt a pinch in her heart and recognized it as a hole in her emotional dam. "You don't have to go in," he said. "I know what Omar looks like."

"I want to," she said, boring into his pellucid eyes. This tattered homeless man, a total stranger only a few days ago, had become as familiar as a lifelong friend.

The uncovered corpses lay in sardine rows on the concrete floor. Susan stepped forward, pushing her disciplined self to the fore. She'd fought in mock battles, killed and been killed, but she'd never seen a truly dead body before, and she'd never thought that her first experience would include so many. She counted the rows and arrived at an estimate of two hundred. "You start from this end, I'll start from the other," she said, the blandness of her voice surprising herself.

Jack took a look at the prospect, and his leathery tan blanched to a mottled gray.

Susan tried to limit her vision to the faces. There were a few women and children, but most were young men who would never see a soccer match again. Some had closed their eyes as in a feverish sleep, lips ajar struggling for breath, the kind of rest that would leave them tired and fretful the next morning. Others were frozen in their last expression of terror, fear shrieking out of their open eyes. The worst, for Susan, were those that had pieces of their faces blown away, for those were the ones she had to scrutinize. A swarm of flies were buzzing in a feeding frenzy. The smell was overpowering. Susan breathed through a small crack between her lips, but even so her tongue could taste the rottenness.

She and Jack converged in the middle of the courtyard. She shook her head no and received the same response from her partner.

Jack led the way out of the labyrinth. Susan had been so preoccupied with identifying the bodies that she hadn't noticed how narrow her path had been. Now that she was aware of it, her knees began to wobble. She spread out her arms for better balance, but the more she minced her steps the unsteadier she grew. One false step and she would be falling into the field of corpses. Jack was already in the clear. Just a few more steps for her. Her pulse quickened; she wanted to run, but next thing she knew the tip of her loafer was digging into a dead man's foot and she was pitching forward. An arm caught her. She started to assure him she was all right, but her throat seized up in a dry spasm. His hand on her shoulder was warm. She laid her head on his chest and wiped her tear-streaked face on his shirt.

Chapter 15

The sweet smell of wood shavings permeated the room. Hamid hunched over a door laid across a workbench, chiseling away furiously. Chips flew out from under him. Squiggles of Arabic letters as refined as handwritten calligraphy etched into the perimeter of the panel, wrapping around it once and twice already. He was starting on the third line, the beginning of a quote from the *Koran*, "God is with those who endure." The saying had taken on a new meaning for him. The ability to endure the passage of time was a requisite for a successful predator, but to have worked up an appetite for a kill and then be told that the wildebeest he'd singled out wasn't to be touched, the frustration was well-nigh unbearable. He'd already seated himself in the car when the last-minute repeal came. No reason had been given, but he'd later learned from his Somali woman that riots had broken out in Mogadishu.

Hamid felt a breeze on his back. Someone had walked in. It could be only one of two people, and he knew which one it was.

"Let's go," the colonel said, breathless from carrying his excessive weight around.

"I haven't had my breakfast yet," Hamid said. That was the least concern on his mind now, but Hamid couldn't stand the colonel's officious behavior, which was worsening with the completion of every job. Hearing him talk, one would have thought he'd been the one to plunge in the knife.

"We didn't pay you to do nothing!" the colonel shouted his favorite line. He pounded his fist on the door Hamid was carving on, flipping up a cloud of dust and chips. Hamid looked placidly at the Somali. The fat oaf was a nuisance, he thought, but this wasn't the time to get even. Not yet. He got up slowly and stretched.

"You're right," he said. "Too much food is not good for you. Makes you fat and lazy."

The barb of sarcasm failed to penetrate the colonel's meaty head. His upper lip stiffening with disdain, he handed the camera to Hamid like an overlord entrusting care of his sword to his valet. Hamid swallowed his pride and slung it over his shoulder. He put the Panama hat on his prematurely gray hair, the result of frequent bleaching, and followed the colonel out. A tire of fat ringed the back of the colonel's neck. Underneath the adipose layer was a column of vertebrae like everybody else. Hamid imagined the pleasure of puncturing the tire with a nick of his blade.

A woman carrying a basket approached. An idea struck Hamid. He aligned the numbers on the combination lock, opened the case, and took out the camera.

"What are you doing?" the colonel said, swiveling his girth around in annoyance.

"Practicing. The American said I must practice." To the woman, he said, "Stand there, don't move," and snapped away. The woman hid her face halfway behind the basket, twittering coquettishly and teasing him on. Hamid danced around her, fondling the devices in his hand the way the American had taught him. Then he spun around and pointed the weapon at the colonel. The fat man ducked, shielding his face with his truncheon arms. Relentlessly Hamid continued to pull the trigger. The *Koran* forbids the capture of the image of the human figure, but these days Hamid had license to violate the rule, and he was taking full advantage of it.

When the shooting finally stopped, the colonel peeked out of his elbow. "Why did you do that?" he shouted.

"I told you, I was practicing. The American said I must learn to hold the camera right."

"Do you have my picture in there?" The colonel advanced, menacing to snatch away the camera.

Hamid decided he'd gone far enough in his little trick. Raising one hand in surrender, he handed over the controversial object. The colonel grabbed it and searched frantically for the film. He was about to rip the camera in half when Hamid reached over and pressed a button on the back. A flap flung out; the chamber was empty.

They drove off to the shooting range. The colonel was quiet and sullen. Hamid, too, was sober. The camera was a powerful weapon. He'd had his picture taken only once in his life, and he'd regretted it ever since. In one click, his American trainer had stolen his face. He could keep it, for Hamid had no use for it anymore.

His captors had performed half the surgery. They'd pulverized his nose, bashed in his cheekbones, smashed his jaws, and knocked his teeth into his skull. The surgeons in Khartoum had a clean slate to work from. They'd molded a straight, well-centered nose, shaped the jaws to a fine taper, pared down his mended cheekbones, and fitted him with a set of dentures arched like a rainbow. It was a picture-perfect face, so flawless that it was hard to describe. No one could call him the man with the hawk nose, or the square jaws, or the rugged cheekbones, or the crooked teeth. It was the kind of face that a person could meet many times and every time he would say, "Pleased to meet you," instead of "Nice to see you again." It was the perfect face for an assassin.

Chapter 16

Jack brought Susan back to the World Bank office. She went straight into Omar's room, hoping against hope that he would be composing telexes at his desk. His chair was empty. Omar wasn't there. How could a man disappear without a trace? Susan wondered. Even if harm had come to him, surely he or news of him would have surfaced somewhere in her extensive search.

The silence in the office was deafening. She'd told Mohammed to stay home, as in her car-less state a chauffeur wasn't of much use. Fatima had taken leave for as long as necessary. During the riots, a number of houses in her Marehan-dominated district had been attacked, entire families massacred, but hers had been spared. Her good fortune, however, might not last, and as a precautionary measure, she'd taken leave to settle her children in Bardere, the Marehan stronghold far away from the capital.

Jack was waiting in her office. She went in and sat down next to him on the sofa. It had been a long day.

"I'm afraid I have to go back to Kurtun Waarey," Jack said. "A consignment of gas is arriving tomorrow. I have to be there to make sure everything's in order."

Susan felt a constriction in her throat. At no time in her life had she felt a greater urge to hang on to somebody. But the greater the anxiety, the calmer was the façade she put up. "Of course, you have to start planting soon," she said.

"The rains are late this year. If we waste any more time, the season will be lost." Jack hung his head and glanced sideways at Susan. "I hate to leave you like this. You don't even have a car—"

"There are plenty of taxis. I'll be fine," Susan said.

"I wish I could help you find Omar—"

"Juergen is on the look out for him. We'll find him sooner or later." Her voice was flat and formal, as though she was leaving a message on an answering machine.

"It's kind of silly to think of putting seeds in the ground at a time like this. Who knows if the country can hold together till harvest? Sometimes I wonder what I'm doing here."

"Well, now," Susan said, peeling back a corner of her shield, "you've got a good project going."

Jack shook his head. "I don't know. Sometimes when I listen to the old men reminisce about the good old days, I feel it's presumptuous of me to tell them how to live. Who am I to tell a nomad he's better off settling down and trying to turn a dust bowl into farmland? His people have been surviving quite well for thousands of years before any of us came along. Do you know, before there was such a thing as a government in Mogadishu, the Somalis were governing themselves by the purest form of democracy?" Jack sat up, his face brightening. It was obviously a subject close to his heart. "I've never heard of a more equitable form of government. They called it the *shir*, a council that ran the affairs of a nomadic hamlet. Everybody in the hamlet was a member of the *shir*, or let's say every *man* was. They usually met under the shade of an acacia tree, sitting in a circle and thrashing out the issues of the day. Now where else can you find such a pure form of democracy?"

"For the men," Susan qualified.

Jack laughed an "I knew you would say that." "I don't mean to romanticize about the old days," he went on. "Life was harsh in the desert, and one group often fought another over water holes and grazing territory. It could get quite violent sometimes, and people speared each other in battle. But still, there were codes of conduct that kept the conflicts from escalating. When the fighting got bad, clan leaders would meet to negotiate a settlement, usually the offering of a camel or sheep to appease the injured group. The standard price for a man's life was a hundred camels and for a woman, fifty." He smiled as Susan wrinkled her nose at the inequity. "The payment of blood money was called the *dia*, and for hundreds of years, it had kept relative peace among the warring groups."

"Siad Barré has banned the *dia*, the *shir*, and all the traditional ways of government," Susan said. "He wanted

134

Somalia to be a modern state. What do you think is going to happen now?"

Jack shook his head. "I don't know. The old rules are gone. There are plenty of new ones on paper, but people don't take them seriously. How can they, when those who made the rules are the worst offenders?"

There was a moment of silence. Susan could feel Jack draw in his breath, arriving at a conclusion. He had to go. She knew all she had to do was ask, and he would stay another day, but she wasn't going to.

"Enough of my rambling. Things have changed, and there's no way anyone can roll back time. We can only move ahead."

Susan pressed her hand on his. "Thanks so much for everything. Next time you come to town, you should stay at my house. I should have moved in by then." In case her offer sounded too forward, she added in a hurry, "You can save the project the expenses of your room and board."

At the door, they stood facing each other for an awkward moment. Susan stuck out her hand, which he grasped and held for a while. The message in the blue eyes was clearer than the desert sky, louder than a carillon of bells. Susan took her hand away. The attraction had taken her by surprise. She hadn't planned or wanted it. Only a few days ago he'd drifted into her life like a spirit from another world, and now he was standing there in flesh and blood, the only person she could rely on.

The door closed, and Jack was gone. Susan wandered over to Fatima's desk and sat down. She stared at the door, then gave her head a good shaking to clear it of the haze. Her thoughts turned back to Omar. Juergen had promised to radio her the moment he had any news. Pestering him wasn't going to help. She looked at the clock. It was five in the afternoon. The lack of sleep and the day of running around were catching up with her. Her head was a muddle, and her heart a raw, malleable dough that anyone could make an imprint on. The next time she saw Jack—if there were a next time—she was sure to see him in the proper perspective. He was just a fellow traveler on this strange and lonely journey. For now, the sensible course of action was to get herself something to eat, a shower and a good night's rest.

She closed up shop and went "home" to the Eden. A group of urchins were hectoring a couple coming out of the hotel. Susan perked up. She hadn't seen them in weeks and had been wondering what had happened to them.

"Jamil," she shouted at the leader, "is that you? Hey!" She ran up to them. "Haven't seen you in a while. Where on earth have you been?"

The children surrounded her. Jamil was grinning from ear to ear. Susan looked over the boy who was now her height and still growing. "You look different. Taller and...more mature," she said, noticing the angles on the once padded face. "What's happening?"

"I am General Ahmed's soldier," Jamil said, bracing like a cadet.

"Oh no, don't tell me they've got you, too." The sight of soldiers rounding up able-bodied men and hauling them into their truck was common in Mogadishu. "So they found out you were just a kid and let you go?"

Jamil tossed his head back. "I ran away," he said proudly. A companion made a remark in Somali, which caused Jamil to eject a string of harsh language. Susan had witnessed his vicious temper on more than one occasion. Jamil was a sharp shooter when it came to spitting, and those who brushed aside his demand for baksheesh did so at their own risk.

"Tell me about it. How did you get away?" Susan said.

"I fly home on General Ahmed's plane." Imitating the wonk-wonk-wonk of a chopper and spinning his finger, Jamil demonstrated how he'd touched down on the spot he was standing. His comrades jeered at him.

"And what you have there is a bug bite, right?" Susan pointed to a sore just above his kneecap. The sauciness vanished from Jamil's face. Susan pinched the hem of his shorts and pulled it up.

"What on earth have they done to you?" Susan exclaimed.

136

"My captain likes cigarettes." Jamil raised two fingers to his lips and sucked on the imaginary smoke. "Every time I run away, he burn me." Jamil stubbed a thumb against his thigh. "I run away many times," he bragged.

"I can see that," Susan said, frowning at the film of yellow pus. "You better come with me. I'm sure Mrs. Giuseppe has something to clean you up with."

As they walked toward the Eden, a man carrying a suitcase came out of the hotel. It was Hoyt Grimley departing for the airport. Susan waved to him. He waved back and got into the waiting taxi.

"He was there," Jamil said. "At General Ahmed's castle. I saw him. He has big black box."

Susan spun around in the direction of the taxi, but it had already pulled off the curb. All she could see was the bald spot on the salesman's dome shining through the rear window.

"His camera. Did anyone see him carrying a black case with a shoulder strap just now?" Susan said to the boys. There was a round of head shaking. "I didn't either," she said. "Jamil, come with me. You and I must have a chat." She looped her arm around the boy's. As she led him into the hotel ground, a forbidden land for the poor and dispossessed, Jamil turned around with a royal grin and flagged "tough luck" to his comrades.

Susan recognized the stout figure pacing in front of the World Bank office. She quickened her gait into a half-run. "Have you found Omar?" her voice shot from one end of the verandah to the next.

"Yes and no," Juergen said. "Let's go in," he added, implying he wasn't going to say another word until they were inside the office.

Susan fumbled for the keys in her handbag. Once inside, Juergen took her by the elbow and led her into her office. After sitting her down at her desk, he dropped his barrel-sized trunk on the chair opposite her. Susan was about to burst with impatience, but she also knew that the security chief had his own set ways, and he wasn't going to change them for a person younger than his daughter.

"Omar's name appeared on a list of people arrested during the riots," he began. "He and forty-five others will be tried tomorrow by the National Security Court. You know what that means."

"No, I don't," Susan said bluntly.

"It means he's as good as dead. The NSC never acquits anyone. He's guilty before proven so. He'll get either death or a life sentence, and I don't know which is worse."

"They can't do that. Omar is a staff member of the World Bank. He must have some immunity..."

"Don't forget, he's Somali."

"I'm sure there's some authority we can talk to. The finance minister—can't he get Omar out?"

"The NSC is a military tribunal. Suleiman has no clout whatsoever with the military."

"I heard he's got a direct line to Siad Barré," Susan pursued. "And he knows Omar. He'll have no doubt the arrest was a mistake—"

"Suleiman is in Rome right now, enjoying his long weekend. Yusuf told me he left town just before the riots. Rather convenient, I must say."

Susan's shoulders sank with disappointment, but they didn't stay down for long.

"Where's this military court? Can't we go there and at least find out what he's charged with?"

"I wouldn't even go near that place. Listen, there's only one way out. You should pick up the phone right now and call Washington. If you can get the World Bank president to contact Siad Barré, you can at least buy Omar some time. The NSC doesn't dilly dally in its deliberations. They can sentence you today and execute you tomorrow."

Susan quickly calculated the time in Washington. It was midnight. She'd have to call Davar at home. He must be in bed by now, but this was an emergency. The moment Juergen left, she started dialing for an overseas connection. Getting through to the building across the street was hard enough, let alone a party across the ocean. It was a matter of chance and probability; like throwing darts in the dark, the more transmissions she sent out, the greater the odds of her hitting a bull's-eye. For about four hours, Susan dialed non-stop. She was glad that there were so many operators and none of them ever said, "You again?"

She couldn't believe her ears when she heard the ring and a sleepy female voice breathed hello. Through the static Susan thought she could hear a man clearing his throat. "Persis Davar," a voice said in a manner that was incredibly businesslike for four in the morning.

"This is Susan Chen—" Another voice bounced back at her. It was her own. Trying her best to disregard the echo, she continued, "I'm calling from Mogadishu." The line crackled as if somebody was crushing a bag of potato chips in her ear.

Persis's voice sounded very, very far away. "Can you speak louder? I can barely hear you," he shouted.

"I'm calling about Omar. He's been arrested," she shouted back.

"Who's been arrested?"

It suddenly dawned on Susan that Omar was too far down the totem pole for the director to know. Bawling like a fishwife to make herself heard, she explained who Omar was, what had happened to him, and what would happen if the bank's president didn't intervene.

"The president is traveling...I'm not sure..." Persis's voice was waning.

"Can you speak louder?" Susan hollered at her director.

"I said the president is touring South America. Besides, this is a matter that should be resolved at the working level. I want you to write me a full report, cc to Security, Legal and..." The last department was blown away by a blitz of static. "In the meantime, I suggest you do everything you can on your end. You must have *some* connections by now. How long have you been there? Two weeks?"

"Yes, I'll do what I can here, but there's not enough time to go through the regular channels. The trial is tomorrow—"

"What? What did you say?"

Susan could feel the heat rise to her ears. She gripped the phone with both hands, something she would like to do to Persis's neck if he were present. The difficulty in communication had little to do with the bad connection. It was the man himself, the man who valued his own ass more than anything in the world, who would never make a move unless a retinue of department heads had been assembled to cover his backside, so that his memo to his superiors could read, "*It* has been decided..."

For Omar's sake, Susan had to try another tack. "You're right. We can resolve this quite easily at the working level. The next auction is only three days away. The bank has four million dollars earmarked for it. If we threaten to withhold the money, I'm sure they'll listen."

"That's preposterous! Aid allocation is a policy issue that can only be addressed in the country strategy paper. It's not something you and I can decide. Speaking of which," Susan sensed a dangerous change in tone, "I still haven't got your input for the strategy paper. The deadline was—"

A long beep sounded, and Persis's deadline disappeared into a maelstrom of crackles. Susan seized the opportunity to put down the receiver.

"Excuse me for interrupting," she said to the group gathered around the table in Juergen's office. Then her eyes zeroed in on the security chief. "I need a name from you. Who's the head of the National Security Service?"

"What do you want it for?" Juergen asked, his bushy brows jumping with alarm.

"I called Washington, like you suggested. But my boss didn't think a minion like Omar was worth bothering the president about. So now, I'm on my own. If I don't do anything, Omar's a goner."

Her audience emitted various noises of sympathy. Griping about headquarters was the favorite sport of field officers, and everyone had a story to tell about having the rug pulled from under his feet by some bureaucratic jerk back home.

"Oh all right," Juergen said, slamming shut his manual. "Let's meet back here first thing tomorrow," he said to his staff and sprang to his feet. In the blink of an eye, he was at the door, holding it open for Susan. She'd always been amazed that such a large man could be so nimble.

Juergen marched into the red brick building of the National Security Service, his apple-shaped chest thrust out even more than usual. Susan tried to match his profile, but knew that Juergen was the only reason nobody had stopped her yet. Through the corner of her eyes, she could see the doorman falter and then it was too late. She and Juergen were deep into the maw of the building already. Juergen stopped a soldier and demanded to know where General Nur's office was. The soldier saluted and took them up a flight of stairs to the general's doorstep.

Juergen bellowed a demand to see the general. The two soldiers in the antechamber stood at attention, replying in unison that the general was away. Juergen whipped out his I.D., announced his title, "Chief of Security, United Nations," and demanded to see the second man in the chain of command. The uniformed secretary left the room. Minutes later, he returned to take them a few doors down the corridor.

A huge bulk of a man towered over Juergen. Susan had always thought of Juergen as bear-like, but if Juergen was an ordinary brown bear, this man was a grizzly. The bulk was more brawn than fat, and his charcoal complexion indicated he was an active military man, not just an administrator. If he so much as sneezed, the buttons on his shirt were sure to rocket into space. He wrapped Susan's hand in his paw, and she stared in amazement as the extension below her wrist became completely devoured.

Even Juergen was awe-struck. His diminished head slightly bowed, he said with the humility of a man conceding defeat,

"Miss Chen here is the World Bank's representative in Somalia. A member of her staff is listed as one of the persons to be tried by the NSC tomorrow. She thinks perhaps there is a misunderstanding, because this man is normally a responsible, law-abiding citizen."

"What's his name?" the lieutenant general thundered.

"Omar Abdi Hashi," Susan piped up. She was feeling very small.

The warrior stared down at her, but when she refused to blink, he called for his secretary. While they waited for the information, they discussed the riots, or rather, the lieutenant general ranted his opinion on the riots. The rioters were hooligans, and nothing but the severest punishment should be meted out as a deterrent to future disturbances. To Susan, it sounded as if a judgment had been passed already. In the course of the conversation, she also found out that the man in front of her was going to be the magistrate for the trials. All forty-six were supposed to take place in one day. She now understood why such judicial systems were called kangaroo courts—"justice" was going to progress in leaps and bounds.

When the secretary returned, Susan was expecting some sort of a file or piece of paper in his hand, but all he carried was a brief message delivered orally.

The lieutenant general interpreted: "Your man was arrested for breaking into a house, raping the women and murdering the men and children."

"There must be a mistake," Susan almost laughed. "Omar isn't capable of any of those charges. If you've only seen him, you'd know. He's a very fragile person. He's just incapable, physically incapable of those crimes."

The lieutenant general glared at her. "This is a matter for the court to decide."

"I'd like to get him a lawyer," Susan said. A pressure on her toes made her look down. Juergen's patent leather shoe was on top of her sandal.

"There is no need," the lieutenant general said. "The court will provide the defendants with lawyers. It is only fair to

142

everyone, don't you agree?" He turned to Juergen and lanced him with a gaze that commanded the one right answer.

"What time is the trial tomorrow? I'd like to be there." Susan received another squeeze on her toes, harder than the last.

"We do not allow observers at the court! This is a military tribunal!"

"We've taken up enough of your time," Juergen said, rising.

"How do I find out the outcome of the trial?" Susan said, gripping the edge of her chair as Juergen's fingers dug into the inside of her elbow.

"Go to the stadium and you will find out," the lieutenant general said, his voice sinking to a low snarl more dangerous than his roar.

On the return trip, the only words uttered in the car were Juergen's. "We've done our best," he said with a touch of apology. Susan looked away, disappointed with the security chief's lackluster performance, yet knowing at the same time that he couldn't have done more. Juergen continued a monologue on how he would file a report to the U.N. headquarters in New York and hopefully—although his subdued tone didn't inspire much of that—somebody with enough clout would intervene. But Susan's mind was elsewhere, planning a program of her own that didn't involve dragging along an elephantine organization. She had Juergen drop her in front of the Ministry of Finance, and went straight to Yusuf's office.

To her relief, the minister had returned from his vacation. Yusuf took her to him at once. The minister rose to greet her, clasping her hand warmly in both of his own. The good life in Italy had tinged his sallow complexion. Despite the disturbance in his country and his attempt at moroseness, his face was flushed with the fine food and wine of southern Europe. It was only after Susan told him Omar's story that a shadow drifted over him, and then he grew more and more somber.

"The next auction is in three days," Susan said. "Omar is an employee of the bank. If he's not released by then, I'm afraid we'll have to withdraw our contribution."

The minister flinched visibly. Susan knew she'd hit where it hurt.

"The auction is very important to our economy," the minister said. "I will have to go to the highest authority, but first you have to give me a letter stating the World Bank's position. Without the evidence, I cannot act."

"No problem." Susan bounced up from her chair. "I'll write you the letter *pronto*."

"We need an official communication from Washington. With all due respect to your authority, my government is too familiar with your procedure. The president knows that recommendations made in the field are not final until they've been confirmed by headquarters."

Shoot. How did a bunch of nomads get so well versed in bureaucratese? Susan wondered.

Susan whacked the ball at the wall. It hit above the white line, but the return whizzed past her face, too high and fast for her to do anything with. She let it go and fished another ball from her pocket. Over at the learner's court, Nick was huddling with his student, imparting what seemed a final tip. Susan waved to him, and he waved back. Rallying at the wall was the agreed upon signal for an emergency meeting.

Nick sauntered over with his bucket of balls. The silly bonnet, sitting on top of him like a head of wilted lettuce, seemed to have grown roots into his brains and become an integral part of the man. He reached for her hand and checked her grip.

"My assistant Omar was arrested during the riots. He's been accused of some ridiculous charges of rape and murder and will be tried tomorrow at the military tribunal. There's only one way to save him, a telex from the World Bank headquarters in Washington, saying if Omar isn't released, the bank will cease further contributions to the auction."

"Hope it works, but what's that got to do with me?" Nick said.

144

"Because my director at the bank is a gutless wonder and isn't about to stick his neck out for anyone. I know a way of getting around him though. If you get in touch with Alex, I'm sure he can finagle a bogus telex from Persis Davar."

"Not so easy. He'll ask what saving Omar's life has got to do with our mission. What am I supposed to tell him?"

Susan thought for a moment. "Tell him Omar is a key informant who may lead us to Hamid."

"He'll say where did this Omar person creep out from? How come there's never been a file on him?"

"He's a developmental then. We're this close to recruiting him," Susan measured an inch with her finger, "and it would be a pity to lose him now. Come on, Nick, have a heart. Omar may be of no consequence to our mission, but I can't just stand by and let an innocent man face the firing squad."

Nick looked at her with a strange smile on his lips. Susan realized what she'd just said. Have a heart. That was what got Nick into trouble in the first place.

"I'll see what I can do," he said. "Now you have to stand farther away from the wall, or the ball is going to hit you in the face." Susan backpedaled two steps. "That's right," Nick said. "About the hair you found. It belonged to a man and was originally black in color. It was bleached and then dyed blond. The DNA analysis didn't match anything on file."

"Thanks, that's all I need to know," Susan said. In the excitement of the riots and the search for Omar, she'd all but forgotten about Hamid. Nick's report was good news. Her theory had been proven. The hair belonged to Park's murderer, who had entered the apartment before Park, dried himself with a towel and positioned himself for the kill. She never expected the DNA to match, because Alex had told her there was no handle on Hamid. But now, she'd touched a part of him, this man without a face, who could kill without a sound.

Chapter 17

One by one, Persis Davar picked up the rings from the night table and slipped them on his third, fourth, and fifth fingers. Emerald was for health, moonstone for love, and diamond for success. He caressed each one to activate its magical power, for this morning, he needed all the vitality he could get. His night had been restless. After Susan's call from Mogadishu, he hadn't been able to catch another wink. What she suggested was out of the question. For a person in his position to be meddling in a client country's politics was suicidal. The government might take offense and declare him *persona non grata*. An ordinary staff member could transfer laterally to another region, but for a person at the pinnacle of his career, the only movement was down or out. What would he do then? He'd worked for the bank since he'd got his degree from MIT. He knew nothing else. Besides, his visa in the States was only good for working in an international organization. The moment he quit, or was forced to quit, he would have to leave the country. Where would he go then? Back to Karachi where he would have to start over from scratch? Getting fired was unheard of several years ago, but in today's downsizing mood, no one could afford to be complacent.

How he wished Andrew Barnett were still alive. Although the Englishman could be gallingly hoity-toity at times, he was impeccable as far as toeing the line was concerned. Susan, on the other hand, was a wild card. She'd been with the bank for only six months, the whole time in Personnel. When he saw her application—unfortunately nobody else was interested—he was inclined to keep the vacancy open until news of the murder had blown over. But that same day the U.S. representative took him to lunch and expressed a desire to see the post filled as soon as possible. When a major contributor made a request, there was only one course of action. He closed his eyes and accepted whoever was willing, and now he'd lived to regret it. After failing to respond to his queries for three days, Susan had awakened him in the middle of the night and suggested killing the Somali program. How preposterous!

He stroked the emerald to calm himself. Anger was unhealthful.

Persis changed into his office clothes. He looked spiffy in his tailored suit, but there was a general crookedness about him, in the way he carried one shoulder slightly higher than the other, and the way he tilted his head, that marred what would have been the paragon of sleekness. After kissing his Chilean wife good-bye, he hit the road. Traffic was dense but not yet bumper-to-bumper. Half an hour later, he arrived in the northwest quadrant of Washington. A block from the White House, his black Jaguar entered a parking lot underneath a glassy building, one of the many owned by the World Bank, and rolled into a space reserved in his name. This was the "J" building, home of the Africa region. The elevator took him to the eighth floor. He negotiated several corridors lined by pink and gray workstations, and entered a spacious room. The morning sun was pouring in through the floor-to-ceiling windows. At eight in the morning, Davar was one of the few early birds. This was the best time to catch up with his reading. Once the clock struck nine, the appointments blackening his calendar would obliterate the minutes and hours of the day.

Persis greeted his first visitor with an exclamation of "*Bon giorno*, Francesco," and a handshake that broadened into a hug. The Italian, a mousy man, accepted the heartiness with a reservation bordering on shyness. As an emissary from the Italian foreign ministry, he visited Washington several times a year to facilitate what was known in professional jargon as "aid coordination."

The two men sat down on the sofa and exchanged pleasantries on the weather in their respective capitals. After an appropriate pause, Francesco came to the point of his visit.

"What do you think of the situation in Somalia?" the Italian said.

Persis hemmed to collect his thoughts. Of course, Francesco wasn't asking for his personal views but the organization's. He hemmed again, this time to switch gears into his business lingo, which was articulated in an Americanized accent acquired from more than thirty years of studying and working in the States. "The situation in Somalia is a pain in the neck, if you don't mind my saying so. The riot is going to set the reform program back, and it's going to make it harder than ever for the government to cut spending. On the other hand," Persis hedged, "it's not the end of the world. Somalia has gone through worse crises, and Siad Barré seems to have come out with his head above water every time. We'll have to watch the situation carefully," he concluded with the noncommittal statement.

"The auction money will be depleted next month. Has the bank decided on the replenishment?" Francesco pursued.

Persis squirmed in his chair. He felt he was being put on the spot. He also knew the foxy Francesco. Unnervingly low-keyed and composed for an Italian—his hands were always folded neatly on his lap—he could drive in the blade at moments one least expected it. "This is one of the things I'd like to discuss with you," Persis said, tipping his head in deference and accentuating the crookedness of his nose. "Since Italy is a major donor in Somalia, we wouldn't dream of making a decision without checking with you first. The Italian grant is coming up for renewal, too. What are *your* plans?"

Francesco greeted the challenge calmly. "My government has been in close consultation with Siad Barré. It has convinced the president that a political solution to the crisis would be the best." He leaned over in confidence. "This hasn't been announced yet, but it will be very soon. Siad Barré has agreed to two points: the release of the signatories of the manifesto, and the re-writing of the constitution to allow for multiparty elections. My government will be sending a team of legal experts to help with the drafting. If all goes well, we hope to avoid any interruption of Italian aid to Somalia. The use of our funds will be carried out in close coordination with the World Bank, of course."

"Of course," Persis echoed with a lopsided smile that belied the twist of sourness in his heart. He hated to be upstaged.

Despite all his trips to Somalia, he still hadn't been able to meet with Siad Barré. It had been a sore point. On his last visit, he'd sworn never to request a meeting again. Siad Barré would have to come to him.

"A hiatus in donor funding can cause an immediate collapse of the ruling regime. I hope you will take this into account in your budgeting," Francesco added almost casually, as if that wasn't the sole intention of his journey from Rome.

"The bank has its own criteria," Persis said, his eyes trained straight at Francesco's to show that he could see through him any time. The Italian was telling him how to do his job and he didn't like it one bit. "Politics isn't one of them. According to our charter, the economic development of a country is our only concern."

"Yes, of course," Francesco said with a coy smile.

"I'll be leading a team to Somalia in the near future. We'll be discussing with the government the measures it needs to take to improve its economic management. If we can come to an agreement on a program, then I can't see any reason for withholding the funds, pending, of course, approval from our board."

"Of course," the Italian repeated. Slapping his thighs with both hands, Francesco thanked Persis for his time and begged to rush off to another meeting.

The moment the Italian revolved out the door, a petite Japanese woman spun in. With a sharp bow, she presented to Persis several yellow slips of telephone messages. Persis vetted them, trashing one, spiking another and frowning at a third. What could the U.S. Senate want from him? It could be nothing but a hassle.

His secretary connected him with the female caller. The woman identified herself as a staff member of the Human Rights Committee. She demanded to know the World Bank's policy on Somalia. Young, abrasive and brunette was how Persis envisioned her as he delivered a carefully crafted statement so broad that his fanny was amply shielded. She listened for a while, and then, like Francesco, she gave him an order, but unlike Francesco, she was totally lacking in subtlety.

"The Somali government's violation of human rights is an affront to the civilized world. Nobody should be giving aid to a dictator who murders..."

Persis held the phone away from his ear. When the screeching had stopped, he mouthed polite, reassuring words into the phone, all the while thinking, what about the arms your government is supplying the murderer?

At noon, Persis escaped for lunch, feeling he'd taken enough abuse to justify his six-digit salary, the tuition subsidy for his children's private education, and the free "home leave" travel he and his family were entitled to every other year. The crap he must take from people high and low was incredible. Sometimes, he wished he'd gone back to Karachi and taken over the family business. He'd be dishing it out on other people now, not the other way around. If he'd known the drawbacks of a bureaucracy, that no matter how high one climbed, there would still be many tiers above him, he would have chosen the private sector. As if the morning's irritations weren't enough, a shrill commotion greeted him as he heaved open the heavy glass doors. On the sidewalk in front of the Bank, a gaggle of dark-skinned people was chanting: "No more aid to Si-ad Bar-ré!" A homemade poster depicted a blood-dripping dagger juxtaposed with a globe, the Bank's logo. Persis skirted around a television crew and walked briskly up the street.

He trotted down several steps into the basement restaurant. His eyes took a few seconds to adjust to the dimness. The popular Peruvian eatery was packed already. Persis nodded to a few colleagues from the bank and to his pleasant surprise, a blond man waved to him. In their twenty-year association, he could count on the fingers of one hand the number of times Erik was on time. His entry was always dramatic—hair disheveled, red tie askew (it was always red), breathless from the dash—and always just a moment before his lunch date walked out in disgust. However, his colleagues always forgave him, for as the secretary to the executive board, Erik was their peephole into the inner sanctum of power. Persis squeezed through the narrow spaces between the tables toward his friend.

The two men ordered their customary aperitif of Piscou Sour. From the wild gleam in Erik's eyes and the evil way the corners of his lips turned up, Persis could guess why the Dane was early. He was bursting with gossip.

"Guess who's coming back as principal VP? Zimmerman." Erik posed the question and answer in the same breath.

"What!" Persis exclaimed. Checking himself, he surveyed the tables within earshot and lowered his voice, "Didn't he resign last month?"

"Yes, but he lobbied the Americans. I heard he spent quite a bit of his wife's fortune on some senators. They're pushing all out for him."

"Oh my God," was all Persis could say. In the last reorganization, he was one of those who'd stabbed Zimmerman in the back, and later in the gut when he was staggering. For that, Persis had been awarded the directorship. Now that the VP was returning to power, would he seek revenge? Persis downed his drink. That was all he needed to hear that day.

Little did he know that there was more waiting for him in the office. An Ethiopian delegation rose to greet him. Still reeling from the bad news and two glasses of Piscou sour, he shook hands with the finance minister and his entourage, cursing them silently for their habit of arriving early. He'd meant to go to the men's room first, but now he'd have to hold it for another hour.

Having heard the worst news of his career, he thought there was nothing the Ethiopians could say to darken his mood, until he realized what the finance minister was doing. The lean, austere man was destroying the bank's lending program in Ethiopia. More state enterprises, more centralized control, more power to the communists...every time the minister thumped his knobby fist on the table, Persis's head ached. There was no way he could agree to finance any of the projects the Marxist government was proposing. Even if he could get past his own VP, the U.S. was sure to exercise its veto once the proposal got to the board. Before the Ethiopian finished his speech, Persis already saw his work program going down the drain. It wasn't his fault that a communist was in the saddle at Addis Ababa, but would Zimmerman sympathize? That would be a bit too much to ask.

After sending off the Ethiopians, Persis told his secretary he wasn't to be disturbed. Alone in his spacious office, Zimmerman's presence surrounded him—his pinched, ratty muzzle, his high, nasal voice, and his small weasel's body that could slink out of any tight corner. The thought of the man filled Persis with loathing, although he was fully aware of the irony: The diminutive tyrant was his role model. Whenever Persis was in a tight spot, he'd always ask himself the question: What would Zimmerman do if he were in my position? So far, the drill had never failed him.

Persis rang his secretary for a copy of the lending program. Sitting back, chin tucked in his bejeweled hand, he studied the fateful piece of paper. Two fifty-million-dollar projects had been earmarked for Ethiopia. Where could he redistribute this money so that people couldn't say he had too little work and too many staff? His eyes scanned down the page to the section for Somalia. Across the line for the item "foreign exchange auction" appeared a figure of a hundred million dollars enveloped in a pair of brackets. Eureka! The arithmetic was simple. He picked up his pencil and scratched off the brackets and the uncertainty they implied. Francesco was right. Somalia was coming around. The international community should redouble its support. To hell with the human rights softies. They had no idea how the world worked.

Across the Potomac, somebody else was fretting over the horn of Africa. Alex Papadopoulos was pacing his office, mulling over the Senate hearing he'd just attended. The session on human rights in Somalia had heard testimony from watchdog groups and Somali dissidents. A couple of former political prisoners had paraded their ugly scars around, and a Somali woman related between sobs the gory details of being gang raped by Barré's Red Berets. The display had been well choreographed and evoked the desired reactions of horror from even the stodgiest senator.

In stark contrast to the impassioned speeches of the dissidents, a colorless State Department officer had delivered a cool, rational statement. War was about to begin in the Persian Gulf. The U.S. needed its military facility at the horn of Africa. Stability in Somalia was crucial. An abrupt withdrawal of aid would plunge the country into turmoil that could lead to the overthrow of Siad Barré and anarchy.

He'd also cited the ideology factor. Since Somalia's defection to the West, it had been flaunted as the showcase of the superiority of capitalism. The G-7 nations had invested large amounts to help the country make the transition. The teething problems had been many, but abandoning Somalia now would drive it back into the arms of the Soviet Union.

The senators, however, suppressed yawns and glanced up at the clock. Several years ago, whenever criticism of Siad Barré's brutality arose, rumors of a Somali *rapprochement* with the Soviet Union would promptly squelch any suggestion of a censure. The Cold War had justified U.S. support for the cruelest regimes, but today, the ground had shifted and the sympathies of the panel were inclined toward the victims of brutality. After *glasnost* and *perestroika*, the Soviet Union was no longer the evil empire that had to be contained at all costs. The tug-of-war for allies was a contest of the past.

Alex walked up to the window and sat down on the sill. Whichever way the coin fell in the Somalia debate, his operation must go on. His agency had created a dangerous killing machine in Hamid, and his agency must get rid of him before he turned against his creator. They had taught him too much and too well.

He turned around and looked out at the green grass on the lawn. December already, and yet the weather was as balmy as spring. He hated warm winters.

Susan had been in Mogadishu more than two weeks now, not a long time by any count, but enough for Hamid to claim another victim. Every day that passed was a new opportunity for him to kill again. So far no American had been hurt, but who knew who was next? Perhaps he'd been rash in letting her cut her teeth on a high-risk mission, and with so little support from the man in the field. Nick Wade had been a good agent, but he'd reached burnout years ago. Alex chided himself for not recognizing the symptoms.

Intelligence was supposed to be Susan's function in the World Bank, but this assignment had extended her far beyond his original intention. Over objections from some quarters he'd chosen her over several more experienced candidates. The reason he gave was that she'd already been implanted in the right place. His opponents had given in reluctantly, unaware that his judgment had been tainted by his partiality toward the Chinese-American.

Some years ago, he'd been the scapegoat for his division's mishandling of a Soviet defector. While being pastured at Translations, he hired a young woman who was fluent in Chinese and French. In the two years he worked with Susan, he discovered that she could not only translate but also interpret events. She wrote analyses for him and was right on the mark on her prediction of the massacre at Tiananmen. The analysts at Intelligence were furious that she should be invading their turf, but he only thumbed his nose at them. He was already on ice; there wasn't much else they could do to him.

What he liked most about Susan was the fusion of the East and West in her psyche. On most days, her American can-doism would carry her through any task. But when her best efforts failed, she would fall back on her Taoist cushion with an "Oh well, I've done my best. Let nature take its course now." He also knew she was a champ in a school of martial arts called *tai chi*, but he never saw her in action until much later.

He'd recommended her to several people at Operations, but the bureaucratic hurdles for such a radical transfer were too daunting. But as Susan would say, nature has its way of getting things done. As inevitable as the rotation of the seasons, the cycle of changes in administration brought on a series of shake-ups. Alex awoke one morning and found himself back in Operations. He set the ball rolling immediately, and a year later, Susan was sent to Camp Peary to be trained to become a spy.

Since then she'd passed every class with flying colors. Her teachers had written in her report card that she had the ability to extract information from the most impenetrable sources. She was resourceful, creative, and indefatigable, quick to learn from mistakes and rally in the face of setbacks. Alex knew she would make a good case officer. In the spy games they played at Camp Peary, people were naturally drawn to her. They trusted her not to double-cross them; they trusted her with their lives, which was essentially what agents did when they sold their souls to a CIA case officer. An agent was a foreign national who, for reasons of his own, was willing to lie and cheat and betray his country's secrets. If found out, he could be imprisoned, tortured, and killed. He must have absolute faith in his handler.

"Charm" came to Alex's mind, but behind that overused word lay a simple explanation: Susan was a "nice" person. He'd been afraid that the year of training had purged every ounce of niceness from her system. To be kidnapped in the middle of the night, tied and gagged and threatened with a pistol to the temple could change a person's outlook very fast, which was the purpose of this portion of the induction. After such an experience, a person could even appear different: a hardening of the eyes, setting of the jaws, sclerosis of facial muscles. He'd seen Susan go through the process, but he'd also caught her off-guard and seen a glimmer of her old self. "Niceness" was a dirty word in the profession, but without it she could turn into the kind of cold-hearted monster that she was hired to protect the country from. The agency had created a few, and unfortunately the minority had come to represent the whole.

On the combat scene, Susan's marksmanship in a variety of weapons had set new records for her class. It was that peculiar Oriental focus of hers, an intensity so strong that he could visualize the rarefied string connecting her with the target. He'd also seen her take on barehanded a couple of butchers, each one large enough to swallow her alive, and give them a tussle to remember. It paid to have a martial arts instructor for a father. A smile came to Alex's lips. She would definitely give Hamid a run for his money.

The smile reversed to a frown. A nagging question remained. When faced with a real-life encounter, could she keep her nerves?

Alex rubbed his forehead. If he recalled her now, that would be the end of her career in Operations. He imagined her going back to Translations, buried in a pile of newspaper clippings. No, he shook his head. He couldn't recall her now, not just yet. Hell, how does one get experience? By doing the job.

Alex looked at his wall calendar. Christmas was coming up in two weeks. The attack on Iraq wasn't likely to begin before then. There might still be time. All right then—Alex fell into his chair, relieved at having stalled a tough call—he would give her till Christmas. If Susan couldn't come up with anything more than a piece of hair by then, he would have to replace her.

Chapter 18

People streamed into the stadium. They were healthy young men, the type who would be yelling and jostling their way to the bleachers during soccer season. Today, however, they were as somber as the retinue of a funeral procession. Silently they shuffled into the bowl, some of them holding hands for mutual solace.

In every direction Susan looked, she met soldiers glowering and toting rifles in such a way that no one would question their willingness to use them. She and Mohammed followed the crowd into a mid-level tier. Below them a block of seats was painted brown by the uniforms of the patriotic young Pioneers. In center field, people were busy setting up a mike on the podium, and to their left, Susan counted nine posts staked to the turf. The trials had been conducted in utter secrecy, and now, less than twenty-four hours after the verdict, the sentences were being carried out. No names had been released.

The sun beat down relentlessly. An electronic screech reverberated through the stadium. Music blared. Everyone stood up for the national anthem. A group of manacled prisoners straggled out to the field.

"Do you see him?" Susan nudged Mohammed. He was considerably taller, but even with his neck stretched like a goose's in flight, he couldn't see over the forest of soldiers surrounding the prisoners. When the music was over, an officer bristling with medals ascended the podium. The mike screeched again. The man leveled a broadside at his audience. Susan didn't bother to ask Mohammed for a translation. The Pioneers clapped with an exuberance that was hardly shared by the others.

Susan's ears pricked up when the speaker read out a name. A cacophonous blast ensued, which Mohammed translated as a list of the man's crimes. A prisoner was dragged to the open. Halfway to his allotted post, he collapsed and had to be carried. Meanwhile, a second name was read, followed by another litany of denunciations. The harsh, strident voice ricocheted back and forth across the stadium; a name, denunciations, another name, overlapping each other, drowning out the nervous twitters of the audience. Susan strained to pick out the Mohammeds and Adurahmans, the only words she needed to understand.

The name reverberated across the field. Omar Abdi Hashi. Susan and Mohammed looked at each other with dread. Two soldiers stepped forward, sandwiching between them a scarecrow man. They hoisted him up by the arms and frog-marched him to the last post. Omar. Susan's heart stopped.

The sound track went dead. The firing squad marched out in a wordless vacuum. In the aftermath of the babbling fury, the silence was deafening. The executioners took their positions. Susan's eyes were glued to the sagging body tied to the stake.

A piercing voice scratched like nails on her skin. A dozen rifles rattled. Susan closed her eyes, the image of Omar reflected on her eyelids, the light and shadow reversed as in a negative. Her ears rang in the silence, as if she herself was tied to the stake, waiting for a bullet to explode in her body, wondering which part of her body, and how much it would hurt. The moment stretched, and then she felt a stirring among the people around her. She opened her eyes. The soldiers were frozen in their ready-to-shoot pose. On the podium, the speaker was bending down to talk to someone on the ground. Susan recognized the narrow, scholarly back. It was Suleiman.

The officers scurried around, then two soldiers ran out to the field. They were headed for the last stake. The scene swam in front of Susan. She was feeling a bit light-headed. The rope came loose. Omar staggered out of the firing range.

Mohammed threw up his arms, Susan thumped him on the back, and the next moment they found themselves crying, laughing, and hugging, mindless of the taboo that separated them in culture, religion, and class.

A salvo of shots rocked the stadium. The patriotic youths applauded, but most people, like Susan, simply clutched a part of themselves.

Omar dropped his chin the moment Susan entered the office. He was sitting at Fatima's desk, his head backlit by the sun's last rays seeping through the venetian blinds. She rushed to greet him, he recoiled, and she pulled herself back. Gently, she invited him into her office. Omar got up and edged along the shadow of the wall. Susan went to the window and lowered the shades. Behind her, a *poof* sounded, a tired body flopping on the couch. When she turned around, Omar was enveloped in the buttery folds of the leather sofa. He seemed so small and fragile. Susan took an adjacent seat. The side of the face she saw wasn't much different from before, but as he tilted his head slightly toward her, she saw the egg-size swelling on his good eye, colored in various hues of blue.

"Let me take you to the American doctor," she said.

"I hate doctors."

The familiar crabbiness unleashed a tide of fondness in Susan. "Oh Omar, I'm so glad to see you," she said, clasping one hand over the other to refrain them from demonstrating her gush of feelings. The blood-spattered grass flashed across her mind. A few more seconds and Omar's blood would have flowed into the others'. "What on earth happened? Why did they let you go? What was Suleiman doing there?" She released a barrage of questions.

"A presidential pardon," Omar muttered. "Suleiman brought it."

"The telex worked! I got Washington to send a telex saying if you weren't freed immediately, we were going to cancel the money for the auction. It must have whipped Suleiman into action."

Omar studied the empty chair opposite him for a while. Then his eyeball rolled under the distended lid and he addressed the chair begrudgingly: "I owe you my life."

"Don't mention it, and *especially*, don't mention it to Persis. He knows nothing about the telex."

"I know who owns the Eastern Horizon," Omar said abruptly. "The son of General Ahmed." He aspirated the "h" so strongly that the name sounded more like "Aha-med."

"The general who's notorious for sending his soldiers to poison water holes, massacre the men and rape the women?"

A corner of Omar's cracked lip quivered. He nodded.

"How do you know?" Susan challenged. "The company's registration lists somebody else."

Omar huffed with impatience and for the first time, Susan didn't have to strain to catch his mumbling. "My eldest brother and Ahmed grew up together. They went to the same school, studied in the same class. Of course I know who owns the Eastern Horizon.

"There's something else—Ahmed killed my brother. Shortly after Siad Barré took power, my brother, Ahmed and several others were arrested and charged with plotting a coup. My brother was innocent—all he did was criticize Barré's policies—but Ahmed 'confessed' and put the blame on everyone else. He got out after three years and became Siad Barré's right-hand man. My brother was left to rot in prison."

Before Susan could digest the torrent of information, Omar forced some more down her throat, saying, "You know who Ahmed's son is married to?" Susan shook her head. "Suleiman's daughter," Omar said.

Susan gave her head a sharp jiggle. "Wait a minute," she said, "let me get this straight. Suleiman's daughter is married to General Ahmed's son, which makes Suleiman the in-law of Ahmed. On top of that, Ahmed's son is the owner of Eastern Horizon?"

"Correct, and the person directing the business of Eastern Horizon is General Ahmed himself."

"What exactly does the Eastern Horizon do? Officially, it's an importer of medicine, but nobody has seen any of it in the country."

"Because it turns around and re-exports the medicine for hard currency. With the money, Ahmed can import whatever he wants."

How clever, Susan thought. No wonder she couldn't find anything but medicine in the shipment.

"And what does Ahmed want?" Susan said.

"He's building his own militia in the desert."

"You mean he's importing arms?"

"Go ask him yourself."

Susan ignored the impertinent suggestion. "Andrew died when he was investigating the company. Do you think the general had anything to do with it?"

"Ahmed is known to have done worse things."

"What about Suleiman? Was he involved in any of this?"

Omar shook his head. "Suleiman and Ahmed are sworn enemies. They both like money and power. That's why they can't stand each other. Suleiman won't even talk to his son-in-law. During the Eid celebrations, his daughter would come home by herself."

Susan was beginning to realize what a small place Mogadishu was. She'd thought only the expat community was suffocatingly close, and now she realized that the city was really a village. If she'd known Omar was the Hawiye elder she was looking for, she could have saved herself a lot of trouble. Now she understood that the main qualification for an "elder" was influence and not age. Her amazement turned suddenly into annoyance. He'd kept this library of information from her all this time. But then, she asked herself, why should he have told her anything? She couldn't have been more alien than a Martian stepping onto his planet.

Things were different now. She'd saved his life.

"What do you plan to do now?" Susan said.

Omar's head drooped. A ghost of his old self resurfaced. "Go away for a while," he said and muttered something about staying with a cousin down south.

"I don't blame you," Susan said, understanding that "down south" meant slipping across the border to Kenya. "But can you stay a bit longer? I need you to do a job for me."

"What is it?" Omar said, a bite in his voice.

"How are your relations with Suleiman?"

"He's good to me because he wants me to tell him about the World Bank." Omar added cautiously, "I only tell him what he already knows."

"I want you to get close to him. Tell him something he doesn't know already; make him trust you. I promise you, once I get to the bottom of Andrew's murder, I'll get you to the States. That's better than Kenya. What do you say?"

Omar turned to face her squarely, but his crooked eye was staring at somebody else in the room. As usual, she had the urge to glance over her shoulder to see who it was.

"Look at me here," Omar said, pointing to his good eye. From the depth of the bruised swelling a shiny pebble gleamed straight at her. There was no question whom he was addressing.

Chapter 19

Jack inspected the new shoots of maize. The field was one of the few that had been plowed before the rain. The seeds had sprouted, covering the field with a frayed blanket of delicate green. In the best of times, about half the shoots would mature to produce cobs of chewy corn; in the worst, starvation was the villagers' lot. A short distance away, a woman sat with her legs splayed out on the ground, holding up her chador to shield herself and her baby from the scorching sun. A stick lay by her side, a weapon she would use to shoo away the goats and baboons prowling about, intent on the priceless crop.

Jack stretched his eyes down the road. A steamy miasma rose from the ground, and there was still no sign of the gas tanker. He threw down his cigarette, ground it under his sandal, and got into his Land Rover.

The fallow fields were a sorry sight. He'd gotten one plow up and running by cannibalizing three others, but if he didn't get the gas soon, he'd be missing the precious *Der* rains and an entire planting season. A group of naked children waved to him. He stopped his car and searched for something to give them. An empty bottle lay on the floor in the back. He picked it up and gave it to a little girl, who clutched the treasure to her chest. Tiny outstretched hands clamored for more. He searched his vehicle again but came up empty-handed. He apologized in Somali and drove on. He'd failed them.

Two years ago, the government had bought the promises of his proposal to settle nomadic tribes. Convincing the gypsy herders to participate, however, hadn't been easy. Nomads had always held the macho attitude that a sedentary life was only for the weak. As the saying went: "A camel man is a man, a goat man is half a man, and a cattle man is no man at all." A man's strength was measured by his ability to endure long-distance hardships. Settled farming was only for women. Then one day, after a severe drought decimated their herds, a number of desperate families yielded to the government's incentives: a one-room *muudul*, a plot of land, and a sack of seeds. In addition, the government would provide mechanized plowing service so that they could farm on a large enough scale to make up for the pitiful yield.

He'd failed them, Jack muttered to himself. Now that the calluses on the men's feet had softened, and the women were sitting around waiting for government machines to do the backbreaking work, he couldn't deliver. The method had worked well in Australia. The dryland farming program he'd directed in the outback had been touted as a great success. How could he have known Somalia was going to be like this? Neither the infrastructure nor the superstructure was there to support him. But the harder he tried to convince himself it wasn't his fault, the guiltier he felt. No, he couldn't let this go on. Making a sharp U-turn, he drove back to his aluminum prefab hut. He ran in, pulled out his knapsack, and stuffed in a rumpled shirt, toothbrush, notebook, tape recorder, and several tapes of classical music. He went back out, threw the knapsack into his Land Rover and rattled down the bumpy road to Mogadishu.

His first stop was the World Bank office. He was going to take up Susan's offer to put him up. She was right—it would save the government the money for his room and board. That was the reason she gave, though not the reason he wanted to hear. Since their night of defending the Eden, his heart had been suffused like the desert after a good soaking. Myriad life forms that nobody knew existed were burgeoning everywhere. The drought had lasted six years since his little Sarah's death. He thought he would never see rain again, that the rest of his days were doomed to dryland management. And then Susan swept along, a monsoon from across the ocean. Her courage had greatly impressed him. She was the kind of aid worker Somalia needed. Andrew Barnett was a good man, but he was too concerned with protocol. Sometimes, to get things done around this place, one needed to barge in and demand action on behalf of the downtrodden. One had to step on toes and risk his neck,

166

and Susan had proved that she had the audacity to put her life on the line.

No matter what the government professed to be its policy, the rich and powerful would always be sucking up the resources. He knew where all the gasoline had gone. Anyone who'd been to the port could see the caravan of army tankers. The military took the lion's share, and whatever was left over would be mopped up by the many contenders in no time. If he didn't act soon, starvation was imminent for the five hundred families in his project.

"Fatima, you're back," Jack said at the sight of the secretary at her desk.

"Of course, I have to earn my salary. I came back as soon as I'd settled the children in Bardhere." She paused to cast him a long look that appraised him from his tangled hair to the dusty toes sticking out of his sandals. "How are *you*?" she added.

"I'm fine, thank you. Is Susan in?" He combed his fingers through the knotted curls, suddenly aware of his disheveled appearance. He'd never cared before.

"Jack, what're you doing here?" a robust female voice sang out.

He turned around and saw Susan radiant in a scoop-necked, mint-green blouse with a garland of lavender flowers embroidered across the front. Her skirt was white and cool. Jack had never been one to pay attention to people's clothes, but every speck of color Susan wore seemed to affect him deeply.

"Have you found Omar?" he asked the moment he found his tongue again.

"Oh yes, we've found Omar." Susan beamed, and her lively eyes batted a signal to Fatima, who rustled into the hallway. A minute later, Omar appeared. The monstrous swelling of his eye had subsided to a puffy violet patch. After a euphoric round of congratulations on everyone's well being, the three went into Susan's office.

As soon as Jack had finished pouring out his grievance, Susan declared with an optimism that might seem cockeyed to some, "I'll take your case directly to the finance minister. He should be able to get you the gas."

"I don't know," Omar mumbled, turning his good eye on her while the other roamed.

"Well, he better," Susan flared. "He still owes us a million dollars. We've been very lenient about the deadline for replacing that money. If he can't even come up with a tank of gas, I'm going to get Washington to shut down the entire project."

"Let's not be rash," Jack interjected. "If you close the project, the people who will be hurt most are the farmers. We must keep on wringing concessions from the government. Whatever it's willing to give, even a barrel, I'll make sure it's put to good use."

"You're right," Susan said, feeling chastened. "I think we should meet with the minister as soon as possible. Can you make the appointment, Omar?"

The Somali got up and left without replying. Jack stared uneasily after him. "Can you make sure he makes the appointment as soon as possible? I have to get back."

"Don't worry," Susan said. "Omar doesn't say much but he's very reliable. By the way, I've finally moved into my house." Jack thought he saw a brush of rouge across her luscious tan. "It has a huge guest room. You're welcome to use it. Abdullahi's a great cook; you'll enjoy his food much better than at the Eden."

"All I need is one reason to stay at your place. Now that you've thrown in so many bonuses, how can I say no?" Jack said teasingly.

Ignoring the innuendo of his words, she busied herself with the etiquette of a hostess. "You must be tired from your trip. Why don't you go to the house and rest up a bit? Oh," she started, "I better get Mohammed to go with you. Otherwise, my housekeeper won't let you in. He's very protective of me." She jumped out of her chair and ran out.

He'd never seen her so skittish before. Could she be nervous about him?

Running over to the Ministry of Finance lest he changed his mind, Omar rehearsed his lines once again. The words came readily, but the feelings didn't. Strictly speaking, Suleiman did save his life, since he was the one who took the telex to the president. However, the intention was absent, for Suleiman was merely trying to save his own hide. If the Bank pulled out of the auction, Suleiman would be out of a job. Most importantly, Omar had never liked Suleiman, who had stashed away millions for himself and never bothered to fight the unwritten rules that kept his clansmen down. His vacation in Italy during the riots was another proof of his selfishness. Why wasn't he here when the clan elders were arrested? And who was he to call a donors' conference to announce their release, gloating as if he deserved the merit? No, Suleiman wasn't a person Omar liked, and if it weren't for Susan, he would never dream of catering to the man.

For Susan, he was willing to do anything, even sell his soul. He had no idea when it had happened, the moment he'd set his good eye on her or later, but one morning, he'd gone in for his daily briefing and discovered that he'd fallen more than a little in love with his boss. While she thought he was looking at something else, he would dwell on her clean innocent face for as long as he could. Most of the time, however, he would hang his head and study her hands to his heart's content. They were strong and sturdy, a working woman's hands, yet the perfectly rounded nails were as pink as a baby's. She'd been delivered like a lamb to a pride of lions, and he was trying desperately to protect her. She was no match for the wily Suleiman, but as long as he, Omar, was around, he would make sure that no harm came to her.

Omar sallied into the minister's office, reached across the desk and grasped Suleiman's hands. "Your excellency, you have saved my life. Without your intervention, I would have turned into worm meat. I'm sorry I have not come earlier, for my bruises were too unsightly for your gaze."

"Sit down, sit down, my friend," the minister beamed proudly, nudging him toward the chair. "We are brothers from the same parents, there is no need to stand on ceremony. I am glad you have recovered. Our military can be rough sometimes."

Omar went on to recite his lines. "I owe you my life. If there is anything I can do to repay you, I will be happy to carry out your wishes."

Suleiman smiled, a crude, sinister smirk that he bestowed only on his countrymen. The other one, meek, sensitive and wishing you the best, was reserved for foreigners.

"You can say a few good things about me to the World Bank," Suleiman said. "And when they give you a job in Washington, you can hire me to be your consultant. I heard they pay very well—many times my poor minister's salary."

"You do not need my recommendation. The World Bank already thinks highly of you."

"You flatter me. If they think so highly of me, why are they dragging their feet on next year's commitment? The auction money is running out soon. Normally, we would have an indication by now."

Omar recognized that the minister was fishing for information. He must do his best to give Suleiman an insider's view. "There are reasons and none has to do with your ability," he said. "One is that the Bank is going through a reorganization. An internal battle is going on. People are busy fighting for their jobs. They have no time to think about Somalia." Lowering his voice to convey confidentiality, Omar added, "But yesterday, I received a copy of the updated lending program. It shows that $100 million has been earmarked for Somalia next year."

"Splendid," Suleiman said, his face opening to a bona fide smile, but the next moment, he was frowning again. "I'll believe it when the first installment is deposited in our account. These donors have a way of breaking their word whenever they want to. Unfortunately, our country is poor," Suleiman sighed. "We have no choice but to put up with them. Will you keep me informed? My door is always open to you."

"I will do my best, but there may be one problem. The World Bank is thinking of cutting back the Somalia mission. My job is not secure."

Suleiman arched his brows. "How can it be? You, Omar, are indispensable. You speak the language, you understand the country. What would they do without you?"

"I'm afraid they don't think so, unless..." Omar hesitated so as not to sound too glib. "Unless I accomplish a difficult task, one that reminds them that I am indispensable."

Suleiman waited, his expression deadpan. Omar felt his courage flag, but he'd gone in too deep now. He heard himself say, "The Australian managing the rainfed project is in desperate need of fuel. If he waits too long, the rains will be over and the season will be lost. Miss Chen has assigned me the job of getting him the fuel. She knows how difficult it is. If I can do this, she'll be indebted to me."

Suleiman was silent. Omar didn't know where to rest his good eye. Had he asked for too much? Why on earth did he take it upon himself to get the fuel? Susan only asked him to get close to the minister, not solve the problems of a group of poor dryland farmers. But ah, if he could get it done, he would be one up on Jack. The Australian was getting too close to Susan for Omar's liking.

"Tell me, what do you think of Susan Chen?"

The question took Omar by surprise. A warning light flickered. He must speak carefully. "She's a good person," he said, then quickly balanced his compliment with, "but rather naive. She still has a lot to learn about our country."

"What's her standing in the World Bank?" Suleiman said.

Omar was relieved. He had something to offer on this, something that didn't require his personal opinion. It was a piece of gossip he'd overheard from some expats. "She was sent here almost directly from the outside, which is very unusual in the World Bank. I heard she was very well connected to some U.S. senators."

"Just as I thought. She hadn't been sent here because of her ability."

Omar racked his brains for something redeeming to say about Susan. He hadn't meant to undermine her credibility, which was what he'd just done.

"Is one tanker enough?" the minister said.

"I beg your pardon?"

"You said you wanted fuel?"

Omar roused himself. "Oh yes, one tanker will be enough."

Instead of going straight to Susan's home, Jack made a detour to a barbershop. The transformation was remarkable. With the Spanish moss on his head sheared back and the mat of bristles mown to their roots, he looked more like the thirty-eight-year-old that he was than the ageless ascetic from the desert. Liberated from the clutter, spaciousness spread over his face, and fresh air breezed in.

It was the first time Susan had ever seen Jack smile, not a wistful or courteous smile, but a smile of genuine happiness overflowing from his sky-blue eyes. Like the sun peeking through after a long spell of overcast, its rarity was all the more precious, and soon everyone in the room was grinning from ear to ear—except Omar. After delivering the good news on the fuel, he'd stepped outside the happy circle, arms twined across his tight chest, lips pressed together as if steeling himself against the surrounding cheer. Not even when Jack pumped his hands in an appreciative shake, nor when Fatima cooed over him with praises in two languages, did he rearrange his features one iota. It was only after Susan slapped him on the back and said, "Good job, pal," that his sullenness dissipated—to give way to outright annoyance.

Susan hated to break up the party, but if she didn't make a move now, she would be late for her tennis lesson. She announced her appointment sheepishly, knowing how frivolous it would sound to a workaholic such as Jack. To her surprise, he volunteered to accompany her. Omar stomped away with such fury that the ashtray on the table jumped.

As Susan and Jack entered the International Club, the poolside smiles told Susan the latest chatter among the expats: Susan and Jack have a thing for each other. Their stares made her face feel even warmer than it was under the torrid sun, and she was heart-throbbingly aware of Jack's arm swinging a hair's breath from hers. After having seen the agony her fellow agents had put their families through, she'd vowed not to marry as long as she was leading a double life. But the vow hadn't included deep-freezing her heart in the meantime. She admired Jack for his dedication, however futile it might seem, and was grateful for his help when she was all alone after the riots. The vortex of events had funneled out the core of each person, and in a matter of days, they'd gained a deeper intimacy than many had in a lifetime. Now the friendship was deepening; she could feel her vitals move whenever Jack was near.

Susan went into the women's room, changed into her tennis outfit and headed for the learner's court. Her coach was walking toward her in the easy lope of a man without a care, a happy-go-lucky gait that bordered on insolence. How deceptive appearances could be. Caring too much had been his fatal flaw.

"Thanks for the telex," Susan said. "Omar escaped the firing squad by the skin of his teeth."

"I heard it was a close shave." Nick's lips twisted. The leer again, but Susan had become inured to it. Besides, by the end of the lesson, he would learn to respect her. She'd finally cracked the shell of a Hawiye elder, and pieces of the puzzle were tumbling out.

As usual, they started the lesson with a refresher on forms. Side by side, they executed the forehand on a hypothetical ball.

"I've got news for you," she cut to the chase. "Eastern Horizon is owned by the son of General Ahmed. It purchases medicines with foreign exchange won at the auction; that much is legal and aboveboard. But after the medicines arrive, instead of selling them on the local market, it re-exports them for hard currency. The money is believed to be channeled to General Ahmed, who uses it to import all the weapons he wants. He's building an army in the desert.

"Another thing—Ahmed's son is married to Suleiman's daughter. But Ahmed and Suleiman are not on speaking terms, which seems to exonerate Suleiman for the time being. All the facts point to Ahmed as the person behind Eastern Horizon and

Andrew's murder. I bet you anything he's the one who hired Hamid."

"I want to see a wider sweep and more follow through, like this," Nick said. In slow motion, he rotated his hips, cocked back his wrist and swept a smooth arc with his racket.

Stunned by the coach's response to her momentous briefing, Susan complied, carrying her swing forward until she couldn't extend any farther.

"I wouldn't 'exonerate' Suleiman yet," Nick said. "The surveillance at his villa has gotten the green light. We'll see what that turns up."

"There's another person I'd like a check on," Susan added. "His name is Hoyt Grimley. He claims to be a salesman of agricultural tools. Looks and behaves harmless enough, but he's been seen hanging around General Ahmed's fortress."

"We know Hoyt. He comes here every few months to sell garden tools—simple gadgets such as howitzers, rocket launchers, and armored vehicles. He also has a record of visiting countries at the peak of civil wars—Angola, Uganda, Zaire, to name a few. We've been keeping an eye on him, but he's as slippery as an eel. So far we haven't been able to pin anything on him. I'm afraid only a sting will get him, but that will take too much time to be of use to us. Let's see your backhand grip now."

Susan twisted her wrist and flattened her thumb on the handle. "Can you get me the coordinates of Ahmed's fortress?" She'd had enough of this fictitious game. Now that she'd identified her enemy, it was time to play hardball.

Nick clenched her wrist and twisted it some more. "Don't even think about it. No amount of training can prepare you for an infiltration like that. It's suicidal, it's just plain stupid."

Susan opened her mouth to argue, but Nick cut her off before she could begin. "As long as I'm station chief, you're not going near that place. That's an order."

Susan struck out with the back of her racket, snapping "yes" on the upswing and "sir" on the down.

"I still think the best bet is to lure Hamid to you," Nick went on. "General Ahmed is a psychopath. He never lets any offense go unpunished. If what you say is true, it won't be hard to get him to target you."

"Yes, yes, I know I'm supposed to dress myself up as a bait. But if you don't mind my saying so, your strategy is taking too much time. How many more people are going to get hurt before he comes for me?"

"Listen, you've got to stay the course now. You've come a long way since the day you arrived. I had my doubts about you at first, but you're proving to be better than I'd expected. Actually the whole town is looking at you in a different light. When you first came, nobody took you seriously, least of all considered you a threat. Now things are different. The way you stormed into the NSC has made you famous, or rather, infamous. Nobody in his right mind would lock horns with the brutes there, but that was what you did and you saved Omar. You're achieving a higher profile than Park and Barnett ever did. You're standing out like a sore thumb."

The man sure knows how to compliment, Susan thought.

Nick went on: "You've got to challenge Ahmed personally. There was a raid of a government armory recently. A gang of masked men stole into the place and cleaned it out. I have information that Ahmed was the culprit. If you broadcast this, I'm sure the general would be eager to make your acquaintance. Okay!" he called out. "We're ready to hit some balls now."

"Do we have to?" Susan said, but Nick had already walked off with his bucket.

"Ready or not, here it comes," Nick warned from the other side.

Susan raised her racket, her eyes stinging from the sweat trickling down her forehead. Her briefing was over; why did she have to stay? But before she could finish her thought, a green object was zipping at her. She struck out in reflex and heard the thud of wood.

"Good try," her coach yelled. "Here comes another."

She stepped forward, opened her body sideways and swung the racket hard. The guts twanged with musical resonance. She watched with astonishment as the ball volleyed deep into her opponent's court. She was improving against her will.

"Great job," Nick shouted.

Chapter 20

Susan watched a sheath of cloud peel away from the banana moon. It was a pleasant night, aired by a gentle breeze that lightened the oppressiveness of the day's heat. Jack sat next to her on the backyard patio, apparently uncomfortable about the fuss over him, while Abdullahi ran back and forth the kitchen, serving dinner course by course. Starters were two plates of spaghetti, each piled mountain high. Susan thought she'd be full after that, but curiously enough the starchy appetizer gave her a larger appetite than when she started the meal. The light Chianti from a local Italian store also helped to wash it down nicely.

After the veal piccata and the scrumptious fruit flan, Susan thanked her housekeeper and gave him permission to retire for the night. Abdullahi cast a furtive glance at Jack, hovered around for as long as he could find reason to, and finally retreated to his quarters after admonishing Susan to lock the patio doors.

They were alone. With the housekeeper gone, the structure imposed by formality lifted, and the moment became borderless, filled with a fluidity that could flow in any direction. Their topics of conversation were no longer locked in square boxes labeled "the economy," "agricultural policies," or "political reform." They could talk about anything in the world.

After a glass of the Chianti, a comforting mist was spreading over Susan's head. She let herself sink into the soft folds of the shroud. Gone were the woes of the world, the impending wars and imminent mayhem. She was only aware of the spot Jack occupied. She held up her glass for seconds, but not without reminding herself that two was her limit. Beyond that, her tongue would be too loose for her own good and that of national security. When Jack left two days ago, she thought she would never see him again. This second chance, like a second wind, promised to carry her farther than the first.

"How did you end up in Somalia?" Susan changed gears as soon as Abdullahi turned off the hallway light, a sign that he was truly done for the night.

"That's an awfully long story. Have you got all night?" His tongue too had been loosened by the wine. Susan was beginning to discover he could be quite talkative.

"An abridged version will do, as I don't want to keep you up. You've got a long drive tomorrow."

"You don't have to worry about me. I know that road so well I can drive home in my sleep. Well now, how did I end up in Somalia? You realize that you're asking for my life story, don't you?"

Susan smiled, wondering how those sheer blue eyes could have ever frightened her. "Go ahead," she said.

"All right then, let's start from the beginning. I was born in Amman, Jordan to Dutch parents. My father was an economist with UNDP, and was stationed there at the time. While I was growing up, he was transferred six times to four different continents, which meant that before the age of sixteen, I moved every two years or so from one country to another. As you can see, I'm one of those U.N. kids who don't know where home is.

"The country I stayed longest in was Australia. That was where my father took up a teaching post after he retired from the U.N. My whole family took up Australian citizenship, but I never really felt I belonged there, or anywhere for that matter. So, after I got my doctorate in Ag Economics—"

"Following in your father's footsteps?" Susan said.

"Yes and no. The old man had a hand in it, but it was mostly my own decision. I had two ambitions at that time—to travel and to be a farmer. Since I was a little boy, I've had this urge to play with dirt." Jack looked down at the brown crescents on his fingernails. "The problem was that the two ambitions weren't reconcilable. A farmer has to stay on his farm. If he travels the way I'd like to, his farm would be a shambles. So to satisfy both ambitions, I went into Ag Econ."

"Have things worked out the way you wanted?"

Jack paused for a nutshell assessment. "Professionally yes, personally," he closed his eyes for a moment, "there's room for improvement."

Their eyes were riveted together, as if searching each other's interpretation of his last words. Jerking himself out of the trance, Jack continued his story.

"My first job was with the Department of Agriculture to lead a dryland farming project in Queensland. The project was rather successful, and after that, the government sent me to Indonesia as a member of a technical assistance team. That was where I met my wife."

Susan could see that he was trying to deliver the last piece of biodata in as straightforward a manner as the rest. He would have made it if not for the winged flutter of his lashes.

"Are you still married?" she asked.

"My wife and I have been separated for five years. We never filed for divorce, because, well, there was no need, I guess. In a way, I still wanted to provide for her, the mother of my child. But several months ago, for reasons of her own, my wife started divorce proceedings. Nobody's contesting, of course, so it should be over soon."

Susan hid her face in her wineglass. It was a welcome piece of information.

"What about you?" Jack said. "What made you come to Somalia?"

"Well, now, that's an awfully long story," Susan said, mirroring Jack's words. They both laughed. To parallel his narration, she began with: "I was born in New York City. My father ran something called the Chinese Health Institute. He was a doctor, the traditional kind." She deliberately left out the other half of the institute, which was a martial arts school. "I was the only child, and spoiled rotten, of course."

"I wouldn't have guessed. You're one of the most unspoiled people I know, Susan." His voice was smoky, and she loved the susurration of her name on his tongue.

Suppressing the flush on her face, Susan returned to her life story. "My childhood was rather uneventful. College was at

Columbia U, and I graduated with a B.A. in political science. That landed me a job in a senator's office." She was reading from her packaged c.v. now. "I got to know some people in the banking lobby, then one thing led to another, a commercial bank offered me a personnel job in New York. I took it, and discovered that the banking institution was too cold a place for my liking. So I went back to Washington and looked up my buddies on Capitol Hill. The World Bank was starting a reorganization at the time and was looking for personnel officers with private sector experience. My connections gave me a push, and I was in.

"A year later, a job in the Somalia resident mission opened up." She and Jack exchanged a meaningful glance to indicate they both remembered the reason for the vacancy. "From the moment I joined the bank, I'd been interested in its operations. The idea of going into the field to help the poor had a lot of appeal, much more than shuffling paper in Personnel. At the same time, nobody seemed to want the job. It was a great opportunity, and I jumped at it."

"You're one of those who want to save the world," Jack said with a hint of amusement on his lips.

Susan felt the heat rise up her cheeks. Was he laughing at her? As far back as she could remember, she'd wanted to do something heroic. She didn't know what, but it could be anything from opening a homeless shelter to foiling a terrorist plot. She'd rather die than admit it to others, though.

"You mean spin around a revolving door and fly out in my superwoman suit? Sure, I've always wanted to do that."

Jack laughed, but when he spoke, his tone was serious: "I admire people who want to save the world. If more of us had that kind of ambition, the world would be a better place. As it is, it's filled with power-hungry, money-grubbing people who care only for themselves."

"Which camp do you belong to?" she said although she knew full well.

Jack smiled. "Come visit me in Kurtun Waarey and you'll find out." He touched her on the arm, sending goosebumps from the crown of her head to the tips of her fingers. "You'll see what marginal lives people out there lead. You'll see that your job isn't just sitting around at meetings with ministers and bureaucrats. It's about improving the lives of people."

"I'd love to, but travel outside Mogadishu is restricted."

"I know, and even if Juergen lets you, he'll make sure a truckload of soldiers escort you."

She laughed. "I bet you anything he's still up monitoring the radio." She picked up the CB and turned it on.

Juergen's voice squawked at them: "What's going on?"

Another voice came on, frantic, and somewhere in the vicinity, machinegun fire stuttered. "They're attacking the Ministry of Transport. I can't see them, but the shots are coming from the back."

"Get away from the windows and stay down," Juergen said.

Another blast of gunfire, louder and closer now. A man cried out in distress, and Juergen was desperately trying to keep in contact with the trapped expat. Susan turned off the radio. She and Jack looked at each other in silence. The world they were trying to save was crumbling around them.

They carried the empty bottle and glasses into the kitchen. Susan locked and double locked the patio door while Jack waited by her side. Together, they drifted down the corridor to the bedrooms. At Susan's door, they mumbled an awkward "goodnight," eyes averted from each other. Susan's hand touched the door handle. Tomorrow Jack would be gone. She would never see him again. She pivoted toward the direction of the guest room. Jack's immediacy startled her. He was still standing by her side, so near that she could feel the spark of electricity on his arm.

The space closed and then there was none at all, just the warmth of his spare body, softer than she had imagined. They stood holding each other for a while, two people embarked on a desperate endeavor in a desperate country. This was their last chance. They could walk away and regret it the rest of their lives, or they could seize the moment and squeeze what they could out of it. Behind Susan, the bedroom door opened, seemingly on its own. She looked up at Jack, who bent down and covered her lips with his own. His sandpaper chin chafed her cheeks, dispatching a chain of tingles throughout her body. The next moment, she was aware of standing in the darkness of her bedroom, as stars swirled above and she tiptoed greedily to reach them.

Jack planted a long, passionate kiss on Susan's lips. She squirmed a little at first, conscious of Abdullahi looking out the window into the driveway. But after a while, her mind blanked out, and her body surrendered.

Jack looked down at her, his eyes shining and his callused hand pressing the small of her back. "Come with me to Kurtun Waarey. We'll send Juergen a message later. What can he do to you?"

Susan laughed, a mischievous laugh at the thought of Juergen's chagrin, but in the next instant the impossibility of the escapade hit her, and her cheer quickly disintegrated. "I wish. But it's not Juergen I'm worried about, it's my boss in Washington. Who's going to answer his telexes while I'm gone? And then there's the meeting with—"

"Tell them you're sick, caught a summer cold. You know how nasty that can be. I'll bring you back in a few days. Come on."

Susan ran the back of her hand over Jack's freshly shaved skin, a smile loaded with longing and sadness on her face. "Another time, sweetie. I've just got too many things on my plate right now"—if he only knew, she thought—"but the moment I'm done, I might take you up on your offer. Don't be surprised if I knock on your door one day."

He held her closer. "You're welcome any time."

They clasped each other for another moment. Then without another word, Jack tore himself away and hopped into his vehicle. Before starting the engine, he fished a tape recorder out of his knapsack and placed it on the seat next to him. The sight of the machine reminded Susan of something.

"Where's your radio? Didn't Juergen issue you one?"

"He tried to, but I told him to save it for somebody else. The moment I leave the city's limits, I'll be beyond help. Nobody can come and save me."

Susan clutched the rim of the rolled-down window and murmured, "Be careful."

Jack's hand reached out and stroked the long silky black hair, still a bit tangled from their night's intimacies. "I'll be back soon."

They let their eyes speak to each other once more. Jack switched on the ignition. Susan stepped aside and waved ruefully as the Land Rover backed out of her driveway. "Safe trip," she whispered.

One hand on the steering wheel, Jack slipped a tape into the recorder. At the sound of the first trumpet, he named the composition as Beethoven's *Ode to Joy*. How could he have known when he left home that this piece of music would be so appropriate for his return trip? His heart was bursting with joy. Making love had always been a serious undertaking for him. It had meant caring, communication, and commitment, but after the experience with Susan, thrilling was the first word that came to his mind. There was a brinkmanship in her that he never knew existed, a dare-devilish streak that enjoyed pushing him farther and farther to the edge, and when he was begging to leap off the cliff, she held him back. Then without warning, she dropped him down the precipice, and he could feel his heart soaring out of his mouth and his body smashing into a million pieces. With an intensity that frightened him, she made him give as much as she gave. Did she think they would never meet again? He'd promised to be back once the planting was done, and even if Somalia were to fell apart and they had to be evacuated, he could always reach her through the World Bank in Washington. Having lived his life as an international nomad, the world was his grazing ground. He could meet up with her anywhere on this planet.

Jack sniffed his shirt. The scent of Susan was still on him. He felt he'd been walking on a beach all day, absorbing into his hair and skin the smells of the sun, sea, and sand. A memory brought a smile to his lips. With her supple body, Susan could twist into all manners of contortions and still fit him like a tailored suit, but when she'd tried to make him flex, his joints had cracked, and they'd erupted in a fit of laughter. He hadn't heard himself laugh as heartily in a long time.

Jack found himself at the fringe of town. From the rearview mirror, he could see the last adobe houses recede behind him. He'd never liked coming to Mogadishu much, for every time an expat looked at him, he knew he was the object of pity. But now, one woman had transformed the city for him. The next trip couldn't come fast enough, but first he must hurry back and complete the plowing.

Jack drove past the Italian-run banana plantation, forded the Shebelle at a shallow section, and came upon a stretch of potholes that jolted every vertebra in his spine and distorted the music into a wriggly belly-dancing tune. He pressed the "pause" button, intending to continue the symphony when he got to the part of the road that had recently been repaired by Italian aid. Having driven back and forth more times than he could remember, the road was as familiar as the back of his hand.

As he turned a corner, the flank of a Pajero came into view. A soldier was flagging him down with an AK-47. Jack braked, glancing around for other men. He registered two irregularities: The soldier was alone, and he was unusually fat for a Somali.

The trooper approached, his fleshy breasts jouncing under the uniform. Jack looked down at the pack of cigarettes in his pocket and was glad to see that it was half full. Soldiers at roadblocks were jittery animals. His every action must be slow and unthreatening. His papers were in the glove compartment, but he mustn't give the impression that he was reaching to grab a weapon. The trooper must have spotted his U.N. license plate by now. It was best to let him speak first.

"Get out," the soldier said, beckoning with his automatic.

"My papers are in the glove compartment. Let me show them to you," Jack said, slowly reaching.

"I don't want papers. Come out," the soldier shouted.

This doesn't sound right, Jack thought. His hand crept toward the recorder, found the twin buttons for "record," and pressed them down. "I work with the World Bank," he said. "We have a project in Kurtun Waarey, that's where I'm based..."

The soldier flung open the door. With the deadly barrel wagging at him, Jack had no choice but to obey. He got out and faced the soldier. Courtesy hadn't worked; now he must be firm. "I have papers signed by the minister of finance *and* the minister of agriculture. If you would only let me..." He saw the soldier make an abrupt move. The butt of a rifle was coming at him. He raised an arm to ward off the blow. *Thwack*! He heard his bones shatter and an explosion of pain threw him to the ground. He struggled to get up, but as he raised his head, an object was flying at him, right between the eyes. This time he heard nothing.

Susan burst into Juergen's office. He immediately wound up his phone call and got up to embrace her. "I'm sorry, my dear. I'm very sorry."

Susan buried her face in Juergen's chest, mumbling, "I should have gone with him." When she finally pulled away, Juergen gave her his handkerchief and sat her down.

"Tell me everything you know, everything!" Susan said, her voice hoarse and eyes rimmed with tears.

"An Italian construction team was traveling south this afternoon. A little past the banana plantation, they found an empty vehicle on the road, a Land Rover with a U.N. plate. They got out and found Jack...lying in a ditch. They radioed us and we got there, fortunately, before the police. We retrieved all his personal items." Juergen got up, unlocked a cabinet and took out a tape recorder, a crumpled knapsack and its contents—a shirt, toothbrush and notebook. Susan flipped through the notebook and found a page dedicated to her name, printed in an elaborate penmanship and decorated with flowers and leaves. Her throat constricted; she closed her eyes and steadied herself.

"The method of killing—is it the same as Park's and Andrew's?" Susan said.

Juergen nodded gravely.

Hamid, this is all out war, she declared silently. She willed her heart to shrivel and freeze into a lump of ice. She'd let it out of her armor, allowed it to encroach and corrupt the purpose of her mission. It was time to put it back where it belonged. From now on, she would be a cold and calculating hunter. She would use any means at her disposal to capture her quarry, dead or alive.

"Where was his body taken?" she said, her voice crusted with frost.

"The morgue. It's being prepared for shipment to Australia. They'll do an autopsy there, but as far as I could see," Juergen frowned, "the incision was in exactly the same spot as Park's. In addition to that..." Susan saw him swallow his words. "It's not important..."

"Tell me. I can take it," she said in a voice so icy that Juergen stopped to assess her for a few seconds.

"He was hit on the head by a blunt object."

"Where exactly?"

Juergen held his breath, but Susan kept the pressure of her gaze on him. She wasn't going to let him exhale until he told her. "Right here," he said, pointing to the gap between the brows.

Susan stared into space, imagining what a blow like that would do to the underlying bone and those beautiful eyes.

Juergen quickly added, "That must have knocked him out. Believe me, it was quick and painless. He didn't know what hit him."

Susan dug her nails into her thigh. Juergen patted her hand. She jumped at the touch, afraid that any bit of warmth would thaw the chilliness she had forced on herself.

"Can I take his things with me?" she said in the same arctic tone.

Juergen hesitated. Susan could see his mind working out the legality of ownership. Jack was still married to somebody in Indonesia.

"I'm his closest friend here," Susan said. Knowing the hyperactivity of the grapevine in Mogadishu, she was sure she needn't explain further. "I just want a few moments with them. I'll return them tomorrow."

"Sure, sure," Juergen said.

"Can I use Jack's car? I haven't replaced mine yet."

The request took Juergen by surprise. "It's been impounded by the police," he said.

"Can I borrow one of yours then?" she said.

"What are you going to do?" he said dubiously.

"I want to retrace Jack's route since he left my house," Susan said.

Juergen studied her. In all his years with the U.N., he'd never met anyone like this young woman. Susan Chen did not know her limits. The world worked because the cogs and wheels functioned according to the way they were supposed to, but when a cog tried to behave like a wheel, the machinery would go haywire.

"What do you hope to accomplish?" he finally asked, disapproval written all over his face.

"I don't know. I just have to."

"I'm very busy right now. I have to meet with the police, inform the community about what's happened, and telex New York. Maybe tomorrow, I can drive out with you."

"It's okay. I'm sure I can find a car somewhere else." Susan got up to go.

"All right, all right, I'll take you."

They picked up Jack's belongings and walked out to Juergen's truck. Their first destination was Susan's home, the starting point of Jack's journey. From there on, they took the most direct route out of town, which was what Jack would have done. Sitting up close to the windshield, Susan saw the passing streets and houses the way Jack had. In the last moments of Jack's life, what did he see? What was he thinking? She

187

blinked the moisture away and turned her thoughts on Hamid. Where was he while Jack was driving along this road? Was he tailing Jack, or lying in ambush ahead?

Susan reached over to the backseat and grabbed Jack's tape recorder. It was a compact, no-frills machine the size of an office phone. Susan opened the tape deck and found that a cassette had played to the end on side A. Written on the label in Jack's neat penmanship was "Beethoven." She pressed the rewind button and played the tape from the beginning. A wind instrument came on.

"*Ode to Joy*, by Beethoven," Juergen said with an expression that was anything but joyful.

Susan noted the volume the recorder was on. She could imagine Jack humming along with the ecstatic tenor. Juergen fidgeted in his seat, obviously disturbed by the incongruity of the music. Susan was tempted to turn it down, but remembering that this was the way Jack had played it, she left it alone.

A soprano was warbling to a climax when the road sank into a crater. Juergen slammed on the brakes and swerved. "*Scheisse!*" he cursed. "I should have remembered that big hole. We're very close now." He rounded the bend, coasted to the edge of the ditch and came to a stop.

"His Land Rover was parked here," Juergen said, stamping his foot on the broken asphalt. "Something made him stop."

Susan studied the crisscross of tire marks on the muddy road. Unfortunately, the police had come by and stirred up the water.

"How were the tires positioned?" she said.

"They were all straight."

"You mean he stopped in the middle of the road?" Susan said. She'd seen Jack do that in front of checkpoints, which were usually temporary barriers made of boulders, a truck or men brandishing AK-47's.

Susan placed herself in Jack's absent vehicle and peered ahead, imagining what he could have seen to stop right then and there, without pulling aside. The scene of a checkpoint kept coming to her mind.

"Where was the body?" she said.

Juergen pointed to the ditch in front. Susan grew taut. Juergen was about to say something, but she shushed him. A man's voice was coming from the direction of Juergen's vehicle, and it sounded awfully like Jack's. She looped her hair behind one ear and pointed it toward the source of the sound. Juergen looked at her, his eyes wide in astonishment. They ran up to the Land Rover.

The tape had gone silent. Susan rewound it a few seconds and replayed it. Jack's voice came on, unmistakable now, and he was saying, "We have a project in Kurtun Waarey, that's where I'm based..."

"Get out!" a shrill voice shouted. It was hard to tell whether it was a man's or a woman's. A hinge creaked, footsteps crunched on dirt, Jack spoke again, something about his papers, a thud, and another. A spell of silence followed, then a man spoke, barely audible. Susan twisted the volume knob as far as it could go and replayed it. This time, the words took shape: "My dear colonel, that was not necessary."

"You think I'm not necessary? I think *you*'re not necessary!" the shrill voice said.

Susan waited for a response, but there was nothing except the crush of hard leather on gravel, the start of an engine and the hush of the empty road.

Chapter 21

The colonel stepped into the dim foyer. The metal door clanged shut, blocking out all light except for a low wattage lamp on the ceiling. A guard announced his arrival through an intercom while another ran a metal detector over him. The colonel stood stock still, his eyes following the wand with disgust. The electronic device let out a scream over the dome of his belly. At the guard's insistence, the colonel unfastened the silver-buckled belt that held up his pants and handed it over. Here he was, the nephew of General Ahmed, subjected to insulting scrutiny by somebody from the rank and file. Who were they anyway? Why should they have daily access to his uncle, while he, the favorite nephew, virtually had to be strip searched before allowed in?

The foyer's inner door opened. Another guard appeared, saying, "General Ahmed has been waiting for you."

"As you can see, I've been delayed," the colonel said haughtily as he pulled his pants up and threaded the belt around his tub of lard.

The thought of his uncle waiting anxiously for his arrival gave him enormous pleasure. His uncle had asked to see him, and he could guess the reason. For once he'd done something on his own initiative, not by anyone's order or suggestion. The idea was completely his. Uncle must be very proud of him.

The colonel followed the guard into the web of windowless corridors. The passage was so narrow that only one person could fit at a time. The colonel's overstuffed shoulders scraped the wall. This was his third visit to the castle, yet every time was as bizarre as the first. He was glad that the guard was in front. After a number of maneuvers in the maze, they went up a flight of steps, down half a flight and up some more, until he was totally disoriented as to which floor he was on, or in which part of the castle. For all he knew, he could be right where he'd started. His breathing was getting ragged, and sweat was pouring down his temples. He was beginning to suspect that the guard was giving him the runaround, but a while later, his guide stopped and ushered the colonel into a room. A blade of light sliced through a slit in the concrete wall. The colonel grinned. He knew where he was now.

A man sat at the desk. He glanced up from his reading, then cast his eyes down again. The lamplight threw shadows around the acute planes and angles of his face, pitching into stark relief the depth of his eye sockets and hollowness of his cheeks. It was a face of unmistakable definition. Without a doubt, this was a man no one would dare cross.

This was the man who had littered his career path with the fallen bodies of men and women, young and old. Once an enemy of Siad Barré, he'd escaped the gallows by selling out his friends. After he came out of prison, his zeal for proving his loyalty to Siad Barré was translated into a merciless persecution of the president's enemies. His tactics were many, but the most notorious was the poisoning of wells and water holes. In the bone-dry country, such an act of sabotage was a crime against man and animals alike. The decimation of a nomad's camel herd, whose rich, creamy milk was his main source of nourishment, was a punishment that promised a slow and agonizing death.

To the colonel, however, General Ahmed was his mother's twin brother, a man who had given him piggyback rides and taught him to shoot his first gun.

"*Haye*, uncle, *warama*?" he said casually.

The older man pierced him with his flinty eyes but said nothing until the guards had been dismissed.

"Who told you to kill the Australian?" the general snarled as soon as the metal door closed.

"Nobody," the colonel said, a smug smirk on his fat lips. "I thought of it myself. The man stole our fuel. That tanker was supposed to be for us. If we didn't punish him, others would think we're weak."

"You fool, there is a time for everything, and this isn't the right time!"

The colonel frowned, more perplexed than mortified. He should be getting a medal for practicing what his uncle always preached—never give an inch to your enemy—but instead he was getting a dressing down.

"Do you know you've been recorded?" the general said. "The Australian had the machine on while you were fixing him. Both of you were recorded, the Afghan and you. Especially you!"

The colonel cringed. His voice captured by the enemy. He felt defiled, violated.

"How careless can you be!" the general fumed.

"It was all Hamid's fault. If he hadn't spoken, I wouldn't need to say anything," the colonel whined, keenly aware of his shrillness. His screechy voice had been the brunt of torment from his peers. While other boys' vocal cords settled into a lower register as they passed into manhood, his had remained in a high state of suspension.

"Enough," Ahmed commanded. "You've done a lot of harm. Somebody is pointing the finger at me, saying I ordered the murder."

"Who says that?"

"The World Bank representative, Susan Chen. She traced the gasoline to me, and now she's accusing me of killing the Australian in revenge."

"But she has no proof!"

"No proof? What do you call this?" General Ahmed reached into a drawer and brandished a small thin box. The colonel looked closer and saw what it was. A tape. "You want to hear yourself order the Australian out of his vehicle? You want to hear Hamid call you 'my dear colonel,' and the two of you argue over what was necessary and what wasn't? It's all in here."

"How did you get it?"

"I have friends at the police station. Here, take it. It's all yours."

Ahmed tossed the tape over his desk. The colonel lurched to catch it, but it slipped out of his thick paws and clattered on the bare floor. He tucked in his belly and bent over to pick it up.

"War is between men, but when a woman interferes, she becomes the enemy as well," the general said. "I hadn't planned on eliminating her, but she leaves me no choice. This time, do a clean job." The general leaned forward, thrusting a sneer at his nephew, "It's only a woman."

The colonel's expression reflected his uncle's, but aside from the attitude, there was no resemblance at all between the two. The difference in weight was so vast that it erased every sign of genetic affinity.

"I will do it with great pleasure," the colonel said. He'd eyed her with interest as she went around town with the Australian, wondering if she would be willing to jump into bed with anybody, including himself.

As if reading his nephew's mind, Ahmed said, "You are *not* to dirty your hands. Let the Afghan do it. That's what I hired him for."

"Uncle, I don't see why you have to spend so much money on this man. What can he do that I can't? I could have taken care of those people just as easily."

"Don't argue with me. Just follow my orders. You've already caused me a lot of trouble. I'm forced to advance my schedule...Go now." The general flicked his hand as if he was shooing away a persistent fly.

Chapter 22

Susan sat down at the long dining table. She couldn't understand why a simple meal of coffee and cold cereal needed to be served, but Abdullahi had a rigid notion of his duties and he was going to perform them whether she liked it or not. It was Friday, the housekeeper's day off, and Susan was dying for him to disappear.

"When are you getting out of here?" Susan said.

Abdullahi was kneeling in front of the buffet, shuffling dishes from one shelf to another. He corkscrewed his head around and replied, "Soon. Are you sure you don't want me to send Abukar here?" His face was creased with worry, but then, it always was. He behaved much older than his fifty-three years, especially toward his employers, who were mere babes in the jungle of Somali intrigue.

"Yes, I'm sure," Susan said, like an exasperated teenager in the face of parental nagging. "I told you, I'm spending the night at a friend's."

The housekeeper rose to his feet, shaking his head. "You have to be careful," he said. "First it was Mr. Barnett, then Mr. Jack. I think this house is bad luck."

"Don't be superstitious," Susan said, although the tremor in his voice gave her the creeps. She quickly finished her cereal and took her coffee to her room.

Andrew, Park, and Jack were alone when the assassin struck. She, too, had to be absolutely alone. The three murders had been tumbling over and over in her mind. The last was the most difficult to dwell on, but she'd forced herself to replay Jack's last moments so many times that she could live and breathe the scene. She'd copied the tape before letting Juergen surrender it to the police.

Living it, dreaming it, she'd given bodies to the voices, feeling to the violent thuds and the vicious silence, in which a blade penetrated the thin film of skin stretched over Jack's neck and severed the cord of life. The shrill voice sounded Somali, and if the address "my dear colonel" hadn't slipped out, she couldn't have been one hundred percent sure that it belonged to a man. The other one, who said, "That was not necessary," was low and flat, devoid of accent, nationality and emotions. Her skin crawled every time she listened to it, and she couldn't quite understand why until a revelation awoke her late one night. The voice was dead. It had none of the timbre or resonance of a human voice. It was the voice of a machine, a robot programmed for one function.

"That was not necessary." The meaning of the words had struck her with lightning clarity. "That" was the blow to Jack's head. "That" was the uncalled for assistance that had offended Hamid, the assassin who took pride in artistic perfection. The crude bash on the skull had ruined his handiwork.

Susan took out her Glock and snapped in the magazine. A knock on the door interrupted her; Abdullahi was announcing his departure. She slipped the gun under the pillow and went out to see her housekeeper off.

As Abdullahi drove the bolt home from the outside, Susan heaved a sigh of relief. At last, the hunt could begin. The first step was to set the trap. She went around checking the window grilles. As expected, Abdullahi had fastened all the padlocks. They were sturdy, made-in-Germany models that Juergen had procured in bulk for all expat homes. He'd touted them as unbreakable, but people knew it was only a figure of speech. Given the right person with the right tools, nothing in the world was unbreakable.

Susan opened the door to the guest room. The row of windows, which was right against a concrete fence and thus shielded from view, was the best place to attempt entry, something Hamid had already discovered on his previous visit. The new padlocks would be an inconvenience but not a deterrent for a professional. After tugging at the locks, Susan left the room and closed the door. She then selected one single strand of her hair, curled it around her fingers and yanked. With a dab of glue on each end, she strung the thread of black hair from door to jamb. She went around the house, performing the same ritual on every door.

The trap was ready. Now, the dressing of the bait would begin. Susan went into her bedroom, put her hair up with a barrette, and changed into her bathing suit. For outerwear, she selected a shocking-pink T-shirt and a pair of equally bright yellow shorts. To top it all, she propped a pair of sunglasses on her head. The image in the mirror made her chuckle in spite of herself. She could have walked right out of a California beach party movie. If Hamid were to see her, he would know exactly where she was going. The house would be empty for at least three, four hours.

Loading the gear was the last item on her list. After checking the safety lock, she placed the handgun at the bottom of her straw basket and piled on it a towel, a bottle of sunscreen and the box of lunchmeat Abdullahi had packed. Now she was set.

A car honked. Susan picked up her basket, surveyed her house once more and stepped into the bright sun. A sporty red coupe was idling outside the gate. She swept a glance down both ends of the street, spotted nothing, and got into the back of the car. In the front were Amanda and Brenda, a middle-aged black American who was in charge of visas at the U.S. embassy.

"How *are* you?" Brenda turned around and said to Susan. Both women were staring at her with round, moist eyes. In them, Susan read their sympathy for her loss of Jack.

"Hanging in there," Susan replied. Then with a deep sigh, she added, "It's too beautiful a day to be miserable. Come on, let's go."

With a roar of the engine that defied the security advisory to travel with an armed escort, the women took off in the direction of the airport.

About a dozen cars were at the cove already. The women carried their picnic lunch to the beach. They found a spot at the foot of a sandy scarp, rolled out a straw mat and stripped down to their bathing suits. Lotions of various degrees of sun block oozed out of their respective bottles. The sweet smell of coconut and pineapple filled the air as the women rubbed the cream all over their skins until they shone with the sheen of a luxuriant varnish.

When they looked up, four men carrying beach chairs were ambling toward them. Susan recognized them as people she'd met at one reception or another. They were Italian, dark-eyed, hairy-chested and overflowing with male hormones.

"*Bon giorno*," said the one with the self-conscious good looks. "Magnificent day to come to the beach."

The three women agreed in the same breath. While the men unfolded their chairs, Susan exchanged glances with her friends and hunkered down for some heavy flirting. The men probably had wives and screaming kids waiting for them back in Italy, but here in the "field," the only token of their ineligibility for bachelorhood was the wedding band on the fourth finger, provided it hadn't been temporarily removed. All of a sudden, Susan was acutely aware of her own body and those of her friends. Amanda's was lily white, fine-boned, and exquisitely appealing to the protective machismo. Brenda's was creamy black, no longer sleek and taut but pleasantly relaxed and confident, like a person who'd got it all figured out. Susan's was a plump brown innocence, still full of the vigor of her cheerleader days.

"Aren't you the one in charge of the mother-infant project at UNICEF?" Amanda said to one of the Italians. Before the man could complete his affirmation, Amanda pounced: "You're just the person I want to talk to."

"There she goes again," Brenda murmured to Susan. "She's such a workaholic." Aloud, Brenda announced that she was going for a swim.

"You're going into that water?" the handsome Italian said.

"Why not?" Brenda said.

"Haven't you heard of the shark attack last year?"

"Sure, but it wasn't here," Brenda said, then adding in a smaller voice, "or was it?"

"It was right here." The Italian flung his arm out and pointed to a particular spot in the sea.

Both Brenda and Susan looked out. A score of heads were bobbing on the water. "There are so many people out there," Susan ventured. "It can't be that dangerous."

"You'll never see me in that water," the Italian said, hiking up his shoulders.

"There are a number of shark attacks every year, but they're all in Mogadishu," Brenda said.

"Nooo," the Italian rounded his eyes, shaking his head so fast that he could be shivering. "This one was right here. The victim's name was Johann, a German. He was wading in water up to his knees and holding a can of beer in one hand. A shark attacked from behind and bit off the hand that was holding the beer."

Susan laughed, glad perhaps it was a joke after all. Amanda smiled, but her brows were wrinkled in a dubious expression. Brenda noted as a matter of fact: "You mean to say it was a beer-drinking shark."

"Believe it or not, it's the truth," the narrator insisted. "Fortunately, other people were there. They dragged the German out of the water. His arm was gone from here down." The Italian chopped at the middle of his own limb. "They flew him back to Germany, and for three months he was in such shock he couldn't speak."

Nobody was laughing anymore. They could see that the Italian wasn't pulling their leg. The women stared at the vast body of unfathomable sea, wondering what monsters lurked underneath.

"Well," Brenda broke the ice. "If you're to listen to every shark story, you'll never get your toes wet." Pulling the rims of her bathing suit over her cheeks, she got up and declared she was going in. Susan stood up to show sororal support. Amanda, on the other hand, had resumed her discussion and was bouncing her golden curls in emphasis of the need for universalizing prenatal care. Susan went after Brenda, and together they headed toward the congregation of swimmers. Safety lay in numbers.

To Susan's surprise, the water was only up to her knees. From shore, the bathers looked as if they were treading in deep water, but in fact, they were only sitting on the sandy bottom, swaying with the waves.

"Doesn't it get deeper?" Susan said.

"You have to go very far out. This should be good enough." Brenda looked around warily before sitting down. Susan tried to swim, but her knees scraped the bottom. She finally found a way of punting herself forward with her hands. It was all right as long as she could scan the seascape ahead, but as soon as she turned toward land, the feeling that something was after her gnawed at her insides. Looking over her shoulder from time to time, she made it back to where Brenda was sitting. Amanda had joined them.

The three friends sat together, the waves lapping at their waists. "Isn't it great that they released the authors of the manifesto?" Amanda said. "Congress has decided to appropriate the funds for my women's project. My consultants are flying in next week. It's going to be really exciting."

"What's the project for?" Susan asked, not so much out of interest as her habit of collecting bits and pieces of information.

"It's to provide technical assistance to the National Women's Association, to help it develop into a corporation-like entity, with an income-generating financial base and a sound accounting system," Amanda said, stirring up whirlpools as her hands gestured underwater.

Brenda glanced at her with the wisdom of every one of her forty years, fifteen of which were spent in the foreign service. Turning to Susan, she said, "You know who the president of the association is?" Susan pleaded ignorance. "Mrs. Ahmed, wife of the general. I can't imagine anything being businesslike under her."

Ignoring the sarcasm in Brenda's statement, Susan seized the chance to involve herself in any business related to General Ahmed. "Women's projects are big in the World Bank now," she said. "We may even be interested in putting in some seed money."

"That's great," Amanda beamed.

While Brenda twitched her nose over her friends' folly, Susan remarked innocently, "General Ahmed seems to be into everything these days, but has anyone ever met the man?"

"Our military attaché has. He said the guy looked like a psychopath. He stares at you as if he never needs to blink and he's got this nervous tic on one cheek."

The women laughed as Brenda convulsed and grimaced like a psycho in a cheap horror movie. Suddenly, Susan spotted a shadow in the water. She bolted to her feet.

"What's the matter?" her friends yawped in unison.

Susan searched the water. The shadow was gone.

"I thought I saw something," she said.

"It's just your imagination," Brenda said, but there was little conviction in her voice as she glanced around the dark blue water.

Susan sat back down, but the mood had undergone a definite change. The eyes that gazed out at the sea were no longer lazy and purposeless but alert, defensive, on guard against danger.

After a while, enough time for any monster to attack if it was present, Amanda said to Susan, "I don't see how you can live in that house."

"Why not? It's been repainted, refurnished, and security bars have been installed on every window and door. It's as safe as it can be," Susan said. Without any warning, goosebumps broke out all over her body. She splashed water over her shoulders to hide the sudden attack of fear.

"Why don't you tell the bank to get you another place?" Brenda said.

"What's the point?" Brenda butted in. "She's not going to stay long. None of us is going to stay long. The place is about to explode, and it's not going to be a pretty sight." Brenda tucked in her legs and shifted to the kneeling position of a geisha. The water licked her belly.

"I think your assessment is too pessimistic," Amanda said, her brows furrowed in thoughtfulness. "The committee is working day and night to get the new constitution into final shape by Christmas. Multiparty elections can take place as early as next April. The way I see it, a peaceful transfer of power is definitely within the realm of possibility."

"I don't know. Somalis have tried their hand at elected government, but it didn't work for them. How many parties did they have at one point? Sixty-four, wasn't it?" Brenda looked to Amanda, who nodded confirmation. "Political parties were drawn along bloodlines. Everyone was looking out for his own family, and the country became so fractured that it came close to anarchy. And then when the president was assassinated, the military had to take over to prevent a total breakdown."

"Democracy isn't something that happens overnight," Amanda said. "Institutions need time to evolve—"

"Yes, but the environment for evolution has been poisoned from the very start. Take, for example, the conflict between the north and south. Before unification, they were living under different structures developed separately by the British and Italians. There was bound to be trouble when the two were brought together under the same roof. The colonialists planted the seeds of contention, and the moment they left, the seeds germinated and blossomed into civil war."

"Come on, Brenda," Amanda said. "How long can a person blame his parents for not raising him right? Sooner or later, everybody has to take responsibility for his own actions. The Somalis have taken stock of their past mistakes and are now headed in the right direction."

"I think it's too little too late," Brenda said. "Politics is like the weather. Once you have the forces gathered in a place, high pressure here, low pressure there, you're bound to have a thunderstorm. What do you think, Susan?"

Susan blanketed her face with a question mark of "Me?"
"It's hard for me to say after only a few weeks here. I'm still trying to digest everything I've seen and heard. How long have you been here?" She put the ball right back on Brenda's court.

Brenda snorted, "Too long. This is my fifth year. I don't know what came over me. When my first term ended, I thought

I was going home. But I took one look at our new ambassador and applied for another term."

The women cooed. Brenda filliped water at her friends. They understood very well whom Brenda was talking about—the dashing, silver-haired Coloradan businessman who had been awarded the horn of Africa for his fund-raising efforts for George Bush. Not the greatest administrator, but the most charming boss a woman could have. In this lighter mood, Susan announced she was hungry. The others agreed that lunch was a good idea.

Around three in the afternoon, the women decided they'd had more than enough sun. They packed up and got into the car. In the comfort of the backseat, Susan fought the contented drowsiness that fresh air and sun had brought on. Her hand reached for the bottom of her basket. The Glock's smooth polymer was warm from the sun. Its touch was reassuring. Her mind drifted away while the others discussed dinner.

"How about you, Susan?" she heard Amanda's voice say.

"What? Sorry, I was daydreaming."

"You want to join us for dinner at the Blue Marlin tonight?"

"What time?"

"Seven," Amanda replied.

Seven, Susan repeated to herself. If she were still alive at seven, it would be cause for celebration. "Sure," she said. "But if you don't see me, go ahead and order. I may be too dead...tired to go anywhere."

"You'll show up," Brenda said, tossing her a backward glance.

At the gate to her house, Susan waved good-bye, shouting, "See you at seven!"

Humming a tune to smother the trip-hammer in her heart, she entered the house. Consistent with a person who'd been out in the sun all day, she went straight for the fridge. Clasping her basket under her arm, she poured herself a long, cold lemonade and quaffed it down. She then pulled out a bag of garbage and headed toward the kitchen. Just in front of the door, the bag slipped out of her hand. She bent to pick it up, continued her

203

way into the kitchen, and dumped it in the trashcan. Still clutching the basket, she entered the cool shade of the corridor.

In those few moments, she'd checked out half the house. Everything was as it should be.

Instead of entering her room, she turned right into another corridor, past the bathroom and guest room and stopped in front of the hallway closet. She opened it, took out a towel, and retraced her steps. The piece of hair glued to the guest room door was gone.

Susan entered her bedroom and started to undress. With the abandon of a person totally alone, she stripped to the part of the skin that had never come in direct contact with the sun. The bathing suit had imprinted zebra stripes on her ribs. She released the barrette, and a cascade of thick black hair tumbled down, covering her from neck to the middle vertebra of her spinal column. She pulled out the soggy beach towel from her picnic basket and took it into the bathroom, kicking the door half-shut behind her. She slipped the gun out of the towel and placed it on the soap caddy under the showerhead.

The temptation to rush to the kill was great, but she mustn't give Hamid cause for suspicion. The semblance of vulnerability was to her advantage. She applied soap, lathering it to a creamy froth on her arm, and spread it to the rest of her body to purge it of sand and salt. She then worked the shampoo into her scalp and massaged her hair into a pile on top, exposing the splendid length of her spine.

After toweling herself rigorously, she wrapped herself in a bathrobe. The Glock sank to the bottom of the roomy pocket. She flipped her hair out over her shoulders and brushed it until it was as smooth and slippery as a thick thatch of wet straw.

She opened the door and walked into her room.

An iron clamp gripped her throat. Her mouth yawned open to cry out, but nothing came. Her windpipe burned. She knew exactly what was going on, had rehearsed the scene many times in her mind, but in the moment of reality, her body was refusing to cooperate. Pain shot down her scalp. Her hair, he was pulling at her hair, pulling it to one side; her neck felt cool, and she saw her nightmare coming true. A rush of adrenalin broke the inertia. She fumbled for the gun in her pocket, found the trigger and fired blindly. The grip loosened. She drove her elbow into him with every muscle in her body. Her assailant belched a harsh grunt, and her windpipe was free. A violent push on her back and she was on all fours. She wheeled around in time to see a hooded figure rounding the corner. She sprang up and chased it into the corridor. A bang came from the left— the guest room door. She hurled herself against it, but the door resisted and bounced her off. It was locked. "Damn!" she cursed as she ran into the living room, skidding round the dining table into the kitchen, where she grabbed the ring of keys in the drawer and fumbled for the right ones, first the back door, then the grille.

Tires screeched; rubber burned. She ran across the backyard, threaded both arms through the bars of the postern, and fired several rounds at the tail of the speeding vehicle. Behind the cloud of dust and fumes, the Pajero careened out of view. *Shit*, she said to herself. She'd lost him.

Chapter 23

A two-storied monolith of masonry stood several blocks from the presidential compound. A legacy from the Italian colonial era, time had painted over the red bricks a stale liver tone. Officially it was an extension of the office of the president, but unofficially it was known to be the interrogation center of the dreaded NSS, the National Security Service. Hair-raising screams had been rumored to emit from its bowels at night. People went to great lengths to avoid it, crossing the street to pass it, or not entering the block at all. But tonight, one after another, shiny black limos deposited altogether ten dignitaries at its doorstep. On entering, each of the nine men and one woman behaved in the same way—after an anxious glance at the dark tunnel of closed doors, they picked up their feet and hurried up the staircase.

A crystal chandelier illuminated the room. Its furnishings, from the imported conference table to the plush cream carpet and upholstered leather chairs, suggested this wasn't a run-of-the-mill government office. On the first Monday of every month, the ruling elites of the country gathered here to advise the president on the state of the nation. However, for two years now, the president had chosen not to attend. Since a suspicious car crash that claimed a number of broken ribs, Siad Barré had withdrawn farther into a cocoon, which only a shrinking clique of family members had access to. Fearful for his life, his once charismatic public appearances had become a thing of the past.

The prime minister sat at the head of the table. He was a cousin of the president's on the maternal side, and a balding man who had grown his hair on one side to thatch over an otherwise bare pate. Although the other ministers went up to pay him their respects, they all knew he was just a figurehead. The real focus of their attention was the person on his right. He was General Nur, the president's son-in-law, who also happened to be the defense minister and chief of the NSS. A willowy man with a pious air, melancholic eyes and a stringy beard that hung down to his chest, General Nur could very well pass for a religious sheikh. Few would have guessed that this was the man responsible for the blanket bombing of Hargeisa, the country's second largest city, resulting in the exodus of three hundred thousand Isaaqs to Ethiopia.

"It's time to begin," General Nur said to the chairman.

"But Faisal isn't here yet," the prime minister twittered nervously. There was nothing worse than being caught between two tussling elephants. Faisal, the president's son, was Nur's archrival, and neither could tolerate a slight.

"If Somalia is to develop into a modern state, the first concept we must grasp is time," General Nur preached. "In the West, a train doesn't wait for a tardy passenger. It runs with the tick-tock of the clock, and according to mine," he flagged the Rolex on his wrist, "it is now five minutes past eight. All the passengers should be on board now. The train is about to leave the station."

Promptly taking his cue, the prime minister blew the stationmaster's whistle and declared the meeting open. Considering his duty done, he handed the platform over to Nur.

"I hope you've had time to study the draft of the new constitution," the general said, his eyes roaming from one face to another. "Before we present it to the people in a referendum, we must be in agreement ourselves. Please, tell me what you think of it."

The ministers directed their gaze at the ceiling, the table, the floor, their hands, anywhere to avoid eye contact. Nur waited patiently, but when the prospect of a volunteer faded, he did what a teacher would to an unresponsive class. "Mariam, what do you think?" he said to the only female cabinet member, the minister of culture.

A large, handsome woman with an aristocratic poise, the minister smiled serenely at the general. "I thought the colonialists went home years ago. How come they're still writing our constitution?"

The men laughed. "I sympathize with your feelings," the general said with an indulgent smile. "But you mustn't forget, we still need their money."

"Let them write what they want. We'll run our country the way we want. They won't know the difference," the cultural minister said.

Laughter rang out again, Suleiman's the loudest. He was waiting patiently for this cat and mouse game to run its course. It was like this at every cabinet meeting—the general trying to ferret out the ministers, and the ministers trying to dodge captivity by convivial banter. A wrong answer could cost a person his head, so the safest bet was to keep one's mouth shut. That had been Suleiman's tactic in the past, but today, he had come with his own agenda.

The door was flung open, and a man sporting a green jacket over an electric-orange bow tie flew in, wailing like a child who'd been left behind, "You started without me?"

"Faisal, I thought you weren't coming," General Nur said. "You haven't missed anything. We just started to discuss the new constitution. I hope you've received your copy."

The heir apparent took the vacant seat on the prime minister's left. Crossing his legs and draping an arm over the back of his chair, he surveyed his future subjects around the table. His long, surly face was a chip off the old man's block.

"I've given it to the servants to burn with the cow dung," he said. "That's what I think of it. We've had multiparty elections before, and there was nothing but chaos. When my father unified the country under one party, he had the support of the people. To go back to what we had before would be like leading a camel to a dried-up well. It will be disastrous!"

The ministers were silent. Nobody would dare contradict Faisal. Thus, when Suleiman spoke, everyone gaped at him with astonishment.

"Our country must exercise its sovereignty, but at the same time, it must maintain good relations with friendly nations. The question is how to achieve both. What I am concerned with are the donor funds that are channeled through my ministry. The greatest pot of money is the auction. We all know how much our government depends on it. The money is fast running out, and the donors are reluctant to replenish it. Why? Because they think our country is politically unstable." Suleiman paused to allow his words to sink in. "It's true that the riots are now under control, and we're confident that General Nur will keep it that way. But what is most troubling is the unsolved murders of the three expats, and the near murder of another." The ministers nodded. Susan Chen's narrow escape was still fresh in their minds. "I read a sense of insecurity among the donors. They think this killer has identified them as targets. Already, they've decided to evacuate their families. I'm afraid their next step will be to cancel their programs."

"Suleiman has a point," Faisal said. Flicking his chin at his brother-in-law, he challenged, "What is the NSS doing about it?"

"Common crime is the jurisdiction of the police," Nur replied with the forbearance of a holy man taken to task by a skeptic. "My department is concerned with matters of national security."

"You don't think this is national security?" Faisal pounced. "Somebody is trying to sabotage our economy, and you think you needn't bother?"

"What do you want me to do, my brother? Catch him with my own hands?" A sharp edge cut into the saintly voice.

"If I let my Red Berets out, they'll round up the murderer in three days," Faisal boasted.

"Please, I have a suggestion to make," Suleiman intervened. "I'm sure the police will capture the murderer sooner or later, but in the meantime, we must do something to appease the donors. A very high official of the World Bank will be paying a visit soon. He has requested to see the president. I think it would be wise to oblige him. If the president can hold a press conference to show the world that Somalia is alive and well, I assure you, the money will flow like water from a tap." Several heads nodded around the table. He could see that his words had

210

struck a chord. The president had barricaded himself in for too long.

"My dear Suleiman, perhaps you have a problem with your hearing," Nur said, stroking his beard. "My brother here has just promised to capture the murderer. How many days did you say?" he said to Faisal.

Backed into a corner, the young Barré slammed his fist on the table. "I will catch him within the week, or I'm not the son of Siad Barré."

Suleiman withdrew from the debate. Pacing was the key to traveling long distances. A person must plant one foot in front of the other, a step at a time. Today he'd whipped his herd to a trot. Pushing it any further would be unwise.

The next day, the corps of presidential guards known as the Red Berets went on a rampage. They pulled people from their cars, roughed them up and ripped off their radios, seats, and tires. As if that wasn't enough, men wearing the maroon-colored berets invaded the homes of several Abgaal merchants and raped the women in front of their husbands.

At the end of the week, the presidential guards apprehended a man of mixed Kenyan and Ethiopian parentage. The mention of Ethiopian blood was enough to prove his guilt, let alone the cache of sharp instruments of various sizes found hidden in the trunk of his car. The man was beaten senseless and dumped in a cell with other criminals. But when his identity was made public, the U.N. let out a howl of protest. The man was a U.N. staffer working for the income-generating project that taught handicrafts to the unemployed. The carving tools were his teaching aids. The protest went nowhere, but when the U.N. produced the suspect's passport, which showed that he wasn't even in the country during two of the three killings, the outcry against the injustice was overwhelming.

The cabinet held a meeting to convince Faisal to free the man. The young Barré gave in grudgingly.

From his ninth-floor office window, Suleiman watched the show. Events had been unfolding faster than he'd anticipated, and if he didn't keep a tight rein, they could easily spin out of control. For his scheme to work, the donors must maintain their engagement till the end. His next move would be crucial. It was time to consult with his own general. A short holiday in Rome would be beneficial to them both.

Suleiman had wanted to show his in-law the nightlife in Rome—dinner at a five-star restaurant, drinks at a nightclub, and afterward, if his in-law so desired, some fun with an escort of his choice. All this could be obtained within the privacy of this exclusive club, where he was the sole Somali member. Safe from the wagging tongues of their own kind, they didn't have to pretend to be enemies. But Suleiman soon discovered that making his in-law relax was harder than chasing the Ethiopians out of the Ogaden. Throughout dinner, General Ahmed sat straitjacketed in his suit, his eyes darting around as if danger was around the corner. The general barely wet his whistle, doing little justice to the selection of wine that accompanied each course.

Oh, how Suleiman loved to eat in an Italian restaurant, with its never-ending dishes and the eternal flow of fine wines. The general's sober company was like a wet rag, but he must forgive his in-law. A man stripped of manhood could find no joy in life. By prostrating himself at the feet of Siad Barré, Ahmed had saved himself from physical torture, but what mental torment he must endure every day. A warrior reduced to a lap dog, tasting the president's food to test for poison, drooling over what scraps his master threw on the floor, and wagging his tail to show the affection that he didn't have—the humiliation must have been worse than castration, and it was repeated over and over again every day, every minute he served his master. Ahmed's hatred was as vast as the sea, an angry sea that would not be appeased until it had swallowed the old man, his wives, offspring and everyone who shared a drop of his blood.

Suleiman had never believed Ahmed's repentance. The president had been too blinded by his own power to see through the theatrics. Suleiman wasn't fooled for a day, and several years ago when he'd learned of a conspiracy to oust him from his lucrative position, he'd quickly arranged for the marital alliance with Ahmed. His enemy's enemy was his friend, and who could be more reliable than a person who had only one thought in his mind? Revenge! Ahmed's hatred for Siad Barré was his reason for living.

Suleiman had loved Barré once upon a time. Serving as a captain under Barré, he'd stormed the palace thirty years ago and wrested power from the inept politicians. With the devotion that only youth could have, he'd pledged to follow Barré to the ends of the earth. He would have carried his pledge through if the lackeys around the president hadn't polluted the old man's mind against him. They were out to get him, to rob him of the riches he'd accumulated through hard work and cunning. A man has to protect himself and everything dear to him.

Instead of the night of carousing Suleiman had planned, they went back to the villa right after dinner. In the security of the heavily guarded compound, General Ahmed finally relaxed. He took off his jacket and, for the first time that evening, rested his spine against the back of his chair. They were sitting in Suleiman's study, a room of rich, warm colors. From the antique Persian rug to the mahogany paneling, the velvet chairs and the intricately carved cherry credenza, every item had been handpicked by Suleiman's personal decorator. Money was no concern, only beauty and comfort. This was Suleiman's principle in all matters related to his lifestyle.

The door opened and in walked a superbly fashioned work of art. Suleiman's face lit up like a hundred-watt bulb. "Ah, Gina. Set the tray down here, please," he said.

Gina approached, her splendid legs swishing against the slits of an ankle-length satin tube gown. Suleiman eyed her with pride. She was as young and fresh as the day she served him dinner aboard Alitalia. A little heartstring had tugged and he'd known he wouldn't feel complete until she was his. Once again,

213

his theory that money could buy everything had been proven. It always pained him to leave her behind, but taking her to Mogadishu was out of the question. His other wives would be so jealous they'd poison her at her first meal. As Gina bent to pour a shot of cognac in each glass, Suleiman glanced at the general. Ahmed was gawking unabashedly at the curvatures under the tight, shiny fabric, but his eyes were like a fish's, cold and devoid of desire.

After Gina left the room, the men raised their crystal snifters. "To the Red Berets," Suleiman toasted, tongue in cheek.

The general tossed back his head and killed the brandy in one gulp.

"Your men did a great job," Suleiman said. "The Abgaals thought they could prosper by minding their own business. Now we'll see what they think!"

"My men did it with great pleasure," Ahmed said, snickering at the memory of his men's enthusiasm as they dressed up as Red Berets and rampaged into the homes of Abgaal merchants.

"How are things at the fortress?" Suleiman said.

"Good, very good. I've been ready since the riots. If we'd attacked then, Mogadishu would be ours by now."

"Well, now, there's no need to rush it. Mogadishu will be ours sooner or later. It will be easier when the old man is out of the way. As long as he's around, he'll try to keep his family together. Faisal alone is no obstacle, but if his father orders him to consolidate with Nur, the union will be tough to beat. Therefore, we must be patient, my brother. We must do this step by step and very soon, you'll have your revenge."

Suddenly the muscle on Ahmed's left cheek started dancing in a spasm. Suleiman looked down at his drink. He'd always found this phenomenon as embarrassing as if his in-law had peed in his pants. When he looked up again, the twitching had stopped.

"By the way, how's the Afghan doing?" Suleiman said.

214

"Forget him." Ahmed gave a fly-swatting wave. "What kind of an assassin is he, who can't even kill a woman? I'm more than ready to send him back."

"Well, now, you can't blame it entirely on him. How would he know she had a gun? She would have surprised me, too." The person Suleiman really wanted to blame was Ahmed himself. Without consulting him, Ahmed had ordered the death of Susan Chen. Fortunately, the assassin had failed, or the World Bank would surely have pulled out, and he would have to go back to the drawing board. However, he must put aside his resentment, for his in-law was a touchy man who would nurse the least barb like a mortal wound.

Aloud Suleiman said, "Perhaps we've overused the Afghan. We don't want him to get caught before the final job."

"What about the woman? She's been spreading stories about me."

"Let her. Nobody listens to her anyway. She's not like Andrew Barnett, who had a high standing among the donors. He could have done our business a lot of harm. That was why we had to get rid of him." Suleiman sipped his brandy. "As for the Korean—well, he dug his own grave. I'm ashamed whenever I think of how our clanswoman could commit adultery with such a disagreeable man. Do you know he was going to dispute our economic growth rate of last year? He thought it was much lower than what our economists claimed." One glance at Ahmed told Suleiman he was barking up the wrong tree. Economics was the least of his in-law's interests. Returning from his tangent, he added, "Then there was the Australian...that wasn't my decision."

"It wasn't mine, either!"

"No harm done. Fortunately, the tape didn't mention names," Suleiman said in appeasement. "Come, let's not harp on it. We're getting closer and closer to our goal, but there needs to be one more push, one more incident that would shake everyone up. I was thinking, a group of expat families are leaving next Sunday. If we can have a little accident there..."

"It can be arranged."

Those were exactly the words Suleiman wanted to hear. "Good," he said, sitting up. "Things are going to move very fast from now on. Are you ready?"

"I'm always ready...well, except for this..."

Suleiman knew what was coming. The request always started with "well" and a twitch of the cheek muscle. Military men were so predictable. He waited for Ahmed to go on.

"I'm trying to close a deal on a longer-range howitzer, but there's a bit of a problem. Ever since that woman started snooping around Eastern Horizon, I've stopped using it to get foreign exchange..."

"How much is it?" Suleiman said.

The general named a six-digit dollar sum. Without a blink, Suleiman said, "It will be in your account tomorrow morning." The general bowed in gratitude. At this point, Suleiman would stop at nothing, and he wanted his in-law to witness his unhesitating commitment to their cause. Suleiman raised his glass as if admiring the golden liquid when he was actually gazing at the upside-down image of his in-law.

"Just give me the word and my attack will begin," Ahmed said with renewed vigor. "My bombers have been streaking across the skies. My troops are well trained. They're itching for action. In one hour, I can flatten the national arsenal, the NSS, and," he added with wicked savor, "the presidential palace."

"Good, good. And when you march into the palace, we will salute you as president."

The general's mouth pulled down into a horseshoe. It was his happiest smile, the smile of vengeance.

"You will be my finance minister," Ahmed said. "You will bring in as much international aid, no, more, much more than before."

Suleiman bowed in acquiescence. Yes, he was content to remain finance minister. The top man was the lone tree at the peak of a wind-blown mountain. He would much rather be a goat foraging under the tree, reaping the windfall of bumper harvests. As long as the tree was healthy and strong, he would nurture the symbiotic relationship.

Chapter 24

The departure lounge at the airport resembled a processing station for arrivals at a concentration camp. Families of expats stood in bewilderment among the litter of suitcases. Children stared round-eyed, too scared to cry. Some people stood in lines that led nowhere while others dream-walked aimlessly in the nightmare. A British woman's wail soared above the disarray, giving expression to the collective exasperation.

"I've got to get on that plane!"

Juergen stretched his sight above the crowd, located the source of the outcry, and bulldozed a path to the counter. "What's the problem here?" he said, flashing his United Nations I.D.

"Her name isn't on the list," the ground personnel said. "The plane is full. I can't put another person in."

"But I have tickets. See here, three of them," the woman said, shoving the pieces of paper at Juergen. Two children bearing miniature duplicates of her auburn hair and upturned nose clung to her skirt.

"Let me handle this," Juergen said and turned to address the airline staff. "You know," he said in a chatty tone, his eyebrows dancing in friendly conspiracy, "Mrs. Smith is the wife of a high-level U.N. expert. It's really best that you let them on the plane. If she lodges a complaint with your government, certain people will lose their jobs."

"He wants me to pay him baksheesh, that's all," the woman shrieked. "I'm not going to pay him one more cent! They've charged me enough for the tickets already!"

Juergen calmed her down while the steward consulted with his colleagues in Somali. Without relaying the conclusion of their discussion, the steward penciled the names of the woman and her two children on the passenger list. Juergen wondered whom he was going to bump but decided he'd rather not know. His responsibility was to evacuate the family members of U.N. staff in as quick and efficient a way as possible. Juergen noted the armed guards patrolling the hall from a platform along the wall. Their rifles were slung recklessly downward toward the crowd. He had half a mind to tell them off but thought better of it.

"Can you please tell me what the check-in procedure is?" he said to one of the crew. "People are running around without knowing what they're supposed to do." A bulging knapsack swiped Juergen on the back. He keeled forward but propped himself back up against the counter.

A discussion in Somali ensued. A few more crewmembers came out from the back to join the conference. Juergen waited patiently. In a way, it was good that he didn't understand a thing, or he might be tempted to barge in and direct the show. The Somalis wouldn't take kindly to that. There were several times when Juergen thought a conclusion had been reached, but somebody always threw in one last word and triggered another round of debate. Inside, Juergen was boiling with impatience, but outwardly, he was a large embodiment of equanimity. As long as the plane was sitting on the runway, nobody was going anywhere.

Finally, one of the stewards turned to him and spoke on behalf of the group: "You check in your bags here. We give you a boarding pass. Then you go around and we open your bags."

Juergen couldn't believe the long debate could be condensed into such simple instructions. "So people should form a line here, am I correct?" he said. The steward nodded.

Juergen did an about-face toward the crowd. "All right, everyone, line up in front of this counter," he bellowed. "This is where you check in your luggage."

Suddenly all was movement. In the rush to be first in line, people collided into one another, crashing trunks and suitcases in their wake. Children cried, and mothers screamed for them to keep up. Juergen watched the soldiers on the platform. From their combative point of view, the commotion must resemble a riot. One of the soldiers butted his rifle against his shoulder and aimed.

218

"Calm down, calm down," Juergen's voice boomed. "No need to rush. Everyone will get his turn. Come on, let's have a line."

Yelling and signaling like a cop, he directed the human traffic into a fat python that slithered around the hall. The orderliness pleased him. There was nothing he hated more than chaos. However, having lived in eight countries, he'd learned that not everyone shared his obsession. People were different. One man's meat may be another man's poison, and he shouldn't expect everyone to behave the same as he. After the years of living abroad, he'd discovered another thing: National qualities can be summarized in a few sentences, but individuals can't. Another individual's soul was as intricate as his own, and he'd learned to judge each person by what he was, not by his race or nationality.

Harsh voices reached him. Juergen could see over the crowd that a Somali family was arguing with a steward. The volume on both sides was rising. Juergen hurried to the counter, a prick of guilt on his conscience. These people must have been bumped to make room for the expats. What the airline should do was announce that it had overbooked and offer a cash incentive for people to take another flight. He would suggest it to the steward when he got up there.

There was the sound of a scuffle, shouts, and Juergen could see the back of a man lunging at a steward. Another body piled into the fray and then, several blasts pealed across the hall. A roaring human tide swept Juergen back as gunfire bounced back and forth. A flux of memories washed over him: his mother's hand clenching his, bombers screaming overhead, and bonfires lighting the place like one fantastic carnival. The noise had been terrifying. He'd wanted so much to plug his ears with his fingers, but his mother had held one hand in a tight grip and the crowds had pinned his other to his side, lifting him off his feet and carrying him away. But today, he mustn't run from the noise, for in the back of his mind, the little word "duty" overrode every other care. He pushed against the wall of bodies and shouldered a path toward the fount of turbulence. The resistance vanished. Juergen found himself in the clear. A little Somali girl lay on the ground. Blood was pouring from her head, a bright match to the holiday dress she was wearing. Juergen looked up mouthing "son-of-a-bitch" and saw a flash coming straight at him.

Everyone was speaking at once. The lame-duck prime minister quacked for silence, but the heated babble went on. General Nur took out his pistol and applied it like a gavel on the table. In the moment of stunned silence, he pointed to Suleiman and commanded him to speak first.

Suleiman heaved a sigh so deep that its vibes could be felt by every minister. "I'm afraid I am of no use to my country anymore. I'd like to tender my resignation," he said. Objections echoed around the table. Suleiman raised his voice to drown them out. "As finance minister, my job is to keep the country's coffers filled. I try, as Allah is my witness, I try. But when the U.N. security chief is gunned down by our own military, there's nothing I can do to stop the donors from fleeing. I have failed." He hung his head in utter depression.

"The fault was the army's, and its leaders must bear the responsibility," Faisal said, his eyes accusing his brother-in-law.

Ignoring the implied charge, General Nur continued to direct his remarks at Suleiman. "It was an accident, like a plane crash, that only the will of divine power could have prevented. Can't you explain that to the donors?" he said, twirling the strands of his beard around his long, slim fingers.

"I've tried. We've held one donor meeting after another to explain the incident. I've assured them it will never happen again, but they don't seem to believe me. They're continuing to send their staff home and stall on new projects. The director of the World Bank has canceled his trip. This ends all hope that the next tranche for the auction will be released any time soon." Suleiman sighed. "It's time the president appoints a new finance minister."

Suleiman's head drooped lower, but he couldn't help flipping his eyeballs up from time to time to watch the ministers defend him. One after another, they extolled him as the country's foremost diplomat. The tips of his ears burned at the fervor of their compliments. The most eloquent was Mariam, the culture minister whom he had helped rake in a bundle of foreign aid for her women's projects.

"Nobody in this country has as high a standing as Suleiman in the eyes of the donors," she said. "Even though they're the givers and we're the beneficiaries, I have seen Suleiman handle them like little birds that feed from his hand. If Suleiman is to leave his job today, our house will collapse immediately."

"All right, all right," General Nur said, indicating he'd had enough of the panegyrics. Turning to Suleiman, he said, "Your resignation is not accepted. You must continue to pacify the donors and get them to contribute as much as before."

"I will stay on one condition," Suleiman said. "I would like the president himself to assure the donors that the security situation is under control. With all due respect to everyone present, we mean nothing to the officials in Rome, Washington, London, or Bonn. The only person they know is Siad Barré, the father of our republic."

The spell of silence was obviously unbearable to the prime minister, for he took it upon himself to say, "That's a good idea." Then turning quickly to General Nur to make sure he'd spoken the right words, he added, "Isn't that so?"

It was Faisal who replied. "You're absolutely right," he said to Suleiman in a gravelly voice that was a passable imitation of his father's. "I'll raise the matter with the president. He's the only person who can speak for the nation."

The other ministers echoed endorsement, but Suleiman knew they were featherweights in the balance of power. The real contest was between Faisal and Nur, who would both rush to the palace afterward to fight for the president's ear. If he knew them well enough, each would claim ownership of the idea. How grand the event would be: pictures of the ancient ruler splashed across front pages, officials from all over the world paying homage at his feet, listening to the wisdom of his words.

Already, Faisal was excusing himself from the meeting. Nur shot him a murderous look. As the man in charge, he couldn't leave until the meeting had adjourned. Suleiman predicted this was going to be a short session.

Chapter 25

Susan seldom bore a grudge for long, but there was one person she couldn't forgive easily, and that was herself. If she hadn't frozen for those few seconds, if she had taken better aim at Hamid, if, if and if. To have come so close to bagging her quarry and missing it was worse than any defeat she'd known. When she was nine and slipped up at a tournament, she was so mad at herself that she broke into uncontrollable tears. Her father sat her down and told her that the goal wasn't to win, but to learn and improve. It was a good consolation philosophy for a loser, and one that had carried her from one match to another, but deep down in her heart, she knew there was only one goal in any contest: to beat one's opponent.

She'd learned from her last round with Hamid, but had she *improved*? There was only one way to find out. She must regain her scent of Hamid's trail. She and Nick played ball over her next move, but just as they agreed on a strategy, the president of Somalia threw in a monkey wrench. Siad Barré issued an invitation to Persis Davar to come to Mogadishu on a fact-finding mission, at the end of which the president would sit down with the bank director and pay personal heed to his conclusions. Susan tried to advise her boss that this wasn't a good time for a visit, but the response was—come hell or high water, and whatever else that hadn't already happened in Somalia, he was flying in.

Susan arrived at the airport in a second-hand Land Rover she'd purchased from a departing expat. Somebody called out her name. She turned around and saw a face that was as familiar as the voice, yet she couldn't place him at once. It took her seconds to realize that the tall rangy man walking toward her was Nick, her tennis coach. Instead of the shorts she'd always seen him in, he was wearing a pair of dress pants and a clean shirt, and for the first time since the start of her tennis lessons, his head was free of the silly blue bonnet. The wisps of gray hairs gave his face an ancient air.

"Hi, what are you doing here?" she said.

He extended his hand and engaged her in a formal handshake. "I'm picking up a friend," he said, still squeezing her hand. "What about you?"

She could feel edges and corners digging into her palm. He was pressing something into her hand. "Same here, except it's not a friend, it's my boss." She withdrew her hand and slipped the folded paper into her purse.

After an exchange of "See you at the club," she went on to the VIP lounge. Suleiman and his coterie were already sitting inside. Susan stepped out of their sight and unfolded Nick's note. "December 8, 10:06, General Ahmed was seen leaving Suleiman's villa in Rome," it read. Susan stuffed it back in her purse and walked into the lounge. What was Ahmed, supposedly an enemy, doing in Suleiman's villa? Did they make up or had they been fooling everyone all along?

Suleiman stood up to greet her with his meek, toothy smile. After reading Nick's note, she couldn't help seeing in him a wolf in sheep's clothing.

From inside the lounge, they watched the shimmering wings of a jet swoop down the sky. Suleiman got up and led the welcoming contingent to the tarmac. The first to appear was a dark-haired, brown-skinned man with a long, crooked nose. Susan recognized her boss immediately. Even if she'd never met him before, she would know this was the author of her daily telexes. He looked exactly the way he wrote—with a caustic twist that would even sour the "Regards" closing his communiqués. Susan would feel more comfortable addressing him as "Mr. Davar," but the bank's protocol required equal first-name basis for managers and staff alike. From now on, she must think of him as "Persis."

Closely behind the director was a slender older man, weighted down by a hefty computer in his hand. He was Attila, the chief economist for Somalia and a sweet-mannered man who had none of the attributes associated with the king of the Huns. Susan always appreciated the way the Turk ended his telexes with "Warmest Regards."

The VIPs were ushered into the lounge, where the finance minister delivered a welcoming speech on behalf of President Barré. After Persis returned the compliment, the one-armed Yusuf passed around copies of a jam-packed four-day itinerary culminating in the hottest event in town—an audience with the president.

"We are most honored," Persis said, tipping his head with a left-leaning curve. "In my four years as director of East Africa, I've met with the heads of states of the countries in my department—Presidents Moi of Kenya, Mengistu of Ethiopia and Museveni of Uganda. President Barré is the only exception. Of course, I understand he's a very busy man."

"Indeed, he has a very busy schedule. To tell you the truth," Suleiman said with a humble bow, "I was the one who suggested the meeting to him. President Barré has not made a public appearance in two years, but I have convinced him that at this crucial point in our nation's history, it is important that he present to the world his vision for Somalia. When a country is going through a crisis, it needs a strong leader to steer the way; otherwise, it can easily fall into anarchy."

The protocol finally over, an official convoy escorted the World Bank team to the Eden. Mrs. Giuseppe and her husband, whose arm was still cradled in a sling, checked them in. It was already evening. Susan was ready to call it a day when Persis started setting the tone of his visit. He announced that dinner meeting was to be held at seven, and asked her to please bring along the latest economic indicators and bio sketches on the ministers they were to meet. Susan looked at her watch and found that she had only half an hour to dash to her office and compile the papers.

"What exactly happened to the office car?" Persis inquiry as soon as Susan plunked herself on a chair, the stack of papers in her arms rising and falling with the upheavals of her chest.

Taken aback by the question, Susan answered a little too honestly, "It got caught in the riots. Mohammed barely managed to escape—"

"What was he doing, driving it around in the middle of the riots?"

"I heard the disturbance broke out suddenly," Attila interjected. "The driver must have been taken by surprise." Persis turned to Susan for confirmation.

"Oh yes, that was exactly what happened," Susan said, silently giving thanks for Attila.

"Well, the situation seems to be under control," Persis said. "The Juergen Klaus incident was most unfortunate, but it was also quite understandable. Given the mass hysteria, an accident of this sort is to be expected. Now,"—he opened his file—"let's go over the issues the loan committee raised." At this moment, the waiter set three plates of spaghetti on the table. "Ah, just the right food for our discussion," Persis said. "Spaghetti is the first issue of the day." He picked up his fork, spun the pasta into a lollilop and brought it into the cave of his mouth.

Was spaghetti to be considered a luxury good or not? That was the sixty-million-dollar question concerning the number one import funded by auction money. The debate started when evidence surfaced that spaghetti imported through foreign assistance was actually hurting the country's agricultural production. It was replacing local wheat as the urban diet, which meant taking the bread out of Somali farmers' mouths. A number of donors were of the opinion that spaghetti should be classified as a luxury good, together with jewelry and tobacco and hence banned from the auction. If Somalis wanted spaghetti, they could very well make it themselves.

The strongest objection came from the Italians, who contended that making spaghetti wasn't as simple as everyone thought. Of course, if one were satisfied with spaghetti of wallpaper-glue quality, then anybody could produce it. But if one had tasted the real noodle, which was clean and crisp and light as air, there was no local substitute. Eventually, the domestic industry might be able to pull itself up to a higher standard, but for the time being, importing the staple was a necessity, not a luxury.

Susan looked around and discovered that the waiters had retired for the night. The three of them could debate the issue till dawn, and if she didn't do something, it could very well happen. Persis was wide-awake, as his body clock told him it was only four in the afternoon. The one on the wall, however, was about to strike midnight. Susan let out a tactful yawn and followed it up with a reminder that the first appointment was at seven-thirty the next morning. Persis got the message and after a final exposition on the subject, he said goodnight.

In the days after, the pursuit of truth in the spaghetti imbroglio brought the team from one end of Afgoy Road to the other. Riding in a government-owned Mercedes Benz, the team braved the hazards of traveling in a city overrun by nervous soldiers and angry citizens. At one road block, Mohammed thought the soldier's wave meant for him to go, but when shouts rang out, he glimpsed at the rearview mirror and found three deadly muzzles pointed at the back of his head. He reversed in a beeline at once. Luckily for him and his passengers, none of the soldiers felt an urge to flex their muscles, even small ones, at that instant.

"What do you want me to say this time?" Omar said gruffly to Susan. They were alone in her office, and in a while he would walk to the next building, climb ten floors and have his weekly tête-à-tête with the finance minister.

"You know," Susan said, swiveling her chair behind the desk, "I'm really curious why Suleiman was so gung-ho about arranging the meeting with the president."

"He wants to please the donors," Omar forced the words through his constricted windpipe. Talking always seemed a painful undertaking for him.

"I'm not sure that's the only motive," Susan said, her chair creaking rhythmically with her swinging. She was about to make a difficult request, and more likely than not Omar would

227

refuse. But first she must make the request. Grabbing the desk to brake her swiveling, she looked into Omar's good eye. "I want you to tell Suleiman that the discussions are going very well. Persis thinks he can wrap things up ahead of time, and as Christmas is coming up, he wants to get home as soon as possible. In short, things are moving along so well there's no need to take up the president's precious time."

"Is it true?" Omar said dubiously.

"Does it matter?"

"Of course it does," Omar shouted. Gone was the obstruction in his windpipe. "If he finds out I'm lying, he'll kill me!"

Previously she would have interpreted "kill" in a figurative sense, but in light of recent events, she was aware that Omar meant it literally.

"You don't have to tell him anything definite," she said. "Just say you overheard Persis talking to me and that there's a *chance* that Persis may leave earlier and that you'll keep him posted. I just want to see his reaction."

Omar shook his head in exasperation. "Why are you doing this?"

"I don't like to be used, that's why. Suleiman's up to something. He's using me to advance his own cause, whatever it is. I have a hypothesis, but I don't want to let it out until I've got more proof."

The scowl never left Omar's face. She could tell her ploy wasn't working. A little bribery might do the trick.

"Come on, Omar, this is going to be the last thing I ask you to do. After this, you'll be off for your training in Washington. There's a course on financial accounting in January. I can sign you up for it."

Omar got up and shook his head a few more times to emphasize his displeasure. With chagrin Susan watched him walk out of the office. The door banged. Omar was gone, perhaps forever. Come next week, he would be sipping tea in a hotel in Nairobi, and she'd still be sweating it out here. She went to the window to catch a last glimpse of her eccentric assistant.

She looked out and saw Omar's truncated body emerge from the atrium. He walked down the steps, turned around and scaled the building with his eyes. Susan raised a hand to wave, but he'd already lowered his head. His body angled abruptly to the left and he was striding toward the finance ministry. Susan clasped her hands together. He'd fallen for her carrot!

Omar's meeting with the finance minister lasted only ten minutes, but its fallout would spawn lengthy telexes and marathon conferences from Mogadishu to the capitals of the richest nations.

Shortly after Omar's visit, Suleiman rushed out of his ministry and arrived at the president's executive office. As expected, Faisal wasn't there. The heir apparent wasn't the desk job type, but still his office was the best place to find him. The one person who knew his whereabouts was stationed there. This was his bodyguard-in-chief, whose main job was to juggle Faisal's active schedule among his four wives and innumerable girlfriends. Releasing the full power of his charm on the Red Beret, Suleiman convinced the man to send an urgent message to Faisal.

He was willing to sit around all day if that was what it took. The young Barré was one of the few who had immediate access to the president, and among those few he was the easiest to manipulate. A pang of regret hit Suleiman. Why was he so accommodating with the donors? He'd made the sailing too smooth for them. They'd begun to think that the Somali government would jump at their every whim. Even a mere director of the World Bank held the delusion that he could walk out on the president of Somalia without repercussions.

An hour later, the door opened. Suleiman sprang to his feet, thinking it was the president himself. On second look, he realized it was only Faisal. Instead of his customary Armani suit and Gucci shoes, he was wearing a plain white shirt and the rawhide sandals that his father was famous for. A man of the people had always been the image Siad Barré wanted to project, and now his son was borrowing it for the day. Somehow it didn't quite fit.

"I almost mistook you for the president," Suleiman said, fully aware of the magnitude of his flattery.

The dour face cracked open into a smile of pure delight. "That's what everyone says. I'm the one who favors my father the most."

The two sat down amiably. Suleiman had invested a huge amount of time and money in cultivating the good will of this favorite son. Every other member of Barré's family had reason to hate Suleiman's guts, but not Faisal, whose Swiss account had been registering handsome monthly transfers from another Swiss account, Suleiman's own. Now was the time to reach out and pluck the fruits of years of labor.

"There's something I need to talk to you about," Suleiman began. "Do you know that at the auction yesterday, the Somali shilling tumbled again? It's now over seven hundred shillings to the dollar!"

"That's not good," the younger man said, his jaw dropping like somebody born with a mental impairment.

Suleiman forged ahead: "Our economy is in crisis, our national honor is at stake. We've got to do something."

"You're absolutely right," he said, responding to all the buttons Suleiman had pressed. But after the arduous outburst, his jaws were left hanging again. "What do you suggest?" he gathered his wits enough to say.

"I think we should stop the auction and go back to our fixed rate. Remember back in those days when gasoline cost only a hundred shillings a liter? It's now a thousand!"

"That's highway robbery," the heir apparent puffed, adding with a perplexed frown, "How did that happen?"

The finance minister gave him a quick lesson in economics. In the simplest language possible, he explained how the rate of exchange among the currencies determined the terms of trade. Using his arm as the plank on a seesaw, Suleiman demonstrated the mechanics. When the value of the shilling dips, represented by his hand, the price of imports, his elbow, flips up. Ever since the shilling was traded at the auction, market forces had pushed its value down from the rate formerly set by the government. The prices of imports, from gasoline to spaghetti, had bounced sky-high.

Faisal straightened up. He understood how a seesaw worked. From the pliant stance of a student, he stiffened into a stern master. "Didn't I tell you to watch out for those foreign capitalists? They're out to cheat us!"

"Yes, yes, you were right," Suleiman said with contrition. "I'd thought the shilling would bottom out at a certain point. Now it seems like it can go on tumbling forever. I hate to see the results of the next auction."

"You're right, we have to stop the auction...Wait a minute, does that mean the donors will stop contributing to our country?"

"Not at all. They wouldn't dare withdraw from Somalia. If they do, who's going to pay all those expats here, and what about our debts? Our creditors wouldn't like to see us default. And if we keep on talking about democracy and multiparty elections, they would never abandon us."

"What 'elections' are you talking about?" Faisal said, wincing at the offensive word.

"You know, our kind of elections," Suleiman said with a wink, and the two guffawed.

"It's all up to you now, Faisal. You're the only person who can convince the president to stop the auctions."

Faisal swallowed the bait, hook, line and sinker. He sprang up. "Let me talk to my father right now. Go back to your office and wait there. If necessary, the president will call you to the palace and you will explain to him what you just explained to me. You know, about the seesaw."

"I am always at your service," Suleiman assured him, bowing to hide his simper.

231

Chapter 26

The bombshell fell the next day. At one p.m., the usual time for the finance minister's monthly briefing with the donors, Yusuf strolled in and seated himself at the head of the table. With the stub of his arm tucked behind his back, he explained that Suleiman had been called away on an emergency. The minister sent his regrets that he couldn't be there to deliver the important announcement. In his self-effacing manner, Yusuf read the statement: "The government of the Somali Democratic Republic, hereby announces, by order of President Mohammed Siad Barré, the termination of the foreign exchange auction."

The gathering froze into a glass of silence, then suddenly, as if on a bullet's impact, the sheet shattered. Everyone was speaking at once. This is outrageous! I'm out on the next flight. What on earth are we doing here?

Ignoring the incensed reaction around the table, Yusuf continued reading: "The government has established an official exchange rate of 100 shillings to the dollar. From now on, all foreign transactions must adhere to this rate. Any deviation from this fixed rate is illegal and therefore punishable by law."

Looking up for the first time at the disgruntled faces, Yusuf said, "Any questions you may have can be raised at the meeting with the president. He looks forward to conferring with you the day after tomorrow, at seven in the evening. Thank you for your kind attention." He gathered his papers with one hand and left.

The room erupted into a cacophony of outrage. Persis grabbed the chair and tried to impose some order on the babble. Comparing Somalia with a derailed train, he tabled his plan for lifting the locomotive back on its track. USAID disagreed, while ODA disagreed with the disagreement, and the Italians agreed in parts with everyone. After an hour of haranguing, the agencies were no closer to a united front than when they began.

A hand placed a note in front of Susan. The large, round scrawl was Nick's. "Your tennis lesson has been changed to Tuesday, 2:30 pm." She looked at her watch. It was almost two.

"I've got a terrible headache," she whispered to Attila. "I've got to run home and take some aspirin. Can you let Persis know?"

"You go ahead. Don't worry about Persis. I'll take care of him," the kind Turk said with a deep look of sympathy.

While Persis was pontificating to somebody across the table, Susan slinked away.

She rushed down to the alley and drove off in her Land Rover. Just past K-4, she ran into a military truck carrying men in spinach-green uniforms. That struck her as odd as most of the other soldiers she'd seen had worn khaki. Registering the anomaly in the back of her mind, she stepped on the gas to pass them. Dozens of bloodshot eyes glared down at her between the glistening AK-47s. Can't slow down now, she hissed to herself, sucked in her breath and floored the pedal.

When she got to the club, Nick was rallying with himself at the board. Susan walked briskly toward him. At the sight of her approaching, he netted the oncoming ball in his racket, dribbled it twice and batted it into the bucket.

There was no playing around with forms this lesson. "Something is happening at Suleiman's villa in Rome," Nick said. "Since last week, about thirty Somalis have arrived at the place. It looks like some kind of mass exodus. See that can of tennis balls over there? Take it to the changing room. It's got some photos you'd be interested in. When you're ready, come back out and let's talk."

In the privacy of a booth, Susan opened the lid and unfurled several blown-up photos of Somali women and children disembarking from a stretch limo. They were aerial views showing incomplete faces from oblique angles, except for one— a huge mastiff's head looking straight into the camera, her eyes closed and mouth open in a reprimanding stance. Susan recognized General Ahmed's wife, the ebullient chairwoman of the National Women's Association, who could ramble for hours to her captive audience. Ahmed's wife, children and grandchildren were shown arriving at Suleiman's house. What was going on?

She turned to the next photo. More faces of Somali women and children. She didn't know any of them, yet there was a familiarity that made her think she should. She picked out one of the women, put a finger on her head to block out the scarf, and traced her profile. A narrow flat plain of cheek rose to a gopher-toothed pucker. Susan smiled in spite of herself. If Suleiman were to dress in drag, he would look exactly like this woman. This was the daughter of Suleiman, and the children around her were his grandchildren.

The tracks were converging on Suleiman. Events had taken a strange twist since she told Omar to pass on the little piece of misinformation. According to Omar's account, Suleiman had taken the news in stride, as if he didn't care whether the president met with Persis or not. Next came the auction's cancellation.

One thing had led to another. Fragments of the puzzle were scattered all over the floor. There *had* to be a pattern somewhere, but right now all she could see were bits and pieces of the same color and shapes that seemed to fit but didn't when she tried to lock them together. They were all there, sprawled under her nose. It was frustrating to know so much and yet not be able to see the big picture.

With agitation Susan swung an invisible racket at the wall. In her mind's eye, the ball traveled in a perfect arc into her opponent's court. Suleiman was standing on the other side in his crumpled suit. And then it struck her. Of course! She'd lobbed the ball over to Suleiman, and now he was volleying back deep into her baseline. He'd been her opponent all along.

She quickly rolled up the photos and went to the wall. Nick was engaged in a brutal duel with himself.

"I know what's happening," Susan said, breathless with excitement. "Something major is going to happen at the meeting with Barré, so major that both Suleiman and Ahmed have evacuated their families. An assassination attempt is what I think. We've got to stop this meeting."

Nick stopped his rally. Sweat was pouring down his bonnet. He pulled up his shirt to wipe his face. Susan couldn't wait for his response; she poured out the story of her tennis match with Suleiman. "If Persis leaves ahead of schedule, the meeting with Barré will be off. So what does Suleiman do to make sure Persis stays? He cancels the auction. Persis can't leave when things are in such a mess. Don't you see?"

"Are you saying that Suleiman is plotting to assassinate the president?" he said.

"Yes, and Ahmed is his accomplice. They're the ones who hired Hamid and told him who to knock off. They picked Andrew because of Eastern Horizon, Park for sleeping around with Suleiman's relative, Jack for taking Ahmed's gas and then me for accusing Ahmed in public." Susan paused for a snatch of breath. "But there's a grander design that connects those murders. It's to flush Siad Barré out of seclusion and get him to appear before the donors. Once he's in the open,"—Susan cocked her thumb and pointed with her index finger—"he's fair game."

It was two in the morning when she got home. A German shepherd charged out, barking at the top of its lungs. A floodlight beamed into Susan's eyes, and she was squinting at a pair of legs shuffling toward the gate. After the attack on her, Juergen had arm-twisted her into contracting a security detail for her house. It was a nuisance to be barked at in her own home, but if she hadn't complied, Juergen would have sent a bodyguard to tail her day and night. Poor Juergen. It was hard to believe he was gone. Behind the overbearing, authoritarian demeanor, she'd come to discover a loyal, well-meaning soul.

The gate opened. Susan drove in, fighting the temptation to swerve slightly to the left at the horrible hound. The barking didn't worry her as much as the gleaming fangs. She refused to get out until the guard had put the beast on a leash.

The house lit up. Abdullahi opened the door, his eyes red with sleep. "You're so late again, madam," he said.

"I was working," she said wearily.

"You can work tomorrow. Why tonight? It's dangerous out there."

"The big boss is here and he wants it done tonight. What can I do?" She threw her briefcase on the couch and kicked off her shoes. Physically she was beat, but her mind was amped up like an electronic game board. The numbers were still clicking in her head. She and Attila had worked all night to quantify the country's balance sheet under several scenarios. A fixed exchange rate would plunge the trade balance into a hole so deep that no amount of aid could keep the country afloat. A flexible exchange rate determined by market forces was the way to go, and they had enumerated its virtues in tidy columns printed on crisp white paper. Tomorrow, they would explain the arithmetic to Siad Barré.

Abdullahi brought a bowl of soup to the dining table. She told him to go back to bed. He grunted agreement but refused to move, worry lines etched deep into his forehead.

"What is it?" Susan finally asked.

"Please, madam. I heard that the World Bank wants the government to raise taxes. Is it true?"

"Where did you hear that from?" Susan said with a tinge of amusement. She never thought her housekeeper would be interested in macroeconomics.

"Everybody is talking about it."

"Well, I guess everybody's right. It's true, we're recommending that the government raise taxes." She paused to think of a simple way of explaining the national budget to a man who'd had three years of education. "Look at it this way. The government has to spend money on building roads, schools, and so on. Where does the money come from? The people, because they're the ones who will benefit from the facilities...you know, the roads, schools and so on."

The forehead smoothed out by a few wrinkles, though not all. Abdullahi nodded and went away, seemingly satisfied by the answer. Some minutes later, while Susan was wiping the bottom of the bowl with her bread, the housekeeper reappeared with every crease once again in place.

"Madam, what happens if the government takes the money from the people but the money disappears?"

"Disappears—you mean into somebody's pocket?"

Abdullahi nodded.

"Then it's corruption. The World Bank is an economic institution. It doesn't deal with that kind of problem. It can give advice and technical assistance for managing the economy, but it can't interfere with the internal affairs of a country." Abdullahi went away as perplexed as he'd come, and Susan hated herself for it. Excusing herself that she was too tired to tackle such a sticky issue, she retired to her room. The hum of the generator meant that the city's power grid was out again. She double locked her door and crawled into bed.

While Susan fought off assassins in her sleep, two people in Washington were playing a game of telephone tag. Since nine in the morning, Alex Papadopoulos had been trying to get a hold of the chief of East African Affairs at the State Department. Between meetings, coffee breaks, more meetings, and visits to the john, they'd managed to miss each other until close to lunch.

"My man in Mogadishu tells me something big is brewing out there," Alex said. "He thinks there's going to be another attempt on Siad Barré's life."

"I haven't heard any such thing from my people. What's the basis for your information?"

Alex told the story as coherently as he could. His phone conversation with Nick had been most frustrating, and he'd become painfully aware that a secure line didn't mean a clear one. After tearing his throat out and Nick's, too, making him repeat every sentence three to four times over the squall of static, Alex had managed to get the main point straight, or so he hoped. He'd done his best to cook up a palatable story from the incomplete ingredients, but the silence on the other end indicated it wasn't going down too well.

"It's kind of hard to put the ambassador out on a limb on such flimsy evidence," the State man said. "A family reunion in

238

Rome doesn't strike me as odd at all. As a matter of fact, I'm surprised that Ahmed and Suleiman hadn't evacuated their families earlier. Mogadishu hasn't been the best place to raise kids."

Alex gave it one last push. "The proof of the pudding is in the eating, isn't it? We can let the meeting go on. If somebody tries to kill Barré, that means my intelligence is right. That's the firmest proof I can think of, but it may be too late. There are enough tensions in the region. We don't want to see a friendly nation go under now."

"Well, let me consult with my staff. I'll get back to you. How's the weather in Langley?"

"Lousy. Sunny and way too warm. Can't believe it's three days to Christmas."

After lunch, a staff meeting, and chiseling away a few inches from the mountain of paper, Alex could no longer refrain from picking up the phone. It was 4:30 p.m., and already a bruised pall draped the sky. The day was the shortest in the year.

"I'm just about to run off to a meeting," he lied to his counterpart at State. "Thought I'd check up with you again on Somalia."

"Oh yes, I was just about to call you," the State man replied with as much candor. "Listen, Alex, I talked to my staff. They think it's important for Siad Barré to meet with the donors. He just reversed his economic policies again. The World Bank is all riled up. It may even pull out altogether. If that happens, Mogadishu's going to collapse within the week, I guarantee you that."

Seeing the nature of the situation, Alex grumbled, "It's a basket case. Why on earth did we get involved in these banana republics anyway?"

"The horn of Africa is a strategic location."

"Yeah, yeah, I've heard that before." Grasping at his last straw, Alex added, "Can't you get the embassy to warn the Somalis so they'll at least beef up their security?"

"I'm sure we don't have to tell them that. There've been attempts on Barré's life before. The old fox knows better than us how to take care of himself. You know how these dictators are. They'll outlive anyone, including you and me," the man laughed.

Alex didn't think it was funny, but for the sake of institutional harmony, he made a guttural noise that could be misconstrued as a chuckle.

Chapter 27

Villa Somalia rose out of the flat landscape, as brightly lit as a space station in a universe of darkness. The presidential citadel never had power outages. Blinding shafts from a necklace of spotlights illuminated the perimeter, while further in, several white cake-box buildings shone from inside out like ivory lanterns. One of them was the office of the president, a Roman-style structure with a grandiose abundance of columns and arches. The president's residence, however, was a humble brick building in the back of the compound, next to a giant acacia under which he'd held many a council in his heyday. That era was long gone, but tonight the city was witnessing one last sparkle of Siad Barré's glory.

A stream of black limos was coming to a stop at the Villa's front gate. A Red Beret opened the door of a Mercedes and invited the passengers to step out. Persis, Attila and Susan emerged in their formal business regalia, the men in crisp three-piece suits, and Susan in a sleek burgundy skirt-and-jacket outfit. When at rest, the pleats of her skirt would collapse in a snug clasp around her hips, but in motion, the accordion folds were capable of expanding to accommodate a wide range of activities. She wore her hair in an elegant chignon coiled pretzel-like around a long, silver hatpin. It was a very special pin, made of sterling silver and as long and sharp as a stiletto, which she wore only on very special occasions. A pearl brooch set in a lily-of- the-valley design was pinned over her heart, just above the blue pen clipped to her breast pocket.

Greeting the World Bank team were Suleiman and a fortyish man with a sullen face that could have been photocopied from any one of the portraits hanging in government offices. Faisal, the president's favorite son, needed no introduction.

"I'm sorry for the inconvenience," Suleiman said, "but we must subject you to a few security procedures. I'm afraid Faisal and his men do not like to make exceptions. Even I was searched before they allowed me in."

"Forgive me, I am only carrying out my duties," Faisal said solemnly.

"I'm all for people carrying out their duties," Persis said, his face tilting in a lopsided smile. "You can ask my staff here; they'll tell you I like it when people do a thorough job. Here, search away."

Persis flashed open his jacket. While the men were frisked on the spot, Susan was taken to a more private location, where two women held up a makeshift curtain, and a third patted her down after admiring her pearl brooch. It was a cursory search, as if they'd already concluded that she carried no weapon.

Susan went to pick up her briefcase. There was only one at the table, a brown leather attaché case just like hers, except that when she picked it up, she knew at once that it wasn't hers. It was too light. Somebody must have made a mistake. She ran after the two men ahead. One of them was carrying a flat case similar to hers.

"Mr. Ambassador," she called out. His Excellency turned around: a combination of Kirk Douglas and Robert Redford but more handsome than either. He beamed a heart-crushing smile at her.

"Susan, how nice to see you." His eyes swept her up. "You look ravishing tonight."

"Thanks." Susan felt a flush in her cheeks. "I think you took my briefcase."

The ambassador looked down at the portfolio in his hand. "No wonder, this thing weighs a ton. I was thinking to myself, what on earth did I stuff in there?"

"It's all the briefing papers," Susan said.

They exchanged briefcases, and with a chivalrous wave the ambassador motioned her to walk ahead of him.

Susan stepped into the office of the president. Chandeliers lit the high-ceilinged lobby. She walked through the cavernous hallway, heels clacking like castanets on the dark green marble floor. It was obvious that the place had been designed to impress, but one important factor the architect had forgotten to consider was the amount of upkeep needed to keep the grandeur alive. Without the periodic maintenance, even the best quality materials would crack, chip, and lose their sheen, which was happening here and there.

Susan walked up to a Red Beret and asked for directions to the ladies' room. With great embarrassment, he pointed down the hallway. She got into a stall and lifted the briefcase on the seat. It was heavy. She took out the ream of computer paper and unscrewed the nuts that held together the secret compartment. The lining opened and there was her Glock, wedged between the hard leather. She transferred it to her pocket.

At the entrance to the conference room, a ministerial group stood in a reception line. One by one, Susan shook the hands of the top brass of the land, everyone brilliantly groomed and polished to a shine. Inside the room, the glitter of leadership refracted into rainbow colors. Ambassadors and heads of U.N. agencies, some in dapper summer suits and others in vivid national costumes, circulated with notebooks in hand rather than their customary drinks.

And where the stars gathered, the gazers followed. Susan recognized the correspondents for Reuters and AP and a freelance American photographer, all of whom had flown in from their Nairobi base to cover the event. Susan knew them by sight and some by intimate details of their extramarital alliances. There were no secrets in the expat ghetto.

Through the kaleidoscope of faces, Susan spotted one she'd never seen before. The man was in the back of the room, and as she moved closer for a better look, he bent over a tripod. Susan waited. Finally he straightened up—she was right. It was a new face, new in more ways than one. Nobody who had spent any time in Somalia could have such an anemic complexion. Somalia was a land of bountiful sunshine if nothing else. He was suitably dressed in a safari suit, but his whole attitude reminded her of winter. His brittle frame was hunched over, chest hollow and chin tucked in, like a person battling against a stiff, cold gust.

243

Susan sought out Yusuf. "Who's that man over there? I've never seen him before."

"He's the man from Tass, the Soviet news agency. I think he arrived only last week."

"I didn't know Tass has somebody here."

"Oh yes, ever since our relations improved. It's good to make friends with everyone," Yusuf said wisely.

No wonder she'd never met him before, Susan thought. The eastern bloc had its own bridge games and sports clubs, separate from the other expats. Susan looked at the stranger again, memorized the features that were symmetrical to the point of being nondescript, the medium height and medium build, and moved on.

A long conference table occupied one side of the hall. On the other were three rows of chairs and then standing room where the photographers had spread out their equipment. Persis had deposited himself at the center of the table. Attila sat behind him, busily sorting through the reams of wide-carriage printouts. She knew she should take the chair next to Attila, so she could jump to produce a figure when called upon. However, a seat in the front would limit her view of the scene. Then she saw Persis swing around to Attila, his lips pursing to form two syllables: Su-san. Clasping the papers to his lap, the Turk rose halfway, rubbernecking in search of the person in demand.

Susan sneaked out the back door. Persis could fume all he wanted, but she wasn't going to be at his beck and call tonight.

Some minutes later, when she reemerged, the last stragglers were filing into the room. Persis was engaged in animated discussion with the bigwigs around the table. Attila hovered behind him, reciting data at the snap of Persis's fingers. She was dispensable, after all, Susan thought.

She took a seat in the back row. Behind her, the photographers were working furiously to set up the klieg light. The Tass man was holding one end of the wire and searching the wall for a socket. At close range, he wasn't as old as his thinning gray hair suggested. His chestnut eyes were hard, and his agility at bending high and low showed little degeneration of the joints.

A troop of Red Berets marched in with great fanfare. The last one clicked his heels together and announced, "President of the Somali Democratic Republic, Mohammed Siad Barré." The assembly rose to its feet. A moment of awed silence followed, then a shadow crossed the doorway. A tall figure appeared, dressed in a simple white shirt and khaki trousers, treading stiff, slow steps on his famous rawhide sandals. Two guards flanked his sides, and although their assistance involved no contact, one could see that they were guiding him to his place. Plagued by advanced diabetes, the president was rumored to have lost most of his sight. Applause rang out. The klieg boomed. The room exploded in a flood of white light.

Susan's system went on red alert. She spun around and saw the American photographer getting ready to pan the scene. His Soviet competitor was stepping up a chair to get a better view. Susan's eyes fell on the motley collection of apparatus scattered on the floor, and then she saw a square black camera case with a four-digit combination lock. She'd seen one like that before—Hoyt Grimley's. What was it doing under the chair?

Grimley's camera was last seen in Ahmed's fortress. Ahmed—

Susan leaped to the side of the Tass man and tugged at a leg of his pants. He glanced down at her, his finger resting on the shutter release. Susan beckoned him to stoop to her level. Siad Barré was taking his place at the center of the table.

As the photographer bent down, Susan grabbed his elbow and whispered into his ears, "Come with me." Smiling sweetly, she slid the handle of the gun out of her pocket to make sure he understood that this was a command, not a request. The president was rasping "Welcome, welcome."

The Tass man hopped down from his chair, the camera and its long-nosed telescope still strapped to his neck.

"This way," Susan said without altering her angelic expression. The bulge in her pocket beckoned. The photographer took a step, and she was behind him, nudging him

245

through the back door. In the hallway, she said aloud for the benefit of the guards, "I knew there was something wrong with that lens. I've got a spare in the car. Let's go get it." She threaded her hand through the crook of his elbow and burrowed her fingers into the nerve under his funny bone.

"Madam, you must be mistaken," the man said with a mildly British accent.

Susan dug in her nails and pushed the hidden muzzle against the pocket lining. "Shut up."

Once they were past the guards, he started again, "Madam, may I talk now?"

She answered with another sharp dig.

The man winced. "Please, not so hard. What are you doing? I'm a journalist from the Tass news agency—"

"I know what's in that camera. Your American friend talked," Susan bluffed.

"I have no idea what you're talking about. Please, can we—"

"You try any tricks on me, and I'll blow your guts out, Hamid." Her prisoner fell silent. They walked down the path under the noses of an array of Red Berets. Susan hung on to her squire's elbow while letting her heels slip-slide on the cobblestones. The soldiers snickered with amusement.

At the gate, Susan looked steadily into a guard's eyes and said, "Can you please open the gate? We need to get something from the car."

"There's a problem with the lens," her prisoner said, pointing with his free hand at the instrument protruding from his midriff. "The glass is broken. I need to replace it with one in the car."

An alarm sounded in Susan's head. Cooperation under duress was one thing, but why was he going out of his way to help her? The gates whined open, and her prisoner led her out. She had a vague, uncomfortable feeling that he had an ace up his sleeve. If she could only make it to the car. The limos were parked two blocks away, their outline visible in the glow of the palace lights. In a minute they would be there, and Mohammed would drive them to the embassy.

"Where are you taking me?" her prisoner asked. His tone was different now, sunk into a deeper, darker realm. She'd heard that voice before.

"How about the U.S. embassy?" she said. "They might give you a visa to visit your old friends at Langley."

"I don't mind, if you go with me. You'll have to undress for me again—"

Susan delved for the nerve again, but before her finger went in all the way, she felt a tingle at the base of her neck, something cool and hard.

"Raise your hands, slowly," a voice breathed on her. For a moment she wasn't sure if the speaker was a man or a woman, then a chill shot down her spine. Her synapses connected. These were the two voices on Jack's tape!

A hand crammed into her pocket and removed her gun. Susan couldn't see the man, but from the thickness of his paw she could extrapolate the rest of his size. This was the "colonel"—the man who had bashed in Jack's face.

He marched her to one of the government buildings, spread her face against a wall and gave her a body search much more meticulous than the one she'd received earlier. The streets had been blocked off, the buildings vacated. Her weapon was gone. She was alone with the murderers.

"Go back there now," the shrill voice said. "I'll take care of her."

"Don't let her fool you. She's from the CIA."

"CIA or not, she's still a woman. You think everyone has trouble handling a woman?"

"The CIA trains its people well. She can give you more trouble than you think, but if I help you, you can have some fun. Come, let's go, there's plenty of time to take pictures."

The burly man snorted, noosed a ham of an arm around Susan's neck and yanked her like a rag doll toward the building entrance. Susan thought of the pen in her breast pocket. She could give her captor a whiff of tear gas and make a run for it. But then, she would lose Hamid forever. The man pushed her into the building. This was her last chance. Once inside her fate was sealed. She could be raped and killed by two men.

Breathe, a small voice in her ordered, and she began drawing in all the oxygen her body could hold, concentrating it on her fingertips and sending it back out through the top of her head. The *ch'i* welled up from her navel and flowed into the hollow of her body, through the locus of her balance, wave after wave, amassing a kinetic force that quelled the tumult and sharpened her awareness of the essence of her surroundings. A window opened on her forehead, and through this third eye, she watched herself as a third person, mounting the staircase in an empty building.

The large man hauled her into a room. From the patchy light filtering out of the palace, she could see that it was a communal office. Half a dozen sets of desk and chair ringed the sides, leaving an arena in the middle. Once again, she was thrust against a wall. Her face and breasts were mashed into the concrete, her shoulder wrenched into a glob of numbing pain. He was tearing at her skirt. With her third eye she studied him and found his weakness.

"I can take it off," she muttered between the crack of her lips. The pressure eased. She plunged out of his grip, snatched the pen from her breast pocket, and crushed the button. A fine spray shot out. The colonel howled, and his arm reared up to shield his eyes. Susan seized a chair and smashed it on his head. The chair broke into many pieces. The man stumbled back, regained his balance and swung around, his eyes red and tearing and raging. "I'm going to kill you," he cried and charged. Susan stood still, seeing him at last, a brute several times her size, overwrought with anger, a savage, sightless bull who could no more change his course than a speeding train. A second before his arms reached her, that point in time where mass and motion peaked, she whipped out the ragged remains of a chair leg and lunged forward with both hands and every muscle and hair, body and soul, to meet the blind, hurtling force. The colonel let out a sigh of "aah," eyes bugging with disbelief, and slumped over Susan in an embrace.

Three cynical claps resounded. "Congratulations, they trained you well."

Susan freed herself from the colonel and stood up slowly. Her head was spinning from the aftershock of the crash, her stomach churning from the stench of blood and sweat. She took a deep breath to steady herself. Her vision focused; the lines crystallized. So this was Hamid standing before her. He'd shaved his beard, shed his turban, and pared down the beak of his aquiline nose. In the clarity of electric lights, he bore no resemblance to his old photo, but in the murkiness of the shadows, his body cut a hungry figure that hadn't changed since his guerrilla days. He reminded her of a wild dog who hadn't eaten in a long time.

"You've done me a big favor," he said. "That man was an ass. I would have liked to get rid of him myself."

Susan's eyes landed on the gun strapped to the fat man's belt. It was her Glock.

Hamid read her gaze. "I don't like guns. They make too much noise. As they say in English, 'Silence is golden.' That was the first rule my American friends taught me. I'm sure they taught you the same?" He took something out of his pocket. In the blotchy glow, it seemed like a comb. He opened it carefully, and Susan caught sight of a glint of silver. "My instructor gave this to me. He would be happy to know that I have found it very useful."

"Just make sure you don't mess up my hair this time," Susan said. With a flick of the hand, she pulled out the silver pin in her chignon. A black waterfall tumbled down. She shook it loose and it settled evenly like a shawl over her shoulders.

Hamid grabbed her mane and flung her on the floor. To his amazement, she rolled off like a ball toward the door. Hamid dashed to keep her from escaping, but when she leaped up and faced him, her back squarely blocking the door, he realized that she considered herself the hunter and he the quarry. For the first time, the fact that he was facing an equal struck home. His desire for a finessed end gave way to a more practical need to finish the job quickly. He'd get her any way necessary, even if it meant spilling more blood than he'd like.

Hamid slashed at her. Every time he thought he got her, she would slip away at the last microsecond. She seemed to be dallying with him, handing over the prize and snatching it away just when he thought it was his. Her movements were big and gusty as the wind. Space was her ally. He saw what he must do—close the gap between them. Wielding his knife in her face, he pushed her into a corner. Her sparring was no longer wide and confident but confined and jittery. He could smell her fear as her space shrank. Unless the walls opened up, she was trapped.

He drew a bead on a spot just below the pearl brooch on her chest. One thrust, and he'd get to the heart of the matter. The burgundy red of her jacket was strangely still. Had she given up, or was she going to pull a fast one, the way she did to the colonel? Her hands were empty; she had no weapon, not even the leg of a chair.

He'd like to toy with her a little longer, but time was ticking away. The president was waiting to have his picture taken.

Hamid drove in with enough force to cut through the layers of clothing, skin, tissue and rib. In the wink of an eye, the burgundy red vanished. Hamid was staring at the wall. Where did she go? Her hair was on his shoulder. He felt her warmth in his arms. He pushed her away. His hand wandered up to his chest and found a hard tip. A sticky wetness met his fingers. He looked down and saw what it was. The warm, pulsing fluid of his heart was trickling out. He gaped at her.

"It's the pin that held up my hair. It's as sharp as your knife," he heard her explain. He staggered up, staring with disbelief at the stiletto buried in his chest. The Glock caught his eye. Pretending to stumble, he fell over the colonel's corpse, grabbed the gun and fired. The thud of a body reached him, but he knew there was something wrong. The body had fallen too fast. Where did she go? He whipped around the room, his eyes straining at the shadows. A rustle sounded from the other end.

250

He sprang over and fired down the row of desks. A wallop on his back sent him skidding on the floor. He swiveled around and she was on him, pinning his thighs and gripping the gun in his hand. He squeezed the trigger. She fell back, but the next thing he knew, a punch on his rib cage knocked the wind out of him. The stiletto drilled into his heart. His chest exploded in flames, and for a moment the pain consumed him. For a moment he was aware of nothing else, neither the gun he was still clutching, nor the two hands bending his wrist inward, turning the gun on him. Then he opened his eyes and knew what was happening. His left fist flew out. She freed one hand to fend off the blow. A shot went off. He smelled the singe of her hair, but she was still at his throat, bearing down with claws and teeth like a tigress. He threw out his left arm again, but this time, she turned her shoulder toward him and absorbed the blow. He pummeled her again and again, but she kept pressing on until the muzzle was staring him in the face and he could feel his trigger finger curling under the force of her hands. His eyes spoke into hers, the word "No!" forming in the kernel of his pupils. The fury in her eyes died.

A shot deafened him. He looked at her once more, a last thought taking shape and solidifying in his lifeless eyes.

"There you are," Persis said as soon as he opened the car door. "We were wondering what happened to you."

"I had an awful stomachache. Must be something I ate for dinner. How did it go?" Susan said, although she could tell without asking. Persis was happy, or he would have bitten her head off for walking out on him.

"Splendid. The president agreed to every condition, in principle, of course. He's not going to work out the details himself. That's the responsibility of the finance minister. By the way, where was Suleiman at the end of the meeting? I was looking everywhere for him."

"I saw him leave the room when we were lining up for the group photo," Attila said. Turning to Susan, he said in a fatherly voice, "You better put on your jacket if you're not feeling well. Shouldn't catch a cold on top of it."

"I'm all right. It's a warm night," Susan said. The jacket lay furled across her lap. Her hair pinned up, her white blouse buttoned to the ruffled collar, she was the paragon of the woman banker. She sat primly, legs locked together at the ankles, a calm, mature person who could conduct a conversation by small adjustments of the head. A larger movement would be unbecoming, aside from revealing the blood stains on the front of her skirt. The darkness also helped hide the evidence of her recent unfeminine behavior.

After dropping the men off at the Eden, Mohammed drove Susan home. The canine flew at her in a frenzy, fangs drawn and nostrils flaring at the smell of fresh blood on her. If Kujo hadn't been tethered to the carport post, she would have had to draw the Glock on it to save her hide. Keeping her eyes on the snapping jaws, she clutched the jacket over her skirt and double-stepped into the house. Abdullahi peppered her with his usual inquiries about her needs, but she bypassed them all and locked herself in the bedroom. She peeled off her clothes and hopped into the shower as if her tail was on fire. She scrubbed herself from head to toe until her skin pinked where it wasn't black and blue. The madness of her energy released, the bruises on her shoulder and elsewhere were crying for attention. She toweled herself gingerly, then pulled a nightie over her head and crawled into bed.

A weight sat on her chest. The blood of two men was on her hands. If she hadn't killed them, they would have killed her. The agency had prepared her for this. Mentally and physically, it had trained her to snuff out the lives of those deemed to be a menace to society, to do it proficiently and quietly, without inflicting injury on innocent bystanders or drawing publicity to herself. She'd followed instructions to the letter. Hamid was dead, the primary goal of her mission had been accomplished, and Jack's death had been avenged. She should be celebrating, yet she could only feel swamped by a sense of failure.

Hamid might be gone, but he'd done his share of spurring the country into a downward spiral. Not even the best pilot could straighten the diving craft now.

Chapter 28

General Ahmed paced the floor of his desert fortress. The strip of carpet he'd been walking on all night was wearing thin. By now the dark sky had ruptured and splattered blood across the sky, yet there was still no news from Suleiman. He peeked through the slit in the wall at the parade ground. What he saw was alarming. The long wait had reduced his men to a group of restless children loafing around a schoolyard. Some had dozed off, while others had laid down their guns and were playing games to pass the time.

He couldn't wait much longer. Making war and love were the same. After the military foreplay of the past few months, he could see the lovesick craving of his men as they handled their weapons like extensions of their manhood. No matter what, the attack must begin. Even if the assassination attempt had failed, victory was still possible if he would only seize the moment and attack with all the firepower he possessed.

But where the hell was Suleiman? Or any of the spies he'd planted around the palace? Had everyone deserted him?

A flicker in the surveillance monitor caught his eye. A car was approaching the fortress. The driver poked his head out. His face appeared on the screen. It was the deputy police commissioner. Ahmed radioed his men to let the visitor in.

"What's the news?" he demanded as soon as the second-highest-ranking policeman walked in.

"General, your nephew..." The commissioner was ashen-faced. Ahmed braced himself. "Your nephew is dead."

Ahmed's cheek throbbed twice and was still. "How did it happen?" he said.

"Two bodies were found in the Ministry of Public Works this morning. One of them was your nephew's. We don't have any suspects yet, but the murderer must have been a large and strong man to be able to cut open the colonel's belly with the leg of a chair. It's most likely there were more than one of them."

255

Ahmed sat in stony silence. No sacrifice was too great for his cause. His sister had ten other children. "What about the other man? Who was he and how was he killed?"

"The other man died of a bullet in his face. A card identifying him as a Tass journalist was found on him."

Ahmed closed his eyes for a moment. So Hamid, too, was dead. There left only one question: "The president is well?"

"Too well," the police chief spat out, the intensity of his sentiment expressed in those two words. "And Suleiman has gone into hiding. He is nowhere to be found."

Ahmed felt a tightness in his forehead. So it had come to this. Their plot had failed, and his ally had fled for his life. Suleiman had never been known for courage. His desertion was no loss, actually a blessing. Power, like a woman, should never be shared.

He laid a hand on his informant's shoulder. "Thank you very much for your help. When I take over the presidential palace, I won't forget you."

"It's not for that. It's for the hatred of the Marehans," the policeman said with a quaver in his voice.

Ahmed walked to his command post and spoke into the PA system. "Attention, everyone," his voice boomed across his hardscrabble kingdom. "The time has come. Allah has given us our signal. Let us march into the capital and give our enemies the trouncing of their lives. Fight with the courage of a lion, the cunning of a fox, and by nightfall, Mogadishu will be ours! Somalia will be ours!"

The jet roared and leaped into the sky. How Susan wished she could be on that flight, even if it meant being cooped up with Persis for twelve hours. Christmas was only a day away. She'd never felt so homesick in her life. Her mission was completed. What more could she do in this godforsaken place?

She walked out to the curb, her hair brushing the back of her safari suit, a feminized version made of a smooth peach percale. Mohammed stood waiting by the Land Rover. His eyes searched anxiously beyond her, half expecting Persis to bustle up and demand to be taken to the ministry of such and such.

"He's gone," Susan assured him. "Look." She pointed to the plane swimming like a minnow high up in the bright blue sky. Mohammed smiled self-consciously, embarrassed to have his unholy thoughts read.

They slowed down at a checkpoint; the guard recognized their U.N. plate and waved them on. It was another clear day, with visibility stretching as far as the horizon. A nice day for a tennis lesson, perhaps her last? Susan was smiling to herself when she noticed a large cloud of dust rising ahead. A convoy of trucks was chugging up the road. Something else caught her attention—a pair of arms flagging, another checkpoint. Mohammed hit the brakes.

The soldiers put them on hold, for on the opposite lane the first truck in the convoy was lumbering to a stop. There were three in all, and each seemed loaded with cargo hidden behind canvas drapes. The driver of the first truck stuck his head out. He was dressed in a spinach-green uniform.

Susan remembered seeing that color before. As she turned to Mohammed to ask him whether he knew what the uniform stood for, a wrinkle in the canvas caught her eye. Sparks flew out of the truck.

Susan flung open the door, yelling for Mohammed to get out. The driver sat frozen in his seat, his eyes about to pop out of their sockets. She gripped his arm and tugged with all her might, but Mohammed was as unyielding as a boulder. A loud *ping* reported; the windshield frosted and crumbled into a million fragments. Mohammed dived into Susan's lap and scrambled out after her. The trucks thundered past, spraying a hail of bullets. Mohammed and Susan huddled in the ditch, hands clasped over each other's head.

Minutes later, when the earth had stopped shaking and the rumble was reduced to a distant hum, Susan pried herself loose from Mohammed's fingers and clambered out of the ditch. Seven bodies lay strewn along the road. No one had survived the close-range barrage.

Mohammed was still hugging his knees when Susan returned. She laid a hand on his shoulder and said, "We have to get out of here." Mohammed lifted his tear-streaked face and allowed himself to be pulled to his feet.

The side of the Land Rover was pocked with holes, but fortunately the engine and gas tank had been spared. Susan used her satchel to sweep the glass from the driver's seat and climbed in. A hole on the passenger side gaped at her. The bullet must have hit the windshield at an angle and lodged itself on the left shoulder of where she'd sat. A twinge dug into the spot on her pectoral muscle where the bullet would have penetrated. Without giving it another thought, she turned on the engine and stepped on the clutch. It was then that she realized her knee was shaking. The magnitude of her luck was overwhelming. If she hadn't been heaving backwards, struggling to get Mohammed to budge, she would be bleeding to death, if not dead by now.

Steadying her knee with one hand, she sped toward Mogadishu. On the outskirts of town, she radioed the U.N. security office and reported the incident. Jean-Paul, the Frenchman who'd taken over from Juergen, ordered her to go home straightaway. Having learned the futility of arguing with that department, Susan signed off with a noncommittal "talk to you later." She detoured to the other end of town, deposited Mohammed at his home, and drove back to the office. She must warn Omar and Fatima.

As she passed by the market, a notion formed in her head. She pulled over and jumped out of her shot-up vehicle. Vendors packed the open-air bazaar. Susan walked briskly past the handicraft stalls, dodging the vines of dangling straw bags, and picked her way around the obstacle course of peddlers with their baskets of bananas and racks of T-shirts and underwear. Then she spotted the two teenagers. They were squatting next to a colorful piece of fabric on which their merchandise was displayed. Susan hurried toward them.

A pair of long faces and high foreheads looked up at her, boys with eyes of men. "Hello, Madame. What you like?" the older youth said with a wizened grin.

258

Susan surveyed the spread before her: a tetrad of hand grenades, half a dozen handguns of various makes, and a rifle boasting a swanky, curved magazine. Her eyes glimmered at the last item as if it was an old friend. She'd been trained in every aspect of the AK-47, and knew that "A" stood for automatic, K for Kalashnikov, its designer, and 47 for the year the gun was approved by the Soviet government for mass production. Since then, the blueprint for the rifle had been circulated all over the communist bloc, resulting in a production of tens of millions of Kalashnikovs that had been used by guerrilla and nationalist movements throughout the world. With a firing rate of six hundred rounds per minute, a single North Vietnamese soldier was said to have used it to mow down seventy-eight Americans at one time. It was a well-designed gun, but there was one fault that Susan could recall. The recoil was violent, making the weapon a monster to control during rapid fire.

"What are you selling that for?" Susan said.

"Three hundred dollars. For you, I give you two for five hundred," the youth said, shoving two fingers splayed into a V at Susan.

"One is enough," Susan said and rummaged her purse for the payment. With the rifle slung over her shoulder, Susan ran back to her car. Several men stared at her, but she couldn't be bothered with appearances now. All hell was breaking loose, and everyone should do what he must to save himself.

The financial district was livelier than she'd seen in a long time. Judging from the number of people crowding the entrance to the finance ministry, the good news from the president's meeting with the donors must have hit the streets. The hopefulness on people's faces stirred up a sadness in her.

After parking her car in the alley, she rushed into the Savoy. Halfway up the first flight of stairs, a boom shook the building. Susan clung to the banister. A fast-moving whistle screamed past and another explosion caromed through the neighborhood. Frantic cries sounded in all directions. Susan dashed up two flights and ran into a handful of office workers who had gathered to watch a mortar draw an arc across the sky.

259

"It's the Radio Mogadishu building," someone exclaimed.

The meaning of the attacks became clear to Susan. A coup was underway—first the seizure of the airport and now the radio station. Susan ran into her office. Omar and Fatima were watching the fireworks by the window.

"Get away from there!" Susan said and herded her staff into her office. She slammed the AK-47 on her desk, noticing the apprehensive stares at the new piece of office equipment. She pulled out her CB and turned it on. A man with an Italian accent was on the air. Gunfire and frenetic shouts were drowning him out, and then through the confusion, Susan heard the word "palace." Villa Somalia was under attack.

The airwaves sizzled. Jean-Paul hollered at the man to respond, but the radio went dead. Moments later, the Frenchman returned and called for calm, although the charge of adrenalin in his voice betrayed his own state. He'd been in touch with the U.S. ambassador, who had promised safe haven for all U.N. personnel. He exhorted people to immediately seek shelter at the embassy compound, but those caught in areas of heavy fighting should stay put and wait for further instructions. One of them was the financial district, where rebel troops were laying siege to the Central Bank and Ministry of Finance.

"What troops?" Susan said. She walked to the window and looked down in time to see a truck plow through the crowd and stop in front of the Savoy. The canvas had been rolled up, revealing the cargo of soldiers and artillery on its flatbed.

"General Ahmed's troops," Omar said beside her.

"How do you know?"

"Their uniforms are green."

Finally, that mystery was solved.

The armed men scattered into the government buildings. People fled, but the troops made no attempt to stop them. A squad of soldiers came out of the Central Bank, dragging with them a distinguished looking, gray-haired man. Susan recognized him as the governor of the Central Bank, a Marehan. They hustled him to the middle of the street and forced him to his knees. A soldier pointed a pistol on the back of his head and fired.

Susan and her crew gasped in horror, but before they could recover, the soldiers were muscling out several more people, one of them a woman.

"I know them. They're all Marehans," Fatima said and fell in a heap on the floor. Susan patted her on the cheek to revive her. Five shots echoed from the street, and a bullhorn blared.

"They're telling everyone to leave the buildings," Omar said.

"I'm not going," were Fatima's first words when she came to. "They know I'm a Marehan."

"We'll find a place to hide until they leave," Susan said. To Omar she said, "You go on to the U.S. embassy. We'll join you later."

"What, you think I will leave you?" Omar's eyelids fluttered furiously as if the greatest insult had been hurled at him.

Flustered by his fierce reaction, Susan stammered, "Well, I thought, as there's nothing you can do—"

"I know where we can hide," Omar said and turned on his heels.

The women followed him. Omar crept under his desk and pulled a panel out of the wall. It was a crawl space that was used as storage for office correspondence. Omar disappeared into the square opening. After a bout of reshuffling, he invited the women to join him. Susan slid her rifle through and scooted in. Around her were boxes and boxes and the tickle of dust on her nose. Omar's breath was on her face, telling her to sit down. He'd rearranged the boxes so all three could squeeze in and seat themselves as comfortably as possible.

The harsh clatter of military boots pounded from floor to floor. Fatima threw aside her reservation, tucked in her radiant black and gold wrap, and scuttled in on hands and knees. Omar reached out for the panel and pulled it back. Night engulfed them. Susan's heart stopped. Her companions were erased, every trace of their existence wiped out. She pinched herself on the arm just to make sure she was still there.

The stampede of boots reached their floor. They were bashing down doors, their door. Now they were inside the office, hurling furniture around. There was banging against a wall. The blows grew to a frenzy and climaxed with an outburst of gunfire. Susan figured they must be working on the safe. She had a thousand U.S. dollars stashed away for a rainy day. Maybe today was the day. She wished they would take the money and leave. The hammering went on for a while, and then came an exultant roar. They'd found the money. *Now leave!*

More shouts could be heard and the crash-bang of heavy objects thrown about. Now what? Wasn't a thousand dollars good enough? Footsteps clomped with growing intensity; they were coming into Omar's room. Bookcases collapsed, voluminous files crashed, and the legs of Omar's desk scraped the floor as drawers were flung out. Voices yelled in angry frustration about "Banka Dunia," repeatedly "banka, banka, banka," until Susan understood what they were agitating about. If this was a bank, where the hell was the rest of the dough?

After a while, the noise waned. The heavy boots stalked around in an unnerving change of pace. They were no longer rushing around, but lingering, settling in. Susan thought she could smell their sweat on the other side of the thin wall.

She started. It was Omar whispering, his lips touching her ear. "They're staying," he said. "Our office has a good view."

"Oh God," Susan whispered back. Of course, she thought, her office was located at a strategic corner. The front faced the Central Bank while the side offered a bird's-eye view into the finance ministry compound.

A moan came from behind. Susan shifted and brushed against a soft, sheer fabric. She reached out and touched Fatima's hand.

The battle raged through the day, sometimes intensely and other times so tranquilly that one would have thought everyone had dozed off. Now and then, Susan pressed the light button on her digital watch. The minutes crawled, and the more she checked on them, the slower they plodded on, a second at a time. Their hideout was getting as hot as a sauna, and it had been long past the half an hour recommended for such an experience. Her pores had opened to their fullest extent, and she was dripping like a burning candle. It was tempting to close her eyes and melt away. Omar was snoring, his head lolling against her shoulder. Fatima seemed to be drifting in and out of consciousness. At least one of them must stay alert.

Sooner or later the soldiers would have to leave, Susan kept consoling herself.   A blast hit the building.   A weight crushed her back and thrust her head against the wall. For a moment, she thought the building was collapsing. The end had come. She pushed and shoved to keep her head up, clawing the pulpy cardboard surfaces and entanglement of limbs, and then she realized the wall was still standing, and the floor beneath her knees was still flat and level.

"Are you all right?" she rasped to her companions.

"I have to get out," Fatima cried. "I can't breathe."

Arms and legs grappled to find their rightful owners. Outside, voices were yelling amid the explosion of shells and gunfire.

"No, you can't; they're still here," Susan said.

"I have to, I have to," Fatima sobbed. The struggle became frantic. A knee or elbow jabbed Susan in the temple. She was stunned for a second, but the pressure of a body climbing over her brought her back. "Fatima," she hissed at the black void. "Do you want to see your children again?"

A slap in the face couldn't have been more effective. Fatima lay still, panting. Susan herself was grasping at every molecule of oxygen she could find. There was more to go around if they'd only stay still. Another shell rocked the building, showering chunks of ceiling plaster on their heads. The din of fighting was rising to a peak. Susan plugged each ear with a finger and kept them there no matter how much the building shook.

When she dared to loosen up, the barrage had abated to a sporadic question and answer. The office squatters were awfully quiet, and then came the sound Susan had been praying for—a thumping of boots, surging, fading. Susan kicked open the panel. The gush of gunpowdered air filled her lungs. She crawled out, choking and tearing.

They ventured out of the Savoy. The time was two minutes past three in the afternoon, six hours after they'd gone into hiding. Looking at the sky, Susan would have thought it was dusk instead of midafternoon. Columns of smoke rose out of the city, billowing and spreading into a gray-black quilt that blocked out the fierce Somali sun.

Susan peered out from behind a pillar. An entire flank of the finance ministry building had been peeled back, exposing a gridiron of cubicles. Kitty-cornered with it were remnants of the Central Bank, riddled with holes like a moldy hunk of Swiss cheese. The U.S. embassy was five kilometers away, an easy walk on a normal day, but today was anything but normal. Their plan was to stop by the Eden to see if they could find help.

Susan looked down the street. Trapped on both sides by multistoried buildings, this stretch of Via Somalia was a perfect sniper's alley. She would have to stay close to the wall and take advantage of the arcades and columns to get herself and the others through.

"I'm going first. Don't come out until I tell you to."

Her companions protested, but she could barely hear them, for her entire attention was focused on the panel of windows across the street. Most of them had been shattered. They were dark and still. Was anyone up there? She would soon find out. She charged out with her rifle at the ready. A slug hit the wall close to her. She dropped behind a pillar, locked her finger onto the trigger and spouted a curtain of bullets at the sniper. "Run, run!" she yelled. A welter of footsteps stumbled past. Her teeth jack-hammering with the percussion of the AK-47, she stepped out of her shelter and crabwalked down the block.

As they dodged around the corner, their vista changed from charred ruins to the grand view of the cathedral. It stood intact, although its front doors were flung open, a sign of looters. Susan heard a rattle behind her, a regrettably familiar sound. She raised her hands, yelling, "Don't shoot," and slowly turned around. A group of bedraggled children extended their cupped hands, but one of them, a moon-faced youth, was pointing an AK-47 at her.

"Jamil," she cried. "What are you doing with that?"

"I found it," he said.

His comrades jeered at him in Somali, and there was a tussle for the rifle.

"Stop it," Susan shouted. "Give it to me. You can hurt yourself." She reached out for the weapon.

"No, it's mine," Jamil said, wagging the Kalashnikov at her.

Susan raised her hands in reflex. "All right, all right," she said, backing off.

"We are hungry. Give us money," Jamil delivered his famous one-liner. His companions joined in a chorus of "baksheesh." Fatima handed over a fistful of shillings, more than she ever would if the beggar weren't carrying a gun. Jamil and his friends whooped and went on their way.

The Eden was deserted. They cut through the empty courtyard to the Giuseppes' living quarters. A curtain stirred. Taking no chances, Susan ducked. The door opened a quadrant and the practical, no-nonsense figure of Mrs. Giuseppe appeared, beckoning them to enter.

"You didn't leave?" Susan said to the couple. Their faces were wrinkled and wan. They'd aged a decade since she'd last seen them.

"Where can I go? This is my home," Mrs. Giuseppe replied. Her husband dipped his stodgy head in agreement. "And you, why aren't you at the embassy?" she added.

"We were stuck in the office when the fighting started. We just managed to get out."

"You must hurry up and go now. Do you have a car?"

Susan shook her head. Mrs. Giuseppe looked at her husband and a heated discussion in Italian followed. As usual, it ended with a slow, ponderous nod from the man.

"Take my car," Mrs. Giuseppe said to Susan.

"Oh no, I wouldn't think of it, unless you come with us."

"No, I'll never leave this country. This is my home. Please, take it. We can use the motorcycle." Mrs. Giuseppe glanced at her husband. Already, he was rummaging in his pocket for the key.

The hoteliers herded their guests out the back door into the garage. As they hugged each other for the last time, Mrs. Giuseppe gave a heart-rending moan. "My father was against giving independence to Somalia. He said the moment the Italians left, the Somalis would go back to fighting each other. I thought he was too pessimistic. He went back to Rome, but I chose to stay. Now I'm beginning to think he was right. The Italians should never have left."

"I disagree," Omar declared, surprising everyone with his unusual clarity.

"Oh of course, I don't mean people like you," Mrs. Giuseppe quickly corrected herself. "You're different; you're educated..."

"Before the Italians came, yes, we fought each other," Omar went on. "We were nomads; we had to fight for survival in the desert, but that fighting was different. After the white man came and taught us to live together under one government, the whole balance has changed. Power and riches became concentrated in one place. Everybody wants to take over Mogadishu, and what people are fighting for is no longer food and water. They want to rule over all the clans."

"Fighting is fighting," Fatima said. "It's bad no matter what. If women were to rule the country, we wouldn't allow it."

"But Fatima, this fighting is different," Omar argued. "This fighting will go on and on until we're all dead."

"I think we better get going," Susan interrupted.

Fatima froze. "I can't. I can't leave my children behind."

"If you want to see your children again, the first thing you must do is stay alive," Susan said.

Fatima's jaws were firmly clenched. She didn't look the least bit convinced.

"Just come with us to the embassy," Omar said. "It will be safer there. When things quiet down, you can find a way to join your family in Bardhere."

Fatima's eyes wandered. Susan could see that Omar's ploy was working. She'd never thought he could be so clever. Without another word, Fatima got into the car. Susan gave Mrs. Giuseppe a tight embrace that expressed the gratitude that no words could convey. Mr. Giuseppe was hoisting the heavy wooden latch off the gates.

"Jean-Paul, this is Susan Chen," she radioed in as she backed out of the driveway. "We're leaving the Eden in a navy-blue Fiat. We should be at the embassy in about ten minutes, *inchallah*." She qualified her estimate with the Arabic for "God willing." "Tell the marines to open the gates wide for us."

The Fiat cruised along the deserted roads. After a dozen blocks, the only life Susan saw was a pack of stray dogs tearing into a pile of garbage. One of them ripped off a piece and scampered away to enjoy its prize in peace. Susan looked closer and saw a set of human fingers flopping from its square jaws.

She swerved to avoid a corpse in the middle of the road. They'd entered an area that had seen vicious fighting. As she turned to inspect the shelled buildings, a group of men entered her peripheral vision. They were running out to the road and waving their rifles at her. She tapped the brake to ease the vehicle to a gentle stop. A dozen men swarmed around. They were in street clothes and looked wild-eyed and strung out. Omar struck up a conversation in that harsh, argumentative tone that she'd often taken for hostility. She was glad to see that she was mistaken again, for whatever Omar said couldn't have been too unfriendly. The men were lowering their guns and ogling her with curiosity.

"Shall I pay them?" Susan whispered to Omar. He nodded.

Susan handed over all the dollars and shillings she could find on her. The men seemed happy, and Susan beamed them her sweetest smile as she slowly placed her fingers on the ignition. Suddenly somebody shouted and everyone began to crowd around the back window. Fatima lowered her head. Omar was talking very fast. Susan took in the word *Marehan*. Somebody had identified Fatima as a Marehan. Hands reached in and pulled them out of the car. Susan's arms were wrenched back and she felt a coarse rope cut into her wrists. A well-known whining of "baksheesh" hummed in her ears. She looked around and saw the beggar children swarming out of thin air. She searched for Jamil, remembering his newfound toy, but he wasn't among them. The men shouted at the urchins and pushed them away, but the beggars persisted in their plea.

The *rat-a-tat* of automatic gunfire ripped the air. The crowd scattered. Susan dived behind the Fiat and looked up at where the shots were coming from. A familiar pumpkin head was silhouetted in the frame of a second-floor window. It was Jamil, happily pumping away and unaware that his noodle was in full view. Her hands still tied behind her back, Susan flicked her head at Omar and Fatima to follow her. They had to get away while the shooting lasted. The moment Jamil took a break, somebody was going to put a bullet through that pancake head of his. Susan bounded up the steps, shouting, "Get down, Jamil!"

The wall of the apartment danced in a shower of bullets. Jamil lay face down on the floor. Susan crouched below the sill and crept to him. The boy flipped around with a grin.

"Cut me loose," she said to Jamil. "Hurry, hurry," she moaned as the boy picked at the knot. It seemed an interminable amount of time, but finally she was free. She grabbed the rifle and moved to a different window. The street was empty, but sticking out of a window of an opposite building, in a way that all students at Camp Peary were admonished *not* to do, was the barrel of a gun.

Susan took out her CB. The Frenchman's voice bleated out of the small box. "Where the hell are you?"

"We got sidetracked. Our car's gone. It's going to take us a little while longer to get there. Can you hold the bus for us?"

"The ambassador's ordered the last airlift. We just spotted some trucks arriving with the big guns. If we don't leave now, we may never." A maelstrom of crackles cut him off. Susan shook the box in a desperate attempt to bring him back. "Jean-Paul, Jean-Paul, are you there? Come back! You can't leave us here!"

"Can you get yourselves to Afgoy Road?" a voice scratched through the static.

"Yes. Which intersection?"

"K-5. We'll see you there." Jean-Paul signed off.

Susan glanced down and saw a figure darting toward their building. "Is there a back door out of here?" Susan asked.

"Yes," the Somalis replied in unison.

Jamil led the way while Susan brought up the rear with the AK-47. They went into a courtyard, through a door into another courtyard and emerged in an alley. Behind them, footsteps were pounding closer and closer. Jamil zigzagged in the warren of stone and mud houses. Susan had no idea where she was going, but she had to trust a street kid to know his way around. The pattering from behind was gaining on them. Fatima was floundering. She couldn't go on much farther.

"We've got to hide," Susan panted. Omar pointed to a plundered shop they'd just passed.

"I go," Jamil said. "I run fast."

Susan's eyes dwelled for a second on the boy, a young man now. "It's all yours," she said and tossed him the rifle. He caught it, his scar deepening into a sassy dimple as he waved *Arrivederci* and sprinted down the lane. Susan and the others ducked into the shop and hid behind the emptied shelves. She could hear their pursuers shouting to each other at the intersection, confused by the sudden silence. A burst of gunfire sounded. It was Jamil taunting them to catch him. The gang raced down the street, past the shop, and beyond. Susan could make out two sets of footfalls—one of Jamil, fleet and light, and the other of a dozen men, heavy and menacing—and both were fading. She came out of her shelter. All was quiet. Time to go.

269

Susan gasped. Outside the shop a figure stepped out of the shadows, a rifle braced against his shoulder. He barked at them in Somali, but Susan needed no interpretation to understand what he wanted. She raised her hands. Fatima said something, the man snapped back, and now Omar was joining in. Susan kept her eyes glued to the muzzle of the gun, hoping that the talking would distract him from his aim. She needed only two seconds. Fatima's hand dug into the layers of her wrap and came out holding a wad of bills. The gunman growled an order. Fatima leaned forward to toss him the money. The man reached out to catch it. The muzzle tipped down. Susan pulled the Glock out of her pocket and fired.

He lay on the ground, whimpering and clutching his guts. Susan bent over him and transferred the strap of his AK-47 from his shoulder to hers. In a while he would bleed to death. She nipped the pinch of regret before it could start. No amount of money would have bought him off. It was either he or they.

Afgoy Road lay to their west. Following the sun at the end of its daily journey would certainly bring them to Mogadishu's main artery. It couldn't be more than six blocks away. If they ran they could make it in a few minutes, but they'd also learned that one false step could set them miles back. They worked their way in cautious spurts, three pairs of eyes watching for signs of marauding bands, so single-minded that they didn't realize that they were growing more and more shortsighted by the minute. Without the interference of man-made lights, night was a fast weaver. By the time they got to Afgoy Road, the cloak of dusk had thickened from a mauve gauze to purple velour.

The three hid behind a wall. A vehicle rolled past, its headlights firmly shut. After a long, intensive gaze, they agreed that it didn't carry their rescuers. Two more cars crept past in the same stealthy manner.

Another vehicle approached—big-wheeled and boxy, a cross-country vehicle but not the popular make in these parts. Its lights were out like the others. Susan was still straining to identify its passengers when Omar ran out. She shouted at him, but the damage was already done. Tires screeched. A rifle pointed out the window, straight at Omar. Susan's heart leaped in her throat, and she gave a small cry. The man was wearing the cap of a marine. She darted out of hiding, quite amazed that Omar's one eye was sharper than her two. The gun retreated, the door was flung open and a hand reached out.

"Welcome aboard," the driver said.

Susan never thought she'd be so happy to hear this voice. "Hey, Nick, thanks for the ride," she said as she scrambled into the Jeep and tucked the Kalashnikov between her legs.

The vehicle made a rubber-burning U-turn. Farther on, bursts of fireflies flew out of the street and met resounding greetings from the embassy's watchtower. The two marines in the car blasted at the invisible enemies. Susan emptied the last rounds of her borrowed gun. Nick spoke into his walkie-talkie: "We're coming in. Open the gates!" The nose of the car reared upward, Susan gripped the seat in front, watching the needle on the speedometer swing to the far right. The iron gates of the embassy loomed ahead. They were only twenty feet away now. If the gates didn't open this instant...she closed her eyes.

When she opened them, the car had stopped—inside the compound. Voices were yelling, "Get out, get out!" Susan scrambled out and saw three marines running from the watchtower. This really was the last bus. The blades of the Sea Knight were whipping up a sandstorm. She looked behind and saw that Fatima was struggling to keep her wrap over her head. She ran to her, put her arm over her shoulders and pressed her on. Omar mumbled something about a man climbing over the wall. Susan looked back and saw only dust dervishes twirling in the twilight.

They stumbled into the helicopter. "You made it," a woman cheered. It was Brenda, and next to her was the ambassador.

"Sorry to hold you guys up," Susan said as the last marines piled in.

The engine roared for takeoff. A marine was reaching out for the door when a fist knocked him center face and threw him back. A Somali leaped on board, wielding a pistol and waving something in the air, something small but significant. A marine

271

stopped another from firing. "Hold it, he's got a grenade!" The engine slowed. Omar stepped forward, saying something in Somali. His hand went out to the man, and then the pistol went off. Omar slumped to the floor. The other passengers shrank back in horror. Susan dropped to her knees beside her assistant. The blood was flowing freely from his chest. The gunman was yelling, "Give me your money, your money!"

Fatima knelt by Susan's side, offering her head wrap. Susan bunched it up and shoved it tightly against Omar's wound.

"Do you want a Mercedes Benz?" the ambassador said, slowly, so there was no misunderstanding.

"Where is it?" the gunman shouted.

"It's parked right outside. The key is here, in my pocket. I'm going to take it out now."

The gunman snatched the key and leaped out. The marines picked up their guns, but the ambassador ordered them back.

"Let's get out of here," he shouted.

Susan felt her heart lift with the chopper. A shell screamed past. She held the makeshift bandage against Omar's chest. Blood was soaking through; her hand was hot and sticky. After a while, the explosions grew distant, the air cooled, and she knew they were over the sea.

Omar's eyelids fluttered. His lips moved. Susan bent down to listen. "It's so dark," he whispered.

"It's just the night falling," she said, patting his hand. "You're going to be all right. In a while, we'll be landing on a U.S. ship. The medics will patch you up. They've got some of the best doctors in the world. Don't you worry, you're going to be just fine." Susan knew it was the greatest lie she'd ever told. A pang of guilt hit her. If she hadn't forced Omar to stay in Mogadishu, he'd be sitting pretty in Nairobi, counting his blessings that he'd gotten away before the pressure reached blowout levels.

The chopper touched down on a U.S. warship. Applause and cheers broke out. Susan couldn't resist getting up to see for herself. The ship's deck was brightly lit, and she could recognize many of the people waving joyously at them. Susan squatted to tell Omar the good news. His good eye stared flatly at her, the other gone its own way. She searched frantically for his pulse, moving from wrist to neck and pressing her ear against his heart, but there was none.

Chapter 29

Susan looked down from her sightseeing promontory. Visibility was fair, a far cry from the early morning when the entire San Francisco Bay had been submerged in a tureen of pea soup. It was now past ten, and the fog had risen to the upper reaches of Golden Gate Bridge. Aside from the stray cottony wisp, her view of the parking lot was unhindered. Tourists were streaming in for photo opportunities at the famous bridge. A bus disgorged a Japanese group into a shack touting a sign that read "Gifuto Shoppu," which Susan interpreted to mean "gift shop."

A radio squawked in the station wagon behind her. Two of her colleagues were testing the sound system. The sea of static and the bodiless voices that surfaced periodically reminded her of another scene, another time. She sat down on the bench and waited.

A gray Toyota van, the kind driven by soccer moms, drove into the lot. It must be packed with kids or something, she thought, for the tires were compressed and the body bucked heavily on the speed bump. It cut a curve and backed in next to a cluster of cars. Susan trained her binoculars on the driver. She could barely see through the tinted glass, but what she saw was enough. Hoyt Grimley's profile, with his head sunk up to his ears between his shoulders, was unique. He remained seated, looking ahead, not budging. Susan looked at her watch. It was twenty-five minutes past ten, five minutes before the appointed time.

A white coupe pulled into the lot and parked several spaces from the van. The driver got out, a dark-haired, mustached man in a windbreaker lugging a bulging knapsack. He strolled over to the van and got in the passenger's side.

"Have you got them?" Susan heard the man say. The bug was picking up loud and clear.

"Sure. First installment, as agreed. (A sigh.) That backpack looks heavy. I hope it has what I think it has." It was Grimley's voice all right, the querulous drawl and sigh.

A zipper scraped the airwaves. "It's all here. Shall we inspect the goods?" The man had a mild Arabian accent.

Doors slammed. Susan watched the men get out. Grimley slid open the side door and disappeared into the van. She couldn't see a thing now, but the Mont Blanc amplified pen continued to pick up the creak of wood and metal, clicks and clacks and the agent's voice counting up to fifteen. "There are twenty in each box?" he said.

"Yep. Fifteen boxes altogether, for a total of three hundred Kalashnikovs, every one of them genuine made in China. (Sigh) I'll contact you about the rest before the end of the week. Here's your key. The rental papers are in the glove compartment. Now, if you'll give me your key, the babies are yours." A demurring from the other party could be heard. "Unless you want me to open every box," Grimley added.

"We don't have time. All right, let's do it. If we have any complaints, we know where to find you."

How clever, Susan thought. She'd wondered why Hoyt had picked a public place in broad daylight for the transaction. Now she understood. The transfer was innocent enough, just an exchange of rental car keys. Nobody would suspect any wrongdoing unless it was conducted in a dark isolated spot. People, especially those having a good time, provided the best cover.

It was clever, though not clever enough. Hoyt Grimley, the arms merchant who'd fed off carnage wherever it raged, had walked right into the trap. Through her binoculars, Susan could see an eighteen-wheeler coast into the parking lot, completely blocking the exit. A couple got out of a car parked two rows behind, armed with the usual tourist gear of cameras and hip packs, and walked toward the van. A split second later three burly Midwestern types in short sleeves trudged out of the gift shop. Grimley was surrounded. The officers drew their guns and sprawled the innocuous-looking man over the hood of his car. Sirens wailed and uniformed men cordoned off the area from curious onlookers.

276

At last, justice had been served. The unscrupulous arms salesman was getting what he deserved. As long as Grimley had remained unpunished, she could feel the irritating scratch of a loose end. Her first assignment was finally over, although she'd often wondered what it was all about. For all she'd done to get rid of Hamid, the country had gone up in flames. Since Ahmed's assault, half a dozen factions had hurled themselves into the fray and carved the country into bloody chunks. Siad Barré had been bunkered down in his palace for a month, but when rebels started scaling the fence, the Red Berets muscled the old man into a car and sped off to his hometown of Bardhere.

Susan had concluded that if there was any utility in her service, it was purely personal. After getting off the U.S. rescue ship at Mombasa, she'd flown to Nairobi with the rest of the evacuees, but instead of getting a seat on the next available flight, she and Nick had stayed to hire daring bush pilots to fly into Somalia and swoop up some of those left behind. Among the rescued were Abdullahi and Mohammed and their families, along with Omar's mother and sister. Susan pulled her embassy strings and secured their passage to America. Fatima's family, however, had retreated to inaccessible territory. Months later, Fatima got word that her husband and children had safely crossed into Kenya. Her youngest, a three-year-old girl, had died during the arduous trek, but the rest had survived and were awaiting clearance for emigration to the U.S. Susan's greatest regret was over Jamil. In spite of all the feelers she'd sent out, nobody could locate the boy. A vagrant with no last name or address was hard to find, more so if he was dead. Did he survive the pursuit? She would never know.

Susan held out in Nairobi for two weeks, but under threat of dishonorable discharge from her superiors on both sides, she returned to Washington. The World Bank was undergoing yet another round of reorganization. With her country of operation in a shambles, Davar didn't have to search far for an excuse to declare her redundant. The parting was cordial, and at a wine-and-cheese farewell party thrown in her honor, he ribbed her about laying waste a country in record time. At her debriefing on the other side, Alex commended her for her performance and promised a promotion in the next annual review. She was now a full-fledged officer, no longer a translator operating undercover. The recognition had meant so much to her before, but now that she'd reached the coveted level of elevation, the view was quite disappointing. Below her lay a patchwork of messy backyards, full of the flotsam and jetsam of human flaws.

The Somalis had tried to live together as a nation and failed. Now they'd lost everything—the old way of life and the new. What pain and suffering the people would have to endure before they could rebuild a civilization. Out of the ashes a phoenix had yet to rise. The rest of the world had also lost. In trying to develop the country, either out of self-interest or altruism, the donors of assistance had cultivated a culture of dependence and lulled the ruling regime into believing that somebody in the world would always prop it up, no matter how rotten its house had become. The repairs had been cosmetic, the donors had known that deep down in their hearts, but for reasons of their own, they'd turned a blind eye until it was too late. In the end, they hadn't helped but merely added to the severity of the disaster. They, too, had lost.

Everyone had lost, and so must this avaricious merchant of death. Susan took one last peek through the binoculars and saw the handcuffs clamping down on Grimley's scrawny wrists.

About The Author

Veronica Li once worked as the World Bank's loan officer for Somalia. The novel, *Nightfall in Mogadishu*, was inspired by her visits to Somalia before it fell into anarchy. During her thirteen-year career in the bank, her assignments also took her to other parts of Africa as well as Asia. She is now retired and fictionalizing her travel adventures. Before joining the bank, she was a journalist for the French news agency, Agence France-Presse, and later the Asian Wall Street Journal.

Printed in the United States
201932BV00001B/1-51/A